"GOD, LOOK AT YOUR SHIRT!"

Haley blinked, suddenly confused. In that instant, the fury she'd felt toward her sister disappeared. All she wanted to do now was rip the skin from her own right arm so the itching would stop. She reached over, ready to rake her fingernails over her skin and froze.

Her right shirtsleeve was soaked with blood, and a bright red trail ran from the hem of the sleeve to her elbow. She looked over at Heather, hoping for an explanation. When none came, Haley carefully lifted the bloody material to peek beneath it.

That's when she saw a droplet of blood fall from the snakes forked tongue—and the slight flicker of its tail.

MORE PRAISE FOR
DEBORAH LeBLANC!

FAMILY INHERITANCE

"The sticky Louisiana bayou comes alive in first-time author LeBlanc's imaginative chiller about family curses and witch doctors....LeBlanc's dialogue is spot-on...riveting."
—*Publishers Weekly*

"Storytelling brilliance...a tour de force."
—*L'Observateur*

"A super-tight suspense tale that features elements that reminded me of several horror film classics....*Family Inheritance* is a sure-fire bet for fans of character-driven horror novels."
—*The Horror Fiction Review*

"What unfolds before the reader is an engrossing—at times terrifying—and altogether enjoyable story that is richly woven and told with passion. Deborah LeBlanc holds the readers' attention and never once drops it."
—*Dread Central*

"*Family Inheritance* begins like the first strong jolt before a climb to the mother of all roller-coaster rides where terror is just around the next curve or over the next hill. Deborah LeBlanc's prose is a flying leap into the labyrinth of madness and self-doubt that stops long enough to catch a breath before the next hurtling plunge into the abyss."
—Celebritycafe.com

MORBID CURIOSITY

DEBORAH LEBLANC

LEISURE BOOKS NEW YORK CITY

For Gervasio—living proof that wolves can dance.

A LEISURE BOOK®

July 2007

Published by

Dorchester Publishing Co., Inc.
200 Madison Avenue
New York, NY 10016

ISBN-10: 0-8439-5828-6
ISBN-13: 978-0-8439-5828-7

The name "Leisure Books" and the stylized "L" with design are trademarks of Dorchester Publishing Co., Inc.

Printed in the United States of America.

Visit us on the web at www.dorchesterpub.com.

MORBID
CURIOSITY

PROLOGUE

He had been forced into closets before, but never by a witch. At least, he thought she was a witch. . . .

Ten-year-old Caster Morbadelli clamped his teeth over his bottom lip and inched his way to the closet door on his knees. In the utter darkness, time and space seemed to go on forever. He stretched out a hand, willing his fingers past his fear to the wooden door that separated him from his father, who he prayed had not left him behind. The scent of mildew, dirty underwear, and old blood swam in and out of his nostrils and roiled through his empty stomach. A tear trickled past the right side of his nose to his mouth, and Caster flicked his tongue over the droplet, capturing it. He needed to pee.

He didn't know how long he'd been in the closet, but it felt like an eternity. When he and his father had first arrived at Madame Toussant's, the sun had been clotted over with storm clouds, which made it feel like late afternoon. But Caster knew better. It had been morning. One of those bad mornings when he woke on his own instead of to the sound of his stepmother's deep, scratchy voice, yelling for him to get out of bed and go fetch her cigarettes in the living room.

She was gone again. He knew it, felt it before he rolled out of bed and crept into the empty kitchen. Knowing the really bad part would come as soon as his father woke and discovered she was gone, Caster quickly poured himself a bowl of stale cornflakes. It would probably be the only chance he'd have to eat today. As usual, there was no milk in the refrigerator, so he doused the cereal with tap water and was about to dig a spoon into the swill when he heard a crash from his father's bedroom. So much for breakfast.

Within a matter of minutes, his father's curses echoed through their small apartment, escalating in volume and vehemence as he hurriedly dressed, pausing only long enough to hurl a perfume bottle, her hairbrush, and a can of shaving cream across the room. Caster knew the drill because they'd been through it so many times before. Once the throwing began, he had about five minutes to dress before his father dragged him outside. The rest of the day would be spent combing the streets of New Orleans, looking for her, something Caster couldn't understand. If the woman didn't want to be with them, why did his father keep begging her to come back? He'd never been brave enough to ask that question aloud.

They'd only walked six blocks this time before his father pulled him into a narrow alleyway that ran between two storefronts on Rue Royal. Caster had balked, tempted to pull out of his father's grasp and run in the opposite direction. He knew they were headed for Madame Toussant's, and he wanted no part of it. They'd been there twice over the last three months, and each visit had left Caster so frightened, he'd had nightmares even during his daydreams. Toussant's house was creepy and always filled with weird people who smelled like they hadn't taken a bath—ever. But willing or not, his father had clamped down on his arm and all but shoved Caster past the white metal door as soon as it opened. He'd gripped Caster's shoulders firmly, steering him down a maze of dark hallways until they'd reached an opening on the left. Over the opening hung long strands of multicolored beads that sparkled, tinkled and pinged when they pushed past them.

Beyond the beads lay a concrete floor and little furniture. Against the back wall of the dingy room stood a small table that looked ready to collapse under the weight of too many burning candles. Their collective glow highlighted a large picture of a scowling, heavyset black man that hung on the wall just above the table. Caster hadn't seen this picture during his previous visits, and he wished more than anything he hadn't seen it now. The man had bushy eyebrows, narrow black eyes, and a wide, crooked nose. A red and gold striped cap sat on top of his head, and it reminded Caster of the hats he'd seen men wearing once at a Shriner's circus, only this one had a black tassel. The picture revealed the man from the waist up, but even dressed in a white, button-down shirt with a high, stiff collar, he still looked dangerous—evil, like the kind of person who'd stick razor blades in kids' candy bars on Halloween.

Even more frightening was Madame Toussant, who sat on a bench in front of the candle-strewn table, babbling words Caster couldn't understand. Her large body swayed from side to side as though to keep time with the sound of her voice.

Madame Toussant didn't wear a pointy black hat or have green skin like the witch from *The Wizard of Oz*. Instead, she wore a dull red bandanna over a shock of wiry black hair, and her skin was the color of roasted pecans. When she finally stood and turned toward them, her dark blue dress billowed around her large body like a wind-worried tent. The whites of her eyes overpowered small irises, and it gave her a stark, wild-eyed look that made Caster think, *Witch!* To make matters worse, her many heavy necklaces swayed and rattled against her huge bosom when she walked, and something about that sound made his teeth hurt, like he'd just bitten into tinfoil. It wasn't until she was only a few feet away that he noticed the ornamentation that made up her necklaces—bits of bone, teeth, shale, and a few beads similar to the ones hanging over the door-way. If wearing necklaces of teeth and bone didn't prove Toussant was a witch, Caster didn't know what would. He turned to warn his father, to beg him to leave, but before he managed to utter a word, Caster found himself alone. His father had already rushed over to Madame Toussant, falling to his knees, crying for her to help him, for her to bring back his wife, his precious Ann Louise. Amid sobs and near hysterical supplications, the short, square-faced man promised to do any-thing, give anything to have the love of his life re-turn home.

As Caster watched his father melt into an emo-tional puddle before the witch, he trembled with fear. He felt abandoned and more alone than he'd ever felt in his life. In one morning he'd lost what little family he'd had. His father knelt only a few feet away, but Caster instinctively knew it was not the same man who'd ranted and wailed through their apartment only an hour or so ago. This kneeling man was broken, too broken to think of his son. Too broken to survive.

Madame Toussant stood, watching Caster's fa-ther with her hands on her hips, the whites of her eyes appearing even brighter, larger than before. She shook her head slowly, like someone disgusted over a pathetic sight. Caster took a tentative step toward his father, but stopped cold when Madame Toussant raised a hand in his direction. She peered over at him, lifting her chin and tilting her head slightly as though to size him up. Caster couldn't read her expression. Was that pity or anger he saw in her weird, large eyes?

Then, without warning, Toussant bellowed, "Renee, Antoine, Marie, *tout le monde, viens vite! Vite!*"

Caster didn't understand what Toussant said, but it sounded urgent, and before he knew it, people began pouring into the room from the beaded doorway. Men, women, most of them black, many of them half dressed, all of them sweaty and barefoot. A few carried strange-looking drums; some held thick cords, each decorated with bone, teeth, and shale, just like Toussant's necklaces. Without instruction, they encircled Toussant and Caster's father, their feet falling into a slow, shuffling march. Three men sat cross-legged on the floor near the table and placed V-shaped drums between their legs. They closed their eyes and began to beat the taut, weathered skin with their fingers.

It was then that Madame Toussant walked up to Caster, snatched one of his hands in hers, and pulled him toward the back of the room. "Dis not for little eyes to see," she said, her voice deep and low.

"Let me go!" Caster cried, trying to pull out of her grasp. Her thick fingers wrapped tighter around his hand, and Caster threw a desperate, furtive glance over his shoulder. "Dad!"

"Hush," Toussant demanded. "You daddy don't hear nothin' no how, not wit' him blub-berin' like a fool idiot over dere. And look at dis, he leave me stuck wit' you. I tell him not to bring de chil'ren, but he don't listen. Dat's not good. Not good for him. Not good for you."

By this time, they'd reached a warped wooden door at the back of the room. Madame Toussant shoved it open with a huff, then pushed Caster inside. He barely had time to register it was a closet before he tripped over his own feet and landed on his butt.

"Now listen up close," Toussant said, glaring down at him with her white witch eyes and rattling necklaces. "Dis gonna have to do 'cause I got no place else to put you. So stay put up in here, you understand? Don't matter what you hear, don't matter what you t'ink you hear, you don't look. You don't come out dis closet 'til I say!" With that, Toussant had slammed the door shut, leaving him to the dark and whatever crawled in dirty, mildewy places.

Whatever time had passed between then and now only compounded Caster's fear. So did the sounds coming from the other room. He heard crying, singing, the babble of nonsensical words, the beat—beat—beat of drums accompanied by the stomp and slap of so many bare feet on concrete. Were all those people dancing? Did anyone even remember he was in the closet? What if Toussant kept him trapped in here forever? He was young but not stupid. He knew Toussant didn't like him. She might keep him in this closet simply because she felt like it, just like his stepmother used to do. He wondered what trapped people died of first—starvation or thirst. Either sounded like a horrible way to die.

Working hard to hold back tears and keep his bladder in check, Caster inched forward once more on his knees. This time he was rewarded with the feel of the closet door beneath his fingertips. The clamor in the next room was growing to a fevered pitch, and the sounds vibrated through his small body. His stomach felt funny, like someone had filled it with bees and creepy-crawly things. He pressed an ear to the door, hoping to hear his father's voice amid the mayhem. What he heard instead was the unmistakable squawk of a chicken, a high-pitched, urgent squall that sounded like a scream for help. What on earth was a chicken doing in there?

Curious, Caster ran his hands along the doorknob, searching for a keyhole he might peer through. There was none. He lowered himself to the floor, lying on his right side, and pressed an eye against the crack beneath the door. It was too narrow for him to make out anything more than an occasional moving shadow, but from down here, the chicken's squawking sounded even more desperate. What were they doing out there?

When his curiosity could bear no more, he scrambled back onto his knees and felt for the doorknob. He was shocked to discover it turned easily in his hand. The door wasn't locked!

As if by magic, the door creaked open a couple of inches before sticking fast. He remembered how Madame Toussant had to push hard against the door when she opened it earlier. Being inside the closet meant he'd have to pull hard to open it all the way, and that would surely get Toussant's attention. No matter, at least now he had a bit of light, was able to breathe fresher air, and could see what was going on with that stupid chicken.

Planting his small body between the jamb and door edge, Caster leaned his forehead against the opening and peered out.

Brown bodies were packed together, everyone jumping and dancing with wild, exaggerated movements, arms flinging in every direction, legs and feet rising and falling to a rhythm far different from that of the drums. Some had their eyes closed and their heads thrown back while others had only the whites of their eyes showing. Sweat ran like golden threads down their bodies, and spittle dripped from the corner of every mouth. Some people were completely naked now, and a few men were thrusting the lower halves of their body against women in gestures Caster knew he shouldn't be watching. But he couldn't turn away. The raw energy radiating from the group seemed to glue his eyes to their every movement. It wasn't until he heard the squawk again that he remembered the chicken.

Squatting a little so he had a better angle from which to see past the bodies, Caster caught sight of Madame Toussant—just as she tore the chicken's head off with her teeth. Paralyzed with shock and awe, Caster watched as the bird's wings continued to flap wildly. Blood splattered over Toussant's face, across the concrete floor, over his father, who lay prone at her feet. No sooner had the bird's wings come to rest than someone exchanged the dead bird with another live chicken. Once again, Toussant, her eyes now completely white, tore the head off the bird with her teeth. This time, however, she captured its blood in a roughly hewn wooden bowl, then drank from it. When she lowered the bowl, her eyes rolled back into her head, and her body began to shimmy and tremble. Pink spittle and blood flew from her lips.

Still writhing from whatever spell had overtaken her, Toussant grabbed a buck knife from the small table bedside her. She let out a barrage of strange words, then dropped into a squat beside his father and with no more ceremony than a loud grunt, Madame Toussant cut the smallest finger off his left hand. The drumming and dancing stopped.

Caster didn't remember gasping, but he must have, loudly, because everyone except his father, who still lay on the floor unmoving and bleeding, turned to face him. His lungs felt vacuumed of air, and for the life of him, Caster couldn't remember how to draw in a breath. He watched as Madame Toussant stood and turned toward him, her eyes bright with anger. Caster felt warm liquid trickle down his legs, and the pungent scent of fresh urine snapped him back to reality. He had disobeyed and witnessed something forbidden, and now there was little doubt he would pay for the transgression.

With a whimper, he quickly pushed away from the door and scrambled to the back of the closet. He was trying to hide beneath a smelly tarp that lay bunched up in a corner when someone kicked the closet door open.

Madame Toussant's large body filled the doorway. The blood on her face, mouth, and hands made her look like she'd just slaughtered and eaten an entire army. She reached for him and with little effort, captured Caster by the collar of his T-shirt. She yanked him to her, and he gagged from the rancidity in her breath.

"What I told you, huh?" Toussant demanded. "Didn't I say dis not for little eyes to see?" Still gripping his collar, she shook him hard. "Didn't I say?"

"Y-y-yes," Casper cried.

"But you gotta look anyway, huh? Curious gotta see, *non?*" She pulled him into the adjacent room, which was slowly emptying of people. "Den Madame will give you somet'ing to be curious about, little man." She grabbed his right wrist so tight he yelped in pain. He wanted to pull free but was too frightened to move.

Toussant took the index finger of her right hand and dragged it down both sides of her face, collecting leftover chicken blood. When her fingertip was covered in crimson, she quickly drew on the back of his imprisoned hand. *"Tu vouloir chercher mais jamais voir!"*

Caster didn't understand her words or the

meaning of the symbol she drew, which looked
like a snake eating its own tail, but somehow he
knew—he *felt*—that Madame Toussant had just
branded him for life—to a fate worse than death.

CHAPTER ONE

Haley Thurston knew there was no turning back, no matter how insistently her twin sister, Heather, tugged on her arm. Not only would they look like idiots if they left now, they'd be throwing away a life-altering opportunity. She wasn't going to let that happen. Not after the crappy year they'd just been through, and if the last three days were any indication, the future appeared doomed to an insurmountable shit pile. As far as she was concerned, telling a couple of lies and wading through a few roaches were small prices to pay for a detour.

The invitation from Karla Nichols came as a shock. The girl had approached Haley and Heather at noon while the two of them sat huddled over tacos and fruit salad in the school cafeteria. When Karla sat beside them, Haley became suspicious. What could one of the most popular girls in school possibly want with them? They

were new to Laidlaw High, as well as to the state
of Mississippi, and Karla appeared to be a land-
mark. She was seventeen, drove her own car, and
always had a group of kids traipsing after her
like hungry puppies. Haley still didn't fully understand how they'd managed to capture Karla's
attention, but why didn't seem important now.
She was just glad they had.

Hoping she appeared braver than she felt, Haley squared her shoulders as they maneuvered
around a coffee table littered with crumpled beer
cans and dirty dishes mottled with dried food and
cigarette butts. A broken trail of small brown
roaches scuttled across the coffee table, down its
legs, then under the green-striped couch beside
it. The mountain of rumpled clothes sitting on
the couch appeared permanent, and she didn't
even want to guess what the long, chunky brown
things were that littered the matted carpet near
the television. The place smelled of stale cigarette
smoke, rotten oranges, and used maxi pads.

"This is *way* gross," Heather whispered as they
followed Karla down a hallway that led to the
back of the mobile home.

Haley scowled. "Shh!"

"In here," Karla said, taking a quick right.

The bedroom looked like the loading end of a
trash truck. The floor was obliterated by clothes,
crumpled paper, dirty socks, Pepsi cans, shoes,
CD cases, and discarded pizza boxes. Lopsided
posters of heavy-metal bands decorated the
walls, along with magazine pictures of hunky
men in Hanes underwear and movie stars in glit-

tery ball gowns. The bed looked like it hadn't been washed, much less made, in years, and the drawers from the dresser beside it were pulled out, each empty and hanging aslant.

Karla walked over to the bed, stepping on whatever happened to be in her way en route, then plopped down on the squeaky mattress. She leaned over, stuck a hand under the bed, and pulled out a large shoebox. "Y'all gonna just hang out there or what?"

Still standing in the doorway, Haley glanced at her sister. Heather was biting the tip of her right thumb, a nervous habit she'd developed in kindergarten and had never outgrown. The trait looked cute on a five-year-old but stupid on a high school sophomore. Haley nudged her, and Heather released her thumb and took a tentative step forward.

Karla opened the shoebox, then aimed her chin at the space beside her on the mattress. "Sit there."

Eager to get started, Haley hurried over to sit beside her, paying little mind to the trash underfoot. Heather stalled at the foot of the bed, and for an instant Haley sensed the fear and doubt swirling through her sister. That was the thing about being a twin—when something good happened, they sometimes got a double dose of happy because both picked up on what the other felt. When things went wrong, however, that occasionally meant double the sadness or fear, which was tough to carry at times. Up until a moment ago, Haley had been dealing with some uncertainty, but she'd been too excited about the possibilities that lay ahead to be afraid. Now, picking up on Heather's vibes, it took all she had not to chicken out of the deal. She shot her sister a *Chill, okay?* look, then turned her attention to their host.

If someone judged by looks alone, Karla Nichols would be the last person anyone would suspect of being popular. She had long, stringy black hair, brown eyes accented with thick, black eyeliner, a fair share of zits, and a tattoo that looked like squiggle art on the top of her right arm. Haley didn't care what the girl looked like or what kind of house she lived in. What interested her most was Karla's tattoo. It was real, not the rub-on kind, and according to Karla it had been the catalyst for her popularity. Haley had to believe the girl was telling the truth because she'd never known anyone to look like that, live like this, *and* be popular.

After removing a pack of Marlboro Lights and a Bic lighter from the shoebox, Karla tapped out a cigarette and lit it. She scrunched her lips into a tight *O*, popped her jaw, and blew out a smoke ring. She held the pack out to them. "Smoke?"

Haley hesitated. She'd never smoked before and wondered which might be worse—looking lame for not taking a cigarette or trying one and possibly puking all over the floor.

"We don't smoke," Heather said, stepping closer to Haley. She had a steely look in her eyes that dared anyone to push the point.

Haley grabbed her sister's arm and pulled her down beside her on the bed.

Karla grinned, a lopsided effort that gave her face a pained expression. She tossed the lighter and pack of cigarettes back into the shoebox.

"Don't your parents care that you smoke?" Heather asked.

Haley groaned silently, wishing her sister back to uncertain and scared.

Karla snorted a stream of smoke through her nostrils. "You see any parental units around here?" She reached for an empty Pepsi can on the floor, righted it on the nightstand that stood near the bed, and tapped ashes into it.

"Parental units?" Heather asked, and Haley jabbed her lightly in the ribs with an elbow.

Pausing in midtap, Karla cocked her head towards her. "Parents. You know, mother, father, shit like that."

Heather frowned, and Haley, fearing her sister was about to ask another stupid question, jumped in. "Okay, so what do we have to do?"

Instead of answering, Karla leaned against the headboard and took a long drag off her cigarette. She closed her eyes when she inhaled, like smoking was the most pleasurable experience in the world. When she opened her eyes again, she studied them for a long moment, then sat up and took two quick puffs on her cigarette. She reached into the shoebox again, pulled out a small notebook and an ink pen, then placed the shoebox on the bed.

"How long's this going to take?" Haley asked.

Karla opened the notebook. "Why, you got a hot date?"

Haley felt her cheeks grow warm. "No, but I told my grandparents we'd be back around four-thirty."

"What else did you tell 'em?" Karla puffed on her cigarette again and squinted through the smoke.

"Nothing."

"They didn't ask why you were going to be late?"

"Well, yeah. I told my grandmother we were trying out for the cheerleading squad."

"Tryouts on the third day of school?"

Haley shrugged. "She doesn't know any different."

"And?"

"And what?"

"What else did you tell her?"

"Nothing else."

"How's she expecting you to get home?"

"I told her a friend would drop us off." Haley frowned and nervously fingered a button on her blouse. "You said you'd drive us home when we were done. You're still going to, right?"

"Yeah." Karla pointed to a pizza box on the floor near the bed. "Hey, see if there's anything worth eatin' in there, will ya?"

Heather leaned over and opened the pizza box. It contained a few crust ridges and two shriveled pieces of pepperoni. She showed the contents to Karla, who made a *pfft* sound, then motioned for her to close the box.

"So what's with the questions?" Haley asked.

Dropping her cigarette into the empty Pepsi can, Karla let out an exaggerated sigh. "Two reasons. One, like I told y'all on the way over here, you can't tell anybody about this. Remember?"

The twins nodded in unison.

"Last person I helped got radared by her parents, and the little bitch wound up ratting me out. I got into all kinds of shit. I don't need another hassle like that."

"We're not going to say anything," Haley assured her.

"Yeah, but what about your grandparents? They snoop around in your room? Dig through your shit?"

"No," Heather said. "Well, except for Meemaw. She comes in our room every once in a while to put clean laundry on the bed."

Haley cringed when she heard her sister refer to their paternal grandmother as *meemaw*. Although the term seemed to be common in Passon, Mississippi, she thought it sounded immature and stupid.

"I had a meemaw like that," Karla said, a heavy note in her voice. "She took real good care of me when I'd go visit her over in Meridian on summer breaks. She died three years ago, though. Heart attack."

"I'm sorry she died," Heather said. "We lost our dad four months ago. Leukemia."

"Where's your mama?"

"In a hospital back in Baton Rouge."

"She sick?"

"Sick in the head," Haley said, flipping over a CD case on the floor with her right foot.

Heather leaned into her, frowning. "Stop. It's not her fault."

Haley waved a hand as though to brush away Heather's words. Living through the drama her sister referred to had been enough. She didn't need to regurgitate the details. For a year, she and Heather had been pushed into a corner while their father struggled with his disease. After he died, they were shipped off to a cousin's, then tossed over to their grandparents a month later when their mother attempted suicide because she couldn't deal with their father's death. And now, because their mother couldn't seem to get her head together, they were stuck in Mississippi until somebody said they weren't. Not that Haley hated her grandparents. Meemaw and Papaw were nice enough, but Passon, Mississippi, wasn't home. Neither was Laidlaw High.

Back in Zachary, Louisiana, she and Heather had attended a small Catholic school, where ninety-five percent of the kids had known one another since grade school, and the graduating classes usually maxed out at fifty. They'd been popular there. But Laidlaw was a different story. The school was huge, holding most of the teens from west Jackson plus some from small farm towns, like Passon, that rode on the hem of the city's skirt. At Laidlaw they were like two ants in an overcrowded mound. Nothing special and easily ignored.

Between losing her parents, her home, and being forced to attend a new school, Haley'd had more than enough. Life had become a runaway bulldozer, and she knew somebody had to grab the controls before the damn thing crashed and left no survivors. If Karla were right and Chaos magic allowed you to gain control, then Haley wanted in big time. She was tired of not having a say in her life.

More determined than ever, Haley turned to Karla. "You said there were two reasons for your questions. What's the second?"

Still holding the notebook, Karla doodled in the corner of a blank page. "When you make a sigil, you've gotta make sure you say what you want in the right way. Sometimes we think one way, but it comes out our mouth different. Just like when I asked you what you'd told your grandparents. You said nothing, but you really had told them something."

"But it wasn't anything important. Nothing that would've given away what we were doing."

"Doesn't matter. The point is you said one thing but meant another. You can't do that in Chaos. You've gotta pay attention to what you're saying. If you don't, you're either going to wind up with only part of what you wanted or the complete opposite. Chaos can be powerful shit. If you get sloppy with the details, it won't work, or even worse—it'll turn on you."

Heather's eyes grew wide. "Turn on you how?"

"Depends on what you're after. The smaller

the wish, the smaller the payback if it's done wrong. Like if you wanted a new stereo, that's small. If you don't do your sigil right or don't take good care of it, the payback would probably be that you lose your old stereo, so you'd wind up with none. Get it?"

Haley nodded.

"It's all by degrees. The bigger the wish or intention, the more serious the payback. Like if you wanted somebody dead, *you* could wind up dead."

Heather gasped. "We don't want anyone to die!"

Karla rolled her eyes. "Whatever. I'm just telling you how the rules work."

"Is that what happened here?" Heather held out her hands, indicating their surroundings. "Payback?"

Karla frowned. "Huh?"

"I mean if Chaos is powerful like you said, you could be living in a mansion, right?"

"Yeah, so?"

"Well, why aren't you? Why are you living in this?"

Karla arched a brow. "You dissin' my house?"

Heather's cheeks turned bright pink. "No, I was just wondering. You said the magic could turn on you if it wasn't done right, and I thought—"

"You thought since I live in a dump, I'd screwed something up, right? Well you're wrong. A house and what's in it isn't important to me. For Chaos to work, you've gotta focus on something you *really* want. I'll be legal and outta here in a few months, so I'm sure as hell not gonna waste my energy or my sigil on this shit hole. All I care about right now is makin' friends and partying."

"Why don't you get Chaos to make you legal now so you don't have to wait to move out?" Heather asked.

"'Cause you can't use Chaos to mess with time, like making yourself older. It won't work." Karla glanced away for a moment, her expression wistful. "Been trying to work it so I can get emancipated, though. It's just taking longer than I figured."

"So why us, Karla?" Haley asked, surprised by her own question. It seemed to pop out of her mouth, having bypassed her brain.

"What?"

"Why'd you decide to show us how this works? There's a ton of other kids at Laidlaw. Why'd you pick us?"

"You complaining?"

"Not even."

Karla eyed her for a moment, then shrugged. "Curious, I guess. I've never seen it done by twins before. I wanna see if you get a double kick. If one person can power up a sigil, I'm thinking twins should be able to make it even stronger. Should be a trip."

"So we're like an experiment?" Heather asked.

"Sorta."

"How'd you know we'd do it?" Haley asked.

"I didn't. Watchin' y'all mope around school by yourselves all the time, though, I figured you might want the help. I remember what that shit's like, being the new kid. It ain't fun."

"Wait . . ." Heather leaned toward her. "You mean you're not from here?"

"Nope. Originally from a hick town in Arkansas. Folks moved out here two years ago and dragged me along."

"But you're so popular," Haley said. "It's like all the kids have known you forever."

This time Karla's grin was wide and real. "I know. Best shit's ever happened to me."

Haley's heart thudded with anticipation. "Chaos made that happen?"

"Yeah."

"How?"

"I don't know exactly how, and I don't have to know." Karla lifted the right shirtsleeve of her blouse, fully exposing her tattoo. "All I have to do is make sure I keep my sigil fed, and it takes care of the rest."

Heather's brow furrowed. "How do you feed a tattoo?"

"The tattoo's not the sigil. It's only a symbol that represents what I want. It's like a focal point I carry around with me all the time. You can't see most sigils because they're energy, kinda like electricity. See what I'm sayin'?"

"But how do you feed what you can't see?" Haley asked.

"You release certain kinds of energy when you focus on your symbol. The bigger your intention, the more energy you have to feed your sigil."

More confused than ever, Haley began to worry she'd never grasp the concept fully enough to use it. "Okay . . . so, like what do you feed yours?"

"Pain."

Haley sat up straighter, taken aback by the answer. "Huh?"

Karla nodded and raised her skirt just high enough for them to see the lower portion of the inside of her thighs. Both had thin red and pink crisscrossing slashes that ran almost to her knees.

Heather gasped.

Haley felt the blood drain from her face. "You're a cutter?"

"Not a cutter like you're thinking." Karla lowered her skirt. "I don't cut to feel. I cut to feed."

"Are we going to have to do that?" Heather asked, her voice trembling and barely above a whisper.

"The way you start up your sigil then feed it is up to you. You can use cutting, sex, bungee jumping, skydiving—anything extreme. The more you want, the more extreme it's gotta be, to start it up anyway. You can back off some when it comes to feeding it every month."

"You mean you did something worse than cutting to . . . to start it?" Heather asked. "And you did all that just to get friends?"

Karla pursed her lips and looked away. "I wanted to make sure it worked . . . and worse is relative."

"What'd you do?" Haley pressed, eager to know.

"It's personal and not important," Karla said,

still refusing to look at them. She tore off the top sheet she'd been doodling on in the notebook, crumpled it, and tossed it on the floor. She finally peered up at Haley. "Y'all still want in?"

Haley glanced over at Heather. Her sister had developed a light sheen of sweat on her upper lip. They spoke eye to eye, neither breathing a word.

I'm scared, Haley.

It'll be all right.

Not if we have to do stuff like cutting!

Maybe we won't have to since it's the two of us.

That *maybe* hung between them like a thick, corded rope. It would either swing them over to a new life or it would hang them for trying. The problem was they'd never know which unless they grabbed it.

Haley gave her sister a short nod, then blew out an anxious breath and turned to Karla. "We're in."

CHAPTER TWO

When Heather heard her sister utter "We're in," she wanted to snatch the words out of the air and tuck them away in a tamper-proof vault. She didn't want in. She didn't want anything to do with Chaos magic, not if it involved something as stupid as cutting. But it was too late. The words had been released, and the determined expression on her sister's face told her that Haley's cast-iron will was locked and loaded. There'd be no changing her mind. Even if she begged and made a scene, Heather knew her sister would simply go through this without her.

Although older by only six minutes, Haley had always been the more aggressive twin, the one most likely to take risks, to speak out, to dream big, to jump from one adventure to the next with hardly a thought. Heather, on the other hand, preferred a more cautious approach to life, but her preference rarely mattered. The genetic tether that had bound the two of them together at conception always managed to yank Heather along. She knew this looming Chaos experiment would be no exception. She'd no more be able to turn her back on Haley now than cut off her own right arm.

With a shiver, Heather scooted closer to her sister and watched as Karla drew four quarter-size circles on a clean sheet of paper, one on each corner of the page. She filled in each circle with a five-pointed star, then wrote Haley and Heather's name between the top two encircled stars.

"What's all that for?" Haley asked.

Karla tapped the pen on the page. "The points of each star represent the elements of the universe—spirit, air, water, earth, and fire. The circle around the star is symbolic, like we're bringing all the elements together. You're supposed to put one on each corner of the paper so they'll protect your sigil while you create it. Now we've just gotta seal them to make them yours." She scrounged through the shoebox with her free hand and pulled out a sewing needle. "Y'all both gimme the first finger of your right hand."

Haley stuck out her right index finger. When Heather didn't follow suit, she nudged her. "Come on."

"Are you going to prick us with that needle?" Heather asked as she slowly extended a shaking finger.

Karla rolled her eyes and dropped the ink pen onto her lap. "Whadda ya think I'm gonna do with it, sew a prom dress?" Without warning, she jabbed the needle into the tip of Haley's finger, and a crimson droplet immediately appeared.

Haley jerked her hand back, sucking air between her teeth.

"Now dab a little blood in each of those circles."

While Haley followed her instructions, Karla motioned Heather closer. "You gotta do the same thing. Just put your blood on top of hers."

Fighting tears, Heather squeezed her eyes shut and stuck her right hand out farther. The prick came swiftly, and pain radiated down her finger. She kept her eyes closed, riding the ripple of pain, wishing it would carry her out of this room, out of this house. Someone grabbed her pulsing finger, and Heather opened her eyes with a gasp.

"Put it here," Haley said, pressing Heather's pierced finger onto the bloodstain that already filled the top left circle. More blood, brighter blood covered the space, and her sister moved her finger from circle to circle until the task was completed. By the time she was done, Heather's fingertip felt numb. And she didn't like the look in Haley's eyes. They held a wild, hungry glow, like someone starved—for anything.

"Now what?" Haley asked. "Do we—"

The sound of a slamming door caused all three of them to jump.

"Karla Marie, you back there?" a woman called from the other end of the trailer.

"Shit!" Karla quickly tossed the notebook, pen, and needle into the shoebox, then slapped the lid back on the box.

"Who's that?" Heather asked, noting the sound of relief in her own voice.

"Parental unit." Karla got up and tucked the shoebox under her arm. "Let's get outta here. She'll be all up in my Kool-Aid in a minute."

"But we're not done, right?" Haley asked, jumping up from her spot on the bed. "You're still gonna show us?"

"Chill." Karla patted the air with a hand, signaling for Haley to keep her voice down. "I'm still gonna show you, but not here."

"Karla Marie?" The woman's voice was louder this time, closer.

"Back here," Karla shouted, then signaled for Haley and Heather to quickly follow her.

She led them out of the bedroom, down the hall, and back into the living room, where a thin, haggard-faced, blond woman stood waiting, arms folded across her chest. A smoldering cigarette dangled between the fingers of her right hand.

"The dishes still ain't done," the woman said, not bothering to acknowledge the twins.

Karla slowed her pace but kept moving. "I'll do 'em when I get back."

"Oh, yeah? And just where in the hell you think you're going?"

Having reached the front door, Karla opened it. "Out," she said without looking back. She hurried down the metal steps and as soon as Haley and Heather cleared the doorway after her, she slammed the trailer door shut.

Within seconds, they were piled into Karla's Neon and barreling out of the trailer park and onto Highway 468.

Heather sat in the back, gripping the headrest of the passenger seat. Her heart fluttered at an erratic beat between her throat and chest as Karla forced the car faster. Haley sat up front, drumming an impatient beat on the dash with her fingers. Wind howled through the open windows and filled the car with the scent of gasoline fumes and freshly plowed fields. They zigzagged through a series of *S* curves, tires squealing, and Heather peered over Karla's right shoulder to check the speedometer. The needle jittered past eighty.

A few miles down the highway, Karla banked the Neon into another curve, then slowed and made a hard right down a narrow, winding road. She swerved past potholes, sped around two bends, then turned left onto a dirt road that eventually led to a large, dilapidated barn. Tall weeds and brambles surrounded the building, and kudzu overran its faded crimson siding. An open loft sat above the two main doors of the barn. To Heather, it looked like a dark, toothless maw, eager for its next meal.

Karla parked close to the barn, killed the engine, then without saying anything, got out of the car. Her expression was fierce, hard, like she wanted to punch somebody.

Heather put a hand on Haley's shoulder, hoping the touch would give her sister pause. It didn't. Haley scrambled out of the car and hurried over to Karla, who now stood waiting near the hood of the Neon, the shoebox tucked under her right arm. Reluctantly, Heather opened the back door and stepped out. The breeze that greeted her only added to her anxiety. Instead of cooling the sweat from her face, it seemed to carry whispered warnings to her ears. They were out in the middle of nowhere. No other buildings, no people. What if someone got hurt? How would they get help?

"Quit dragging ass," Karla said, motioning for Heather to hurry. She turned on her heels and headed for the barn. Haley trailed close behind.

By the time Heather caught up to them, they'd already reached the barn. A heavy chain and padlock bound the main doors together, but that seemed to be the least of Karla's concerns. She leaned her body against one door while pushing the other one out with her hands. The effort took up the slack in the chain and created a two-foot gap, which she easily squeezed through. She nodded for them to follow.

The vast room smelled of hay and dirt and old manure. The afternoon sun peeked through various cracks and holes in the building's plank walls, giving them plenty of light. A tractor with a missing front tire stood in the far right corner of the barn, and a dust-covered engine, trapped in chains and linked to a pulley, hung beside it from the ceiling. The other side of the room held three empty stalls and a set of wooden stairs that led up to darkness.

"Whose place is this?" Heather asked, then flinched at the volume of the echo.

Karla shrugged. "Don't know. Been coming out here off and on for about a year, and I've never met up with anybody. Nothing changes either, you know, like someone would be coming out here to take care of shit."

"Don't you get scared coming here all by yourself?" Haley asked.

A conniving smile spread across Karla's face. "Who said I came here alone?" She headed for the stairs. "Come on. I've got stuff we can sit on up there."

The loft was smaller than the lower section of the barn and just about as bare. On the floor to the right of the loft opening lay a narrow, stained mattress with a rumpled brown blanket at its foot. Beside the mattress sat a plastic crate that held a stubby candle, a box of matches, a can of Pepsi, and a crumpled Snickers wrapper.

"You sleep up here?" Heather asked, looking about warily. She imagined rats darting out of the shadows near the back of the room, snakes slithering out of the chinks in the walls, massive black widows creeping across the spiderwebs overhead. What she couldn't imagine was anyone sleeping in this barn at night on purpose, especially a girl.

"Sometimes, when I need to get away for a while." Karla placed the shoebox on the crate, then grabbed the blanket and spread it out over the dusty floor near the mouth of the loft. After straightening one of the corners of the blanket, she did a double take at the loft opening, then pointed. "Damn . . . look, you can see the Fest grounds from here."

Haley crept up beside her, Heather right behind.

"What's a Fest?" Heather asked. As she closed in on the hay portal, a chill zipped through her. One wrong step and she'd be free-falling twenty feet to a bed of weeds and hard-packed earth. She grasped a wooden beam that was nailed to the wall near the opening, then peered out. Way off in the distance, past the road they'd turned in on and a patch of piney woods, she caught the shimmer of what looked like silvery poles, many of them bunched together.

"Craft Fest. It's like a big hick show. They do shit like mule pulls and square dancing, fiddler contests—they even have a liars contest. That one's kinda cool. And there's lots of booths where people sell shit or show you how to make stuff, like quilts, flower arrangements, jewelry, crap like that. Almost everybody from Laidlaw goes."

"Why?" Haley asked. "It sounds sort of boring."

" 'Cause it's a place to hang out on the weekend, and there aren't many of those around here. They usually have a band or two, and someone's always shoving free food samples at you, so it's not so bad." Karla shook her head as though to clear it of thoughts, then picked up the shoebox again. "Anyway, let's sit over here where there's more light."

After they'd settled onto the blanket, legs

crossed beneath them, Karla opened the shoe-box and retrieved the ink pen and notebook. She placed the box beside her on the blanket, then opened the notebook to the page with the bloodstained stars. "So what do you want?" she asked, aiming the ink pen at Haley.

Haley's face brightened. "You mean we're gonna do it now . . . here?"

Karla tsked. "Duh."

Glancing over at Heather, Haley moistened her bottom lip with her tongue. "You first. What do you want?"

The sparkle of anticipation in Haley's eyes made Heather look away. She plucked a thread from the blanket. What she wanted was to get out of there, but she knew that wouldn't happen until this was done and Haley's curiosity was appeased. Maybe if she pretended to participate in the ritual and said something, anything, it would be over quicker. Then they'd be able to leave, and Haley would soon figure out all this crap was crap and drop the matter. Just in case there was any validity to Chaos, though, Heather figured she might as well give the pretense a decent shot. She looked up at her sister. "Okay, I want everything to go back to the way it was before Dad got sick."

Karla shook her head. "You can't do that. Remember what I said back at the house? You can't screw with time by asking for it to go backward or forward."

Heather frowned. "Okay, then I want our mom to get better."

As Karla started writing the request on the center of the page, Haley held up a hand. "Wait, what about the rest of it?" She turned to Heather. "I mean, I want Mom to get better, too, but if we're going to do this, it needs to be bigger. Mom'll need a job, money to pay the bills, and even if she got better, who's to say how long that will take? We could still be stuck here for a while and have to deal with a new school and no friends. Know what I'm saying? We've got to think of everything, not leave anything out. Like . . . we want to control everything and everyone that touches our lives."

Karla blew out a breath. "Girl, that's some really big shit. You need to start small. Don't forget the payback part of this deal."

"Yeah, but you said payback only came if it wasn't done right."

"So?"

"You plan on screwing this up?"

Karla shot her a hard look. "I'm not gonna screw up shit, but you might."

"How, when you're the one doing it?"

"I'm just showing you. Y'all still have to do the actual charging and feeding."

Haley pursed her lips.

"She's right," Heather said, kneading her fingers nervously. "We might mess up." She knew siding with Karla would delay them further, but she hadn't expected Haley to come up with such a huge request. Suppose Chaos *did* work and payback *was* real?

"We won't."

"I don't want to take the chance."

With a frustrated sigh, Haley dropped her head back and stared up at the ceiling. The silence that followed made Heather even more nervous. Their collective breathing sounded too loud, as did the wind blowing through the loft and the creaking, groaning wood that surrounded them. Time seemed to elongate, and they'd been here far too long already. She had to come up with a compromise, quick.

"What about this?" Heather said.

Haley eyed her wearily. "What?"

"We want everything and everyone we know to be fixed so no one will be unhealthy, unhappy, or poor."

"And you don't think *that's* big?"

"Yeah, it's big, but it's good big, right?" Heather looked from Haley to Karla, then back to her sister. "It's not like we're trying to be selfish and control everything for ourselves."

"Wait up," Haley shot back. "You saying I'm selfish?"

"No, no. I'm just saying if we focus on something that's good for everybody and we screw up, the payback might not be so bad."

Haley looked over at Karla. "That true?"

"I don't have a fucking clue. All I know is y'all are makin' me tired, so whatever. Just agree on what y'all want. The rest of the shit's gonna be on y'all anyway, not me."

A strange look crossed Haley's face, as if something significant had just occurred to her. "Okay, then we'll go with what Heather said."

Taken aback by her sister's sudden consent, Heather sat up straight. Needles of caution pricked the back of her neck. Haley never gave in that easily.

"All right," Karla said. "Say it again so I get it right."

Haley nudged Heather with an elbow. "Go ahead."

Heather clamped her hands together. Her thoughts volleyed between confronting Haley about her sudden agreement and simply repeating the request so they could leave. Leaving won. "We . . . we want everything and everyone we know to be fixed, so no one will be unhealthy, unhappy, or poor."

Karla wrote the request in the notebook. "Now I don't wanna hear no shit from y'all later if this comes back to bite you in the ass. I warned y'all, and that's the end of it." She started drawing lines through the sentence, crossing out all duplicate letters. When she was done, she wrote the remaining letters beneath the original request, capitalizing each one.

EVRYTHINGDKWBXSLOPAFU

"Shit," she said, drawing a circle around the letters. "This is too long. It's damn near the whole alphabet."

"What are you supposed to do with it?" Haley asked.

"Make a word from it that'll create an image in your head. It's like a secret code, a secret sign that represents your sigil. This just looks like fucking jumble, a word snake that doesn't mean—" Karla's eyes grew wide. "Whoa, that's it!" She pulled the notebook in close and began to scribble earnestly. After a minute or two, she turned the notebook around so it faced them. "Whadda ya think?"

Heather shrank back reflexively. Even drawn in ink, the image of the snake with its diamond-shaped head and protruding forked tongue looked ominous, ready to strike.

"Wow!" Haley reached for the notebook. "This is awesome."

Karla grinned. "You like?"

"Big time."

"It just kinda came to me when I was lookin' at that long-ass line of letters."

"You're really good. You should be like an artist or something."

"Yeah, well . . ." Karla reached into the shoe-box and pulled out a black permanent marker. "We'll have to use this since I don't do tattoos. My boyfriend, the one who taught me Chaos, did mine. I can hook y'all up if you want to make yours permanent later. He won't ask for IDs or nothing."

The look on Haley's face as she smiled at Karla was just short of adoration.

Karla uncapped the marker. "Who's first?"

"Me!" Haley scooted closer to her.

"Where do you want me to draw it? It needs to be someplace not too obvious. A place you can cover up quick if you have to."

"You mean you have to draw that snake *on* us?" Heather asked, aghast.

"Well, yeah."

"Why?"

" 'Cause you're not asking for a new pair of shoes. If you were, all we'd have to do is draw an image on this sheet of paper, chant, maybe smear a little more blood on the page, then burn the paper. Shoes wouldn't take a powerful sigil. All you'd have to do is make one, then forget about it. The sigil'd take care of the rest. This is different, though. It involves other people. Anytime you do that, you need to keep the image of your request, your sigil, close so you'll remember to feed it. Fewer chances of screwing up that way."

Heather chewed on her bottom lip. Instead of making the situation better, her request had only made things worse. Snakes drawn with a permanent marker? She wondered how long it would take for the black ink to fade from her skin. Maybe she could use one of Meemaw's Brillo pads to scrub it off once they got home.

"Put mine here," Haley said, rolling up the right sleeve of her blouse.

Karla studied her arm. "Since y'all are making the request together, y'all should put the symbol in the same place." She glanced over at Heather. "You okay with it going on your right arm, too?"

Heather didn't remember nodding, but she must have because Karla immediately started drawing on Haley's arm.

As the tip of the marker glided over skin, Karla's eyes narrowed and her voice took on a slow, deep cadence. "I call on the powers of earth and air, fire and water and spirit—give life to Haley and Heather's request. I invoke you, Dorchone, Gebura, Zamelle, spirits of want, need, and desire, to join forces with these sisters so life may be given to their request."

Heather glanced nervously about the room. It appeared darker now, colder.

"Now stand," Karla commanded.

A huge smile played over Haley's face as she got to her feet. She seemed wobbly, almost drunk.

Karla motioned Heather closer.

Fearing she would bolt from the room if she moved, Heather only stared at her. Karla tsked, got to her knees and inched toward her. Instead of asking Heather to lift her right shirtsleeve, Karla simply jerked up the material and started drawing. The marker tip felt cold and slick as it moved over her arm, and when Karla started chanting again, Heather tried blocking out her voice and the words by thinking about ice cream and puppies. The next thing she knew, Karla was telling her to stand.

Sensing the ritual was almost over, Heather quickly got to her feet. She stumbled back a step and gasped when she found herself only a couple of inches from the loft opening. With a whimper of fear, she held a hand out to her sister. Haley grabbed it and pulled her close.

"Okay, now comes the important part," Karla said. "You need to decide what you're going to do to charge your sigil. After that, y'all need to concentrate hard on what you want while repeating what I say. You're gonna have to stand side-by-side but facing opposite directions so your symbols touch. When you hear me say, 'So shall it be done!' repeat those words, then do what you need to do to charge your sigil. Got it?"

"Yeah, but I know I don't wanna cut," Haley said. "What else can I do?"

Karla pursed her lips and scanned the room. "You have to do something that either brings big-time pleasure, like wild sex, or something painful. Even doing something that scares the shit out of you would work. Since there're no guys here, though, and I'm not AC/DC, you're kinda limited to pain or fear." She peered into the shoebox. "My lighter and smokes are in here. I could fire up a cig, and you can burn yourself a few times with it if you want."

Heather felt her heart shudder to a stop. "Haley, no!"

Her sister scowled at her. "Quit being such a baby. For what we're asking, I think I can handle a few cigarette burns."

"I can't."

"You don't have to," Karla said. "That's one thing that doesn't have to match. You can pick whatever you want. Doesn't look like you're into pain, so pick something that scares you."

Heather immediately thought about her near fall from the loft a moment ago, but kept the thought hidden away. For all she knew, Karla would suggest she do a head-dive through the opening. "I'm scared of spiders and stuff, like those dark corners at the back of the loft."

"That's so lame," Haley said. "No way you're going to charge a sigil by walking into a dark corner."

"If it scares her enough, it'll work," Karla said.

Heather bit her tongue to keep from sticking it out at her sister like she used to do when they were kids. She wasn't exactly thrilled about creeping around the back of the loft, but she could manage a dark corner or two if she had to.

Karla pulled a cigarette out of the shoebox and puffed it to life with her Bic. After taking two deep drags, she nodded at them. "Okay, y'all stand right side to right side."

Heather quickly turned to face the loft opening so she could watch the dwindling afternoon instead of facing what was about to happen. Haley faced the opposite direction, her right arm touching Heather's right arm.

"Here," Karla said, and Heather glanced over in time to see her hand Haley the smoldering cigarette. "When I say, 'So shall it be done,' you burn whatever you've gotta burn. Heather, when she's done, you take off for the dark at the back of the loft. Both of you understand?"

Heather faced the afternoon, hoping the movement would pass for a nod. As she turned, she caught a glimpse of Haley nodding enthusiastically.

"Now y'all close your eyes and concentrate on what you want," Karla said. "Concentrate hard."

Closing her eyes, Heather listened to the drone of the voice beside her.

"Think about your request in as much detail as you can, then picture your symbol in your head. Think of your symbol and your request as one. Your symbol *is* your request. Your request *is* your symbol. One can't be separated from the other. Now repeat after me and repeat it like you mean it. . . . All elementals and desired spirits, we command you to gather now."

As Haley echoed the words, Heather squeezed her eyes shut tighter. Within seconds she heard Karla's voice near her left ear. "You gotta say it, too, Heather. Not just Haley."

Heather bit the inside of her left cheek and nodded.

"All right then, we're gonna start over." Karla's voice kicked up a notch in volume. "All elementals and desired spirits, we command you to gather now."

This time Heather repeated the words with Haley, but she focused hard on her old life. On her mother happy and dancing across their living room floor—

"To leave your present receptacles . . ."

—her father picking pecans with them in the park—

". . . and enter this world to perform your task according to my will."

—family vacations at the beach—

"Heed our voices and go forth as commanded."

—sleepovers with friends—

"So shall it be heard."

—Christmas parties and ham.

"So shall it be done!"

As their echoed response reverberated through the barn, Heather felt Haley twist to the left, then she heard the sizzle of fire against flesh and her sister sucking air through her teeth. Heather's eyes welled with tears as the horrible sounds came again, then again. She was about to scream for Haley to stop when she heard her sister's voice, ragged and breathless, near her ear. "Your turn."

Heather opened her eyes but didn't move. Cigarette smoke and scorched meat—the union of those scents was the breath of monsters. Monsters who lived in the dark. She wasn't going back there. She couldn't go into the dark.

"Go!" Haley insisted.

"I . . . I can't."

"You have to, or it won't work!"

Heather glanced down at her feet. "I don't care. I—"

Someone suddenly shoved hard against Heather's back, and she pitched forward. In an instant, she saw the lip of the loft opening rise up to meet her.

Then she was falling . . . twisting, screaming, falling . . . seeing sky and trees, dirt and the loft—

And Haley smiling down at her.

CHAPTER THREE

Bane Road wound past a large cow pasture, two alfalfa fields, and an oxidation pond that was capped with puke-green algae before it met up with Buck and Nadine Thurston's graveled driveway. A couple hundred feet beyond the drive stood a beige clapboard house with a wide front porch flanked by crepe myrtles. Haley chewed a fingernail when she spotted her grandfather leaning against the porch railing, his hands in his overall pockets. They were well over an hour late, and Buck Thurston looked none too happy about it.

Karla braked at the end of the drive, and the Neon shuddered to a stop. She nodded toward the house. "That your papaw?"

"Yeah," Haley said, opening the front passenger door.

"He looks pissed."

"He always looks that way." Haley turned

toward Heather, who sat in the back. "Think you can walk?"

Heather gave her a pained look. "Yeah, I can walk, no thanks to you. I still can't believe you pushed me like that. I could've broken my neck."

"But you didn't break your neck. Besides, I had to do something. You wouldn't move."

"Of course I didn't move, not after the stupid—"

"Hey, y'all need to hold the arguing for later," Karla said. "Looks like Papaw's on his way over here."

Haley looked back and saw her grandfather lumbering down the porch steps. Stump, an old coonhound with one blue eye, one brown eye, and a deformed tail the length of a hotdog wiener, trailed after him. Not wanting to chance a confrontation in front of Karla, Haley scrambled out of the car, then waited for Heather to do the same.

As soon as the car doors slammed shut, Karla backed the car onto Bane and sped away. Haley watched the cloud of dust in the driveway diminish and wished they were back at the barn. She wanted to try charging the sigil again. Although Karla had tried to convince her otherwise during the drive over here, Haley was certain the first charge hadn't taken. Other than the burns above her right hip, she felt no different from when they'd started. A little more brazen maybe, what with her shoving Heather out of the loft. She still didn't know what had come over her

back there. One second she was listening to her
sister's protests about going into the dark, and
the next she sent Heather flying out of the barn.
The weirdest part was she didn't even feel bad
about pushing her. Weird or not, though, she
was thankful that the only damage Heather appeared to suffer was a few scratches, a sprained
ankle, and a bad case of the red-ass.

The sudden blast of a car horn made Haley
jump, and she spotted Mark Aikman taking a left
into his driveway across the street. He waved,
and she quickly smiled and waved back. Mr. Aikman wasn't only a neighbor; he was the hunkiest
art teacher at Laidlaw High. He had collar-
length blond hair, dark chocolate eyes, a slender
build, and a smile that turned just about every
female in school into a puddle of melted butter.
As far as Haley knew, Aikman had only two
strikes against him. He was twenty years older
than she was, and he was already engaged to and
living with Jasmine Deshotel, a petite brunette
who worked at Laidlaw as a gym teacher.

Letting out a heavy sigh, Haley turned her attention back to her grandfather. When she noticed his deep scowl, she inched closer to
Heather until their shoulders touched. Papaw
had never laid a hand on them before, but she
was all too aware that there was a first time for
everything.

Even at seventy-three, Buck Thurston looked
intimidating. He stood well over six feet tall and
had a barrel chest and thick white hair that he

combed straight back. His weathered face carried deep lines and liver spots and one wrinkly dimple on his right cheek. Arthritis caused him to limp slightly, and Haley suspected that the pain was responsible for the perpetual pissed-off look in his lake-blue eyes.

"Sorry we're late, Papaw," Heather offered as he drew nearer.

Buck grunted, his eyes fixed on the Neon now disappearing around a bend. "That girl from 'round here?"

"Not far from here, I think," Haley said. She poked Heather in the ribs with an inconspicuous finger, eager to get out of questioning range.

Buck eyed her. "Not far where?"

Haley shrugged. "All I know is she goes to our school, so I guess she lives somewhere between there and here. You know, not far."

The three of them stood in silence for a moment, and Haley looked away, unable to handle the probing in her grandfather's eyes. They reminded her so much of her father's, only older, wiser, and equipped with a bullshit meter. Sweat trickled down her sides from under her arms.

Stump broke the silence with a loud chuff, and Haley smiled, grateful for the distraction. She held out a hand to him. The dog glanced up at Buck as though to get permission, then ambled toward her. After only a few steps, he came to an abrupt halt, and the stiff hair on his back stood on end. He lowered his head, and a deep growl rolled from the back of his throat.

Haley frowned. "What's wrong, boy?" She squatted, intending to meet his eyes. The movement evidently startled Stump because he yipped as though slapped, then tucked his tail between his legs and ran back to the house. She saw him disappear behind the crepe myrtles.

"What's with him?" Heather asked. "I've never seen Stump act that way before." She limped forward a couple steps and whistled for the dog. He didn't respond.

Buck's eyebrows knitted into one white, hairy caterpillar. "You wasn't gimpin' like that this mornin'. What happened?"

Heather looked up at him, wide-eyed. "Huh?"

"You're walkin' all hunched over, like a cat tryin' to pass a peach pit, and I wanna know how come." He aimed his chin at her legs. "And them scratches wasn't on your legs this mornin' neither. What happened?"

"She fell at cheerleading practice, Papaw," Haley said quickly. "The school nurse checked her out, though. She's all right."

Buck's eyes bore into them as if searching for truth. Another long, silent moment passed before he finally sucked on his front teeth and nodded once. "A'ight then. Guess you two bes' go inside and wash up. See if your meemaw needs help with supper."

"Yes, sir." Before he had time to say more, Haley grabbed Heather by the hand and pulled her down the drive to the house. Her sister hissed in pain as they hurried along.

As they reached the porch, Haley caught the

aroma of fried chicken and blackberry cobbler, and it made her mouth water.

"That was close with Papaw," Heather whispered.

Haley nodded. "Too close." She opened the screen door, then held a finger to her lips, signaling for Heather to be quiet as they went into the house.

Nadine Thurston stood near a counter in the kitchen, cutting cornbread into single-serving squares. She hummed as she worked, her eggplant-shaped body, decked all in pink polyester, swaying from side to side. Haley didn't recognize the tune, but she would have bet money it was a gospel.

Heather dropped her book bag on a chair near the kitchen table, and Nadine gasped and whirled about. The dark gray hairpiece she wore to give her bouffant more height jiggled, then settled on top of her head slightly askew.

"Merciful Lord, y'all scared me!"

Heather quickly snatched up her bag as if doing so would reverse the effect. "Didn't mean to, Meemaw. Sorry."

Nadine leaned against the counter and patted a hand against her chest. "It's all right, puddin'. Your ol' meemaw's ticker'll settle down here in a minute." She pointed toward the archway that separated the kitchen from the living room. "Where's y'all little friend? Didn't she come in?"

"What little—"

"Karla couldn't stay," Haley said, shooting her

sister a warning glance. "She had chores to take care of at home."

Nadine's jowls drooped with disappointment. "Well, next time be sure to tell her she's welcome to stay to supper. Wouldn't've been nothin' for me to throw more chicken into the deep fryer."

Haley knew more chicken in the fryer meant enough food to feed a tri-state area. If there was one thing Nadine Thurston believed in, it was 'just in case' cooking. There always had to be enough on the table, just in case Brother Gerald from Passon Baptist dropped by, just in case those hoity-toity ladies from the prayer group showed up—just in case a battalion of starving marines popped in. Even now, the table held enough food for the entire population of Mississippi and a decent swath of Louisiana—golden brown chicken, buttered corn on the cob, mustard greens sprinkled with bacon bits, fried okra, sweet peas, and cornbread. Two pans of blackberry cobbler sat on the side counter near the can opener and coffeepot.

"We'll make sure to tell her," Haley said, and Heather nodded in agreement.

Nadine smiled broadly, showing off a set of dentures with wide, fake gums. "So how'd y'all do with your cheerleadin'?"

Heather lowered her head and hobbled off toward the refrigerator.

"Heavens, you hurt?" Nadine's face crumbled into a pile of worry.

"I'm all right," Heather said. "Just sprained my ankle a little. No big deal. We have any Coke?"

"No Coke, honey. Sweet tea's in the clear pitcher, and root beer's in the plastic jug, but it ain't got no fizz like you young'uns are used to. It's the extract kind. You sure you're okay?"

"Positive."

Nadine gave her a little nod, then turned her attention back to Haley. "So y'all done good at your practice?"

Haley adjusted the straps of her book bag so she wouldn't have to look directly at her grandmother. Her right arm suddenly began to itch, right where Karla had drawn the snake. She rubbed her left hand over the spot, being careful not to lift her shirtsleeve in the process. "I guess so. We won't know whether we made the squad, though, until next week."

"Anybody else want some?" Heather asked from the fridge. She held up the clear pitcher.

"Me," Haley said, jumping on the diversion. She went to a cupboard near the sink, removed two glasses, then joined her sister at the fridge. They exchanged eye rolls.

"Need any help with supper before we go start on our homework, Meemaw?" Haley asked as Heather filled the glasses with tea. Homework was another lie, but a necessary one. It was the only excuse that carried enough weight to get them out of chores, and Haley wanted to get her sister alone so they could talk about what had happened at the barn. If she handled the discussion right, she might be able to talk Heather into trying to charge the sigil again. Only this time it would be just the two of them, and they wouldn't have to do it in a creepy old barn.

Nadine waved a dismissive hand. "Y'all go on and tend to your schoolin'. Supper's about done anyway. I'll call y'all when it's time to eat."

Haley nodded, smiled, then grabbed Heather by the arm and yanked her out of the kitchen.

As soon as they reached their bedroom at the opposite end of the house, Heather pulled out of Haley's grasp. "You've gotta quit dragging me around like that." She dropped her book bag on the floor near the dresser, then sat on the edge of one of the twin beds and peeled off her right sneaker and sock. A blue-black knot the size of a walnut sat on the inside of her ankle. She ran a finger over it. "Man, I still can't believe you pushed me out of that loft."

Haley threw her bag into the closet, then gave her right arm a good scratching. "Do we have to get into that again?" She lifted her shirtsleeve and noticed a red, scaly patch had formed around the snake's head.

"What if I'd done that to you?"

"So you can do it to me next time."

Heather's head jerked to attention, and she wagged a finger at her. "Huh-uh, sistah, there ain't gonna be a next time. Why would you even want to go through that again anyway?"

" 'Cause I don't think the first time took."

"Good."

"Don't say that."

"Too late, already did." Heather pulled off her other sneaker and tossed it in the direction of the closet. It bounced off the wall with a loud *thunk*. "You know, I can't believe I even let you talk me into getting involved with that stupid crap in the first place."

Haley glared at her. "It's not stupid."

"Yeah, it is, and so was burning yourself and pushing me out of the loft. Can't you see that? All that yak about powerful sigils and look what we've got—cigarette burns, a twisted ankle, and now that ugly red splotch on your arm that's got you scratching like Stump when he's flea-bit. You're probably allergic to the damn ink that was in that marker."

"So I'll take some Benadryl."

Heather let out an exasperated sigh, then leaned back on the bed, propping herself up with an elbow. "Fine, whatever, but all that's going to change is the itching—if you're lucky."

"Whadda you mean?"

"I'm saying Chaos magic is whacked."

"No, it's not!"

"Look, I know how much you wanted it to work and everything, and I understand why, but, Haley, it's not real. All that's going to change if you keep messing with it is you—and it won't be in a good way. You're either going to wind up seriously hurt or dead from all the stupid stuff Karla says you have to do to keep up with it. You hear what I'm saying?"

Anger thudded in Haley's chest like an extra heartbeat. "If Chaos isn't real, then how do you explain Karla being so popular at school? It sure isn't because of her looks or her family's money."

Heather shrugged. "Maybe she puts out a lot, or maybe people are just scared of her because she's weird."

"That's stupid. If they were afraid, they'd stay away from Karla, not hang out with her."

"Not if they thought she'd cast a spell on them or something if they didn't do what she wanted."

Haley blew out a raspberry. "Get real."

"That *is* real. Karla could easily be screwing with other kids' heads like she did with ours."

Not wanting to hear any more, Haley stormed over to the bedroom window and slapped her palms down on the sill. She rested her forehead against the pane, trying hard not to cry. Chaos had to be real. It *had* to be. Without it, she'd be back to where she was before she'd met Karla, having no hope of ever returning to her old life. Haley refused to accept that. No matter what it took, she'd find a way to make her sigil work, and she figured the best place to start was back at the beginning. What had they messed up? What had they done or not done that kept it from working the first time?

She turned to Heather. "Over at the barn, when we had to repeat the chant Karla gave us, did you concentrate on what we wanted, like she said? Did you really try?"

Heather dropped her gaze and stretched out flat on the bed. "Yeah, I concentrated."

The words zapped Haley's ear like a bee sting, and she instinctively knew Heather was lying or telling a half truth. It didn't really matter which because either would have kept the magic from working. Knowing her sister, her own flesh and blood, had sabotaged the conjuration made Haley tremble with rage. She balled her hands into fists, wanting to pound Heather, split her lip for lying, bust her teeth for making her believe she'd go through with the Chaos ritual in the first place. The need to feel blood and teeth against her knuckles became so strong it forced a groan from Haley's lips. She headed for her sister and was halfway across the room when Heather sat up on the bed.

"What's the matter with you?" Heather asked, frowning.

Haley paused midstep. *What the hell am I doing?* She'd fought with Heather before but never with blows, no matter how heated the argument. And they'd had some mega-battles in the past, many much bigger than this. So why was she all wired up to hit her now?

Because she screwed up the plans you had to take control of your life, that's why.

The thought seemed to come out of nowhere, and it urged Haley forward. Why couldn't her sister see they needed to take absolute control over their lives? Haley *knew* that was the answer to all their problems. Control had been all she'd focused on when they'd chanted—control over everything and everyone. To her, the request was only a shade darker than the sappy one Heather had made, so she'd concentrated extra hard, hoping they'd end up with what she wanted. But that didn't happen. Nothing happened. And all because Heather hadn't bothered to live up to her part of the deal. Her sister's selfishness had left her with nothing—except more anger.

As she drew closer, Heather's expression shifted from confused to fearful. "Haley, what's wrong?"

The fear in her eyes sent a bolt of energy through Haley that nearly made her stumble. She'd never felt anything so exhilarating. Causing fear in someone, now *that* was power . . . *that* was control. She grinned and stepped up to the foot of the bed. "What makes you think something's wrong?"

Heather scooted back on the bed, her eyes wide and worried. She pointed, her finger stabbing the air again and again. " 'Cause look—God, look at your shirt!"

Haley blinked, suddenly confused. In that instant, the fury she'd felt toward her sister disappeared. She no longer wanted to hit Heather. All she wanted to do now was rip the skin from her own right arm so the itching would stop. She reached over, ready to rake her fingernails over her skin, and froze.

Her right shirtsleeve was soaked with blood, and a bright red trail ran from the hem of the sleeve to her elbow. She looked over at Heather, hoping for an explanation. When none came, Haley carefully lifted the bloody material to peek beneath it.

That's when she saw a droplet of blood fall from the snake's forked tongue—and the slight flicker of its tail.

CHAPTER FOUR

Mark Aikman stood under his carport, scratching the light stubble on his chin. He'd meant to shave right after breakfast but had gotten sidetracked when he heard the persistent yap of a dog. He'd peeked out his kitchen window to see what the ruckus was about and saw Stump, Buck Thurston's hound, running erratically in their front yard while Buck slammed a shovel against the ground. Five minutes later, when he'd peered out the window again, Stump was still barking, and Buck was still hammering dirt. Curiosity had forced Mark outside, but even from here, he couldn't make out what the two were after.

He thought about going over to see if Buck needed help but hesitated. They'd been neighbors for the past six years, and if he'd learned anything during that time, it was that Buck

Thurston didn't take kindly to anyone sticking their nose in his business unless asked. And he rarely, if ever, asked.

A few high-powered expletives flew from the Thurston yard as Buck repeatedly stabbed the ground with the shovel blade, all the while yelling for Stump to shut up. Mark had heard Buck curse before, but nothing stronger than a shit or damn. Whatever was going on over there had to be serious.

He decided to chance a reprimand. "Need help?"

Instead of acknowledging him, Buck pivoted and batted a crepe myrtle with the shovel. The momentum of the swing nearly turned him completely around. Stump danced beside him, yapping and snapping at the ground.

Mark stepped out from under his carport and cupped his hands around his mouth so his voice would travel farther. "You need help?"

This time Buck's head snapped up, and he turned toward him. "You got a machete or a pistol?" he shouted.

A pistol? "No, but I've got a shovel."

"Bring it!"

Dressed only in gray sweatpants and a white T-shirt, Mark hurried to the storage room at the back of the carport. He dug past old bicycle parts, scraps of crown molding left over from last summer's remodeling project, two empty gas cans, and a half-bald broom before he finally found his shovel. The blade was rusted, the top of the handle chipped. Certainly not worth squat for digging, but slamming? Definitely. He grabbed it, spotted a pair of tattered deck shoes, shoved his feet into them, then ran over to Buck's.

As soon as he reached the Thurston property, Mark came to a sliding halt in the graveled drive. Buck, dressed in jeans and bare-chested, was stabbing the ground again, only this time Mark saw what he was after—a diamondback rattler, at least six feet long. It had already been chopped in two, but both halves writhed and twisted in and out of tight coils. Buck did another bayonet thrust and severed its head.

Although the rattler was impressive, it wasn't the only thing that had yanked Mark to a dead stop. It was the twenty to thirty other snakes of varying colors and lengths squirming in the yard. Some had already been cut into pieces, others had smashed heads, and still others looked whole and very much alive.

Not bothering to wait for instructions, Mark took off for the slithering reptiles that had yet to meet up with Buck's shovel. He whacked and stabbed with his own weapon, feeling the give of flesh and bone travel up the handle. He soon felt like a pinwheel, spinning in place as he tried to see everywhere at once. A black-and-gray striped ribbon snake slithered over his foot, and he kicked out with a loud grunt and sent it flying toward the road. As he watched it sail, Mark felt a heavy crawling sensation around his left ankle. One glance confirmed his fear. A milk snake was wrapping its four-foot-long body around his an-

kle and lower leg. Under different circumstances, like viewing it through a glass cage,
Mark might have marveled at the deep red and
brown splotches covering its thick, gray body
and the black-and-white checked pattern of its
belly. But right now he didn't give a damn if
those shiny, keeled scales were swirled in bright
purple and chartreuse. He just wanted the sono-
fabitch off his leg.

Instinctively, he thrust the shovel blade into
the section of snake still on the ground, severing
it, then stomped and kicked and bashed the
back of the shovel blade against his leg until the
top half of the reptilian bastard let go. Once
freed, a rush of adrenaline sent Mark hunting
for more. This time he didn't bother checking
whether a snake was alive or operating on nerve
impulse. He just slammed and jabbed until nothing moved anymore. Only then did he allow his
gaze to leave the ground.

"I think we got 'em all," Buck said. He stood
near the porch, his face and chest glistening
with sweat, his shovel blade on the head of a
multicolored snake. Stump sat on the porch,
panting.

Mark went over to Buck and toed the lifeless
tail beside his blade. "Jesus, that looks like a
coral."

"Could be a king. Some's got the same colors."

"I don't think so. See how the red and yellow
bands touch? That's how you can tell it's a coral.
I learned a rhyme in Boy Scouts that helped me

remember—red touch yellow, kill a fellow; red touch black, venom lack."

Buck turned his head and spat a stream of saliva on the ground. "A'ight, guess it's a coral then."

"You just walk up on all this when you came out this morning?"

"Nope." Buck pointed to a flowerbed that circled a pine tree in the middle of the lawn. "See that right there? Came out to put fertilizer 'round it, and that's when I seen the first one, all curled up tight in the pansies. I hadn't finished up killin' that one 'fore another comes slitherin' 'cross the yard. 'Fore I knew it, they was everywhere. Only up here, though, not the side yards or out back."

"Any idea where they came from?"

"Nope. The varmints just kept showin' up, all of 'em headin' for the house. It was like somebody was tossin' 'em in the yard from the road every time I turned my back. Thing is, I never seen a one of 'em *on* the road." Buck shook his head. "Dang if I can fig're it." He pulled the shovel out of his last victim, then scooped the limp body into the blade.

"I can help clear the yard if you'd like," Mark offered, knowing full well he'd be late for work if he stuck around much longer. Being late didn't seem to matter, though. He felt a kinship to Buck, one forged by battle.

"Nah, I got it," Buck said, scooping up another snake. "Bes' you go check your yard, too. 'Preciate you comin' and all."

"Anytime."

Looking slightly embarrassed, Buck nodded and turned away, his attention already on another corpse.

Mark didn't press him for more conversation. He headed back to his house, all the while wondering where the snakes might have come from and knowing if he *ever* saw another one it would be too soon.

As soon as he crossed over to his own property, Mark scanned the lawn, then breathed a sigh of relief when he didn't see anything slithering. He glanced back at the Thurstons'. Except for Buck scooping up dead snakes, everything appeared normal. He was about to turn away and head into the house when something on their roof caught his eye.

A silvery-white haze wavered above the center of the roofline, like heat waves on sun-baked asphalt. Puzzled, Mark rubbed his eyes with his palms. It was barely seventy degrees outside, how could it be a heat wave? Dropping his hands, he squinted for a better look.

It was still there—a gauzy veil—quivering, shimmering, distorting the world beyond it.

Haley winced as she pressed another wad of toilet tissue against the cut in her upper right thigh. She'd cut deeper than she'd intended, and the wound wouldn't stop bleeding. But she didn't care about the blood. *Something* had happened when she'd cut. Something real and unquestionable. Not like yesterday, when her sister had spent an hour trying to convince her that the blood on her arm was the result of excessive scratching and the twitch of the snake's tail a figment of her imagination. This was definitely different, although Haley wasn't quite sure why.

Maybe her concentration level had been greater this morning, more so than yesterday at the barn. Maybe being alone instead of with Karla and Heather had allowed her to focus more intently when she'd chanted. Whatever the reason, the moment the broken end of the disposable razor tore through her skin, Haley's vision had blurred like someone had thrown cheesecloth over her eyes. Then something coiled up tight in the center of her gut until she felt like a windup toy poised for action. Her fingers had grown cold, too. So cold it had been difficult for her to hang on to the blade and keep cutting. But she had, and as the wound widened, the chill had traveled throughout her body, making her teeth chatter. She was much warmer now, and her vision had cleared, but she still felt the coiling sensation in her stomach. Surely that had to mean the sigil was charged now.

Eager to see if she looked any different, Haley held the tissue against her thigh and went over to the mirror above the sink.

Dressed only in panties and bra, she cocked her head and examined her reflection. Same muddy brown eyes. Same unruly, strawberry-blond hair. Her nose was still too small for her face and her lips too thin. Her right collar bone still stuck out a little farther than the one on the left and even with the aid of pads, she still barely managed to fill a B cup. Everything about her body looked the same, incredibly boring—until she turned slightly to the left.

The swelling that had started yesterday around the snake's head was much worse now, giving the drawing a near 3-D appearance. It no longer itched, and the tongue didn't drip blood. But the body—God, the body was changing. Instead of the soft, flowing lines of yesterday's drawing, the snake's body now had deep curves, like it was preparing to coil, to pull itself in tight. Grinning, Haley ran a finger over it and felt intense heat pulsing from her skin.

A knock at the door startled her.

"Haley, I need to get in there," Heather called, knocking again.

"Go away, I'm busy."

"What're you doing?"

"Nothing." Haley checked the wound on her thigh and saw the bleeding had finally stopped. She tossed the tissue into the toilet and flushed.

"I need to get in there."

"Go use the half-bath by the kitchen."

"My brush and hair gel's in this one."

"Use my brush. It's on the dresser." Haley opened the medicine cabinet and found gauze for her wound but no tape.

The knocking grew persistent. "You know I can't do my hair without gel. It gets all frizzy."

"I *said* I'm busy. Go—"

"Girls, y'all get on over here. Them grits is gettin' cold." Meemaw's shrill voice sounded insistent and not far away.

Haley heard a loud *tsk,* then the squeak of sneakers hurrying down the hall. She went to the door and pressed an ear against it. Low voices filtered in from a distance, but no sound came from the hallway.

Gauze in hand, she opened the bathroom door, peered out to confirm all was clear, then sprinted across the hall and into her bedroom.

It took a while before she found Scotch Tape, and Haley worried her grandmother would come barging in at any moment, looking for her. She quickly bandaged her thigh, looping the tape around her leg a couple of times to make sure the gauze stayed in place. Then she threw on her school clothes, ran a brush through her hair, and hurried out of the bedroom.

Right before she reached the entrance to the kitchen, Haley adjusted the sleeve of her blouse to make sure the snake was covered. Her thigh burned and ached horribly, but she gritted her teeth and forced herself to walk straight and even as she made her way to the kitchen table. No sooner did she settle into a chair beside Heather, than Meemaw handed her a small bowl of grits.

"Where's Papaw?" Haley asked, noting the empty chair at the head of the table. Ever since the first day she and Heather had moved in, their grandfather had insisted everyone eat together during meals. She didn't care about the break in mandate, but she wanted him here so she could test-drive her sigil. She planned on starting with something simple, like getting Papaw to say yes when she asked to go to Craft Fest. If most of the kids from Laidlaw were going on Saturday, she wanted to go, too, especially with Karla. She hadn't discussed Craft Fest with Heather yet, but Haley assumed she'd go as well since they rarely went anywhere separately. That made her a little nervous. Given her sister's current negative attitude toward Chaos and Karla, she hoped Heather wouldn't turn into a giant pain in the ass and ruin their fun. As for Chaos, getting their grandfather's permission for Craft Fest would be her first proof that her sigil worked.

"I seen him diggin' 'round in the shed out back earlier," Meemaw said. "But that was a while ago. Don't know where he went off to after that." Her blue polyester pants made swishing sounds as she carried eggs, bacon, and biscuits from the stove to the table.

Trying not to let her disappointment show, Haley spooned grits into her mouth. The food had barely passed her throat when the tight, coiled-up feeling in her stomach returned, stronger than before. It took all she had not to double over.

"Why you askin'? You need him for somethin'?"

Fighting nausea, Haley kept her answer short. "No."

Heather's face suddenly appeared in her periphery. "You all right?" she whispered.

Haley shook her head slowly. She felt like crap.

"What's wrong, hon? You sick?" Meemaw peered at her from across the table. "You lookin' a bit green around the gills. Want me to get you some med'cine?"

The thought of swallowing anything, even saliva, made Haley's stomach cramp even more. She felt her throat tighten and tasted a hint of bile. With a groan, she bolted from her chair and ran for the bathroom.

She only made it as far as the hallway.

Bile and undigested grits shot from her mouth and splattered across the hardwood floor. She leaned against a wall, retching over and over until she thought she'd vomit a kidney.

"Oh, you poor baby!" Meemaw's voice sounded distant, but Haley felt her wide, warm hand on her shoulder. "Heather, go fetch a towel, honey, quick. Grab one of them old ones down in that little cabinet by the commode. Oh, and fetch a wet washrag for your sister's face, too."

Haley heard the pound and squeak of sneakers as Heather rushed off. She felt her grandmother's hand, strong yet gentle as she rubbed soothing circles on her back. The motion quieted the nausea, and Haley closed her eyes, grateful for the respite. She wondered if she'd caught some kind of stomach flu or if she'd picked up an infection from the cigarette burns. She thought of the swelling on her right arm and how fevered it had felt to her touch. Had her arm gotten infected somehow? Was that why she felt so bad? Karla hadn't mentioned anything about Chaos making a person sick, unless it was part of a payback. But that couldn't be her problem. She hadn't done anything yet to deserve a payback—or had she?

More pounding and squeaking, coming toward her this time.

"Here."

Haley opened her eyes. Heather stood in front of her, holding out a wet washcloth. Meemaw was already sopping up vomit from the floor with towels, humming all the while. Haley took the washcloth and pressed it to her face. The cool dampness felt wonderful against her skin. She held it there, breathing in deep. It wasn't until she heard a sharp, short gasp that she lowered the rag.

Heather was leaning against a nearby wall, bug-eyed, one hand clamped over her mouth. The finger she pointed trembled so badly, for a moment, Haley wasn't even sure what she was pointing at. Then she felt it, a squirming, crawling sensation at the top of her right arm. Fear sent her pulse rate into quadruple digits, and she had to make herself look down. What she saw damn near stopped her heart. If this was a figment of her imagination, then, judging from Heather's horrified expression, she was having the same delusion.

The snake's body still hid beneath her shirt sleeve, only now it pushed against the material, its squirming, writhing outline all too visible.

CHAPTER FIVE

It hadn't washed off. Hadn't even faded.

Not that he really expected it to disappear, but hoping it would had become a habit, something he'd done every day for the last seventeen years.

And old habits died hard.

Caster reached for a towel and dried his hands. As usual, he gave the image on the back of his right hand a hard rub, knowing full well it wouldn't make a difference. Wet or dry, freshly scrubbed or left to the wear of years, it always looked as vivid as the day Toussant had drawn it—crimson, crude, and constant. Or so it would seem to the average person, one who saw only the surface of life and defined it by appearance. In truth, he bore an ouroboros of unrest. A sigil of atrocity. The necrosis of hope.

He wondered, as he did every time he washed his hands, what his life might have been like had Toussant never marked him. Would he be mar-

ried? Have his own home and children? Would
he have friends to laugh with, dreams to cling
to? Would his father still be alive? Or would
Caster have shot him anyway?

Sighing, Caster tossed the towel into the sink
and shook off his musings. Just like scrubbing
his hand, dreaming of what might have been was
useless, and it depressed him. He didn't want to
be sucked into those dark shadows today. If anything, he should be celebrating. According to
the message left on his cell phone this morning,
a long overdue adventure awaited him, and it
was only ninety miles away. All he had to do was
drive out there and set up shop. His clingy, self-
appointed protégé would handle the rest.

Thinking about the possibilities that lay ahead,
Caster left the bathroom with a spring in his
step. He had one item left to load up, and then
he'd be set to go. If his van didn't give him problems, he'd easily make the trip in an hour and a
half, two hours max, which would put him there
ahead of schedule. He'd have plenty of time to
toss his little protégé a thank-you bone. In fact, if
she did as good a job as she claimed she did, he
might toss her that bone a couple of times. *Got to
keep the help happy.*

Once in the living room, he collected a
gallon-size jar that sat on the floor near the
couch. Inside the jar, a three-eyed cat sloshed
around in formaldehyde, its small face settling
against the glass. Caster tucked the jar in the
crook of his left arm, quickly scanned the room

to make sure he hadn't forgotten anything, then headed outside.

Humming a mindless tune, he had just reached the front steps of the duplex when he heard the twang of his landlord's voice.

"What the hell you got there, Morbadelli?" Ray Talbot waddled toward him from the opposite end of the long porch, hands perched on mountainous hips. His head bobbled as he ducked and stretched to get a better look. "Sumbitch! That there's a cat, ain't it? You got a cat in that jar!"

Caster's shoulders slumped. He hadn't been prepared for Talbot. Normally the man stayed glued to his couch in the adjoining apartment and only came out of hibernation on the first of each month, when the rent was due. Caster turned to him reluctantly. "Yeah."

Ray came to an abrupt halt, a look of disgust settling over his face. "Why the hell would you put a cat in a goddamn jar?"

"A vet did. I just bought it."

"Why?"

Caster cocked his head, feigning confusion. "Why'd the vet pickle it, or why'd I buy it?"

Red streaks grew on Ray's cheeks like mercury strips on a thermometer. "Like it makes a shit bucket's bit of difference! Who'n the hell'd do either?"

"Me. It draws people to my trade booth." Stifling a grin, Caster took hold of the jar with both hands and aimed it at him. "Wanna closer look? It's got three eyes."

Ray threw his hands up. "Oh, *hell*, no! Get that shit outta my face!"

With a laugh, Caster hopped off the last step and walked toward his van, which was parked under the side portico of the duplex.

"You're a weird sumbitch, Morbadelli, you know that?" Ray shouted after him.

Caster snorted. Weird wasn't even the half of it. If his rotund, shit-for-brains landlord ever figured out just how 'weird' his tenant was, he'd probably summon every cop in Forrest County.

County. The term still seemed strange to Caster. Up until a year and a half ago, when Hurricane Katrina had forced him to grab his few meager belongings and flee New Orleans, he'd lived in a parish, listened to street jazz, and ate food that assailed the human tongue with near orgasmic power. Hattiesburg, Mississippi, offered no such luxuries. Here one lived in counties, suffered through endless country-western music, and ate haute cuisine that held all the allure of Elmer's glue. He supposed he should have been grateful, though. Katrina had ripped close to a million people out of the Big Easy, and many of them were still roaming the country seeking permanent shelter. At least he had a place to live. Chance and a partially clogged fuel filter had led him to Ray's roach-infested duplex. He'd been stuck there ever since.

Having reached the van, Caster opened the back cargo doors and placed the jar into a Styrofoam-padded crate. He shoved the crate against a side panel, then took inventory of the surrounding boxes, ticking their contents off with his fingers.

Candles, shrunken heads, posters . . . jewelry, in-cense, powders, leather chokers . . . ceramic totems . . . doodads, doodits, blah, blah, blah . . .

Satisfied that he had everything loaded, Caster closed the cargo doors, then went around to the front of the van, opened the door, and slipped into the driver's seat. He sat for a moment, soaking in a bit of satisfaction. He wasn't going to another festival or flea market just to sell trinkets. This trip was different. It would be like the old days, when he'd worked at Curious Goods.

Thinking about the little curio shop made him ache for the hustle and bite of the city. New Orleans had been his home since birth, and he understood the rhythm of her heartbeat as well as he knew his own. He loved how she'd coaxed tourists onto her uninhibited, neon-lit streets—the same streets he'd lived on since age eleven, not long after he'd killed his father. He'd spent years trying to convince himself that the shooting had been an accident, but he knew better. He always had. Some dogs had to be put down, that's all. *Especially ones that kept pining for bitches who wouldn't come home, despite the sacrifice of a finger. Especially the ones who took their pain out on their sons.*

Moments after he'd pulled the trigger, Caster instinctively knew he had to disappear before the police or social services found him. So he'd taken to the streets of New Orleans and hidden in her large bosom. There he'd suckled hungrily, eager to absorb whatever nourishment she offered. From his street siblings, most much older than he, Caster learned how to dance so people threw money at his feet, steal clothes from Goodwill and Laundromats, find food without mold, sleep in deserted, rat-infested buildings, and avoid the cops. He'd also learned to keep certain questions to himself, especially the ones that seemed to come out of nowhere, then fester like an overripe boil on his brain until he found the answer. Those special questions had always made the siblings nervous. . . .

"If I stick a water hose down a dog's throat, then turn the faucet on full blast, will the dog's stomach explode?"

"If I shove a pencil up a man's nose hard enough, will it reach his brain and kill him?"

"If I cut off a woman's left tit, will that throw off her balance and make her walk lopsided?"

Over time, Caster discovered some of the answers on his own. No, a dog's stomach won't explode if filled with water, but it does distend to remarkable proportions—and of course the animal drowns in the process.

Yes, a pencil can kill a man if it's long enough and shoved up his nose hard enough—but then you're left with a dead body and the need to haul it away, which wasn't easy for a scrawny seventeen-year-old.

Caster still didn't know whether a woman with

only one tit would walk lopsided, but he was confident he'd find out sooner or later.

Not long after his teen years ended, a few of the siblings began to take greater interest in him, specifically because of the mark on his hand. They took its invariable presence as a sign of Caster's worthiness to learn more. So they taught him secrets, cabalistic truths that had leaked into New Orleans from Haiti decades ago. According to them, those secrets had the power to alter fate if the person who possessed them believed strongly enough and practiced them with diligence. So Caster believed and practiced, but it took years before his labor bore any fruit.

The first indication that he might be making headway came by way of a job at Curious Goods. The little shop was one Caster passed daily when working the streets in the French Quarter, and he occasionally stopped in to browse the merchandise. It was on one of those browsing days when Mr. Fremoir, the shop's owner, offered him a job. It included a salary that was far below minimum wage and a rent-free, rundown apartment above the shop. Since he had no experience, no references, and no home, Caster could only attribute the windfall to the secrets.

It didn't take long before Fremoir gave him the run of the shop, and Caster used his knowledge of the streets to help push business to an all-time high. People expected to see raunchy and raw in New Orleans, especially in the French Quarter, and Caster did his best to deliver. For the faint of heart, he stocked the front of Curious Goods with milder merchandise like candles, powders, leather-wear, and totems. He kept the hard-core items at the back of the shop behind a black curtain with a sign attached to it: ENTER AT YOUR OWN RISK. MUST BE 21 YEARS OLD OR OLDER. The warning helped keep minors at bay, but it also attracted the curious like a magnet, just as he'd hoped it would.

Caster understood the need some people had to see and touch the forbidden because he had the same need. Only his went way beyond gawking at three-eyed cats and detailed posters that portrayed every form of sexual atrocity known to man. He not only had to see the forbidden and touch it, he had to experience it fully so those special questions could be answered—like he had with the dog and the water hose, the man and the pencil—like he had with Thomas.

Remembering Thomas sent a shiver through him. Caster had caught the strung-out twenty-two-year-old stealing a copy of *WHAP* magazine from the back of the shop. Once confronted, Thomas didn't run out of the shop as Caster suspected he would. Instead, the guy came on to him, offering sexual favors in exchange for amnesty. That sudden, blatant proposal had piqued Caster's curiosity. He had little interest in sex, whether homosexual or heterosexual— his experience with both had proved boring and unsatisfactory—except when it served as a means to an end. Like answering a special question. *Just how far would Thomas go to save himself?*

He'd found out how far later that night. A small pill dropped into a jigger of tequila, and Thomas had been more than willing to let Caster lead him to an abandoned building and experiment on his body. He'd been a willing participant even to the end—when Caster castrated him to see how quickly he'd bleed out. As far as he knew, Thomas's body still fed fish at the bottom of Lake Pontchartrain, where he'd dumped it.

It had been nearly two years since that last outré adventure, that last conquest—far, *far* too long.

Smiling, Caster started the van. The rumble of the engine sent a bubble of excitement through his body. It wouldn't be long now. Soon he'd know the answer to another special question, one he'd conceived about a week ago, when he last saw his raven-haired protégé. She'd mentioned the twins only in passing, but it had been more than enough to prompt the question, and now it sizzled in his mind along with the others that still craved answers.

Since raven-hair had easy access to the subjects in question, he'd made ridiculous promises of everlasting love and inside knowledge of the secrets if she helped him get what he needed. And like any lovelorn loser, she jumped at the chance. Now, based on her recent account, it appeared he might have promises to keep. Then again, maybe not. He could circumvent the issue by using her to answer one of the questions that had plagued him for years—*Would a woman walk lopsided if she had only one tit?*

Just the notion that he might get answers to

two special questions at one time made him
tremble with excitement. It also gave him an
erection, which he adjusted before putting the
van in gear.

Only ninety miles to heaven—to Craft Fest—
to his next prey.

Chapter Six

Heather shivered, her mind trying to wrap around yet another impossibility. An ink drawing wasn't supposed to move by itself, yet she'd witnessed one doing just that only moments ago. Her sister wasn't a cutter, but there she stood with a deep gash in her right thigh. A bloody bandage that had obviously slipped out of place hung just below the wound. "J-Jesus H. Christ! What the hell did you d-do? The th-thing on your arm, now your leg! What's going—"

"Shut up before Meemaw hears you!" Haley yanked the bandage up over the wound, then quickly stepped into a fresh skirt.

"But—"

"I said shut the fuck up, bitch!"

Heather's head snapped back in shock. They'd never used words like that on each other before.

Haley glared at her, nostrils flaring, hands

rolled into fists. "If your big mouth brings Meemaw in here, I swear I'll close it permanent. And as for this . . ." She lifted her skirt and pointed to the wound on her thigh. "You're god-damn right I did it, and I'm going to do a lot more than that. Wanna know why?"

Afraid to speak, Heather only stared at her, tears stinging her eyes. From deep inside her chest, she felt something give, like a taut rope had suddenly loosened. It frightened her more than the wild, desperate look in her sister's eyes. She inherently knew what was loosening. It was the bond between her and Haley. She was losing her sister, and it was happening right before her eyes.

"Because the shit works when you do it right, that's *why*. And I'll prove it to you!"

With that, Haley grabbed Heather by the arm and pulled her out of the room. Before they were halfway down the hall, a shrill scream stopped both girls cold. It sounded like it had come from the kitchen. They exchanged a fleet-ing, questioning glance, and another scream blasted through the house, louder this time, fol-lowed by Meemaw's frantic, "Get it! Buck, get it! Get it! Sweet Jesus of Nazareth, *get it!*"

The girls bolted for the kitchen, Heather yanking free of Haley's grasp.

They burst through the archway side by side and saw Meemaw standing on one of the kitchen chairs. She faced the refrigerator, and her hands flapped wildly about, her body bobbing up and down like a cheerleader with her feet glued in place. Papaw was on his hands and knees, peering beneath the fridge, jabbing under it with a broom handle.

"What's wrong?" Heather asked.

Meemaw glanced back, wild-eyed, her hairpiece flopping along the side of her face. She threw a hand up like a traffic cop. "Y'all stay put! Stay, ya hear?"

Haley cocked her head to one side and walked toward the table. "Why? What's going on?"

"No, no, stay! Snake!" Meemaw shouted. "We got us a snake crawled up under the fridge!"

Heather gasped, a hot flush of panic rushing through her body. She jumped back, one foot poised near the archway, ready to sprint to safety. Haley, on the other hand, crept closer, easing around the table toward the fridge.

"What kind of snake?" she asked, sounding no more concerned than if their grandfather had been searching for dust bunnies.

Meemaw's face turned bright red, and her arms pumped at her sides like she was trying to fly. "Go back, pud! Lord of Moses, go—"

Papaw let out a loud, harsh grunt. "She's out," he said, lumbering to his feet. The broomstick bobbed in his hand, a heavy sword for a weary soldier.

"Out? No!" Meemaw slapped a hand to her chest so hard Heather thought she would topple out of the chair. "Where? Oh Lord, get it! Get it!"

Papaw crept along one side of the fridge, wooden sword aimed at the floor. He jabbed, grunted, took two quick steps toward the back of the fridge and jabbed again.

Haley darted from one side of the refrigerator to the other, her arms held out at her sides as though she were herding cattle. Her eyes, shining with excitement, suddenly widened, and she shot around to the opposite side of the refrigerator. With a loud, "Yeah!" she did a swooping squat, and before anyone knew it, she was upright again, triumphantly holding up a green-and-white striped snake. With its head trapped between her thumb and finger, she grinned. "Got it!"

The thin, three-foot-long body thrashed and curled until the tail latched on to her arm and began to coil around it.

Heather stood motionless, feeling like a spectator at a horror movie in which her sister played the leading role. The skin on her arms crawled as she watched the snake winding around Haley's arm. She imagined—no, *felt*—the cool slickness of its belly against her own skin, the slight scratch of its scales, the squeeze and tug of its body milking itself into position. In that moment, she wanted more than anything to tell everything she knew. Tell her grandparents about the barn, the burns, the cut—all of it. Meemaw hadn't seen the snake move under Haley's shirt because she'd been cleaning vomit when it happened, but they needed to hear about that, too. If her grandparents understood all that was going on, maybe they could do something before Haley flipped completely over the edge.

Heather took a step forward and was about to open her mouth and blurt out every word when Haley shot her a hard, threatening look.

Her glower lasted only a second or two before she turned to their grandfather and smiled. "Snake's kinda cute, huh?"

Meemaw groaned loudly. "B-Buck . . ." Her voice was little more than a raspy squawk. She stooped slowly, her eyes glued to Haley, her hands blindly seeking the table. When they found it, she used the table for leverage and lowered herself off the chair and onto the floor. She walked backwards in cautious, small steps until she bumped into the nearest counter. Her breath came out hard and wheezy. "Sn . . . B-Buck . . ."

Papaw stood with one hand on the fridge, his face red from exertion, his hair tousled as though he'd just rolled out of bed. The brown shirt he wore was only partially buttoned and in the wrong holes. Heather had never seen him look so disheveled.

He walked toward Haley, his eyes moving steadily between her and the snake. "That ain't no pet. Put 'er out."

Haley's grin widened, but her eyes held no mirth. "It's only a garter. See?" In a few quick steps, she stood before him, arm thrust out, the snake's head only inches from his face.

Heather gasped and jerked back reflexively.

Meemaw's scream could have been heard in the next county.

Papaw grabbed Haley's outstretched arm, and

their gazes locked. His face held the determination of a man ready for battle, hers an impish smirk. The snake, evidently perturbed by the pressure from Papaw's grip, tightened its coil and flicked its tail.

"What's the matter, Papaw?" Haley asked. "Don't you like snakes?"

Although Heather stood at the other end of the kitchen, there was no missing the taunting challenge in Haley's voice.

Papaw towered over her, unflinching. "Thought you was s'pose to be sick?"

"Was. Feeling a lot better now."

He nodded slowly, his eyes narrowing.

Heather watched the standoff, hugging her arms to her body to ease the trembling. She had the distinct impression Papaw's nod had nothing to do with Haley's health. It was more like he was sizing up the situation and carefully considering his next move. The sound of a sniffle caught her attention, and Heather looked over to see Meemaw shifting from foot to foot by the counter. She stared at her husband and granddaughter, the fingers of her right hand tapping nervously against her lips, and her other hand clutching the front of her blouse. Her expression held all the makings of disbelief, and tears slid down her plump cheeks. Heather took a step toward her, wanting to offer some comfort, but Meemaw suddenly ducked her head and hurried out of the kitchen.

Papaw tossed a glance at his fleeing wife, then sucked on his front teeth and turned back to

Haley. He aimed his chin at the door that led outside from the kitchen. "Backdoor's in the same place it was yesterday," he said, still holding on to her arm. "Bes' you go to it and put 'er out . . . *now.*"

Haley's tongue flicked over her lips, moistening them. "Okay, I'll put the snake outside . . . but I wanna ask you something first."

He arched a brow.

"Craft Fest starts tomorrow, and me and Heather want to go—by ourselves."

Heather gaped. She remembered Karla talking about Craft Fest when they were in the loft, and she'd mentioned it again on the ride home. She'd even offered to pick them up in her car if they wanted to go. Heather didn't remember agreeing to anything, though. She wouldn't have, not after what had happened in the barn. Even then she'd considered the whole Chaos magic thing stupid. Now, with Haley acting like a masochistic maniac, the last thing they needed was to be hanging around Karla Nichols.

Papaw didn't even blink at Haley's request. "No."

Haley angled her body so she stood almost nose to nose with him. "All the other kids from school are going."

"Ain't worried 'bout no other kids."

"But we wouldn't be like alone-alone at the Fest. We'd be with them."

"No."

Haley opened her mouth like she wanted to say more, then snapped it shut. She lowered her head a little, and her nostrils flared as she took in deep, long breaths.

The snake wrapped around her arm suddenly jerked into action, and only then did Papaw drop his gaze, appearing uncertain about whether to maintain or release his grip. Frowning, he pressed his lips into a thin, hard line and held on as the snake writhed—undulating, coiling, loosing under and around his hand.

The snake jerked its head first one way, then the other between Haley's fingers, yet she seemed oblivious to the movement, her focus solely on Papaw. Its tail whipped about wildly and appeared to grow longer with each twist. Then in one swirling loop, it wrapped around Papaw's wrist, binding him to Haley.

For an instant, Heather thought she saw fear flicker across her grandfather's face. The fingers he had wrapped around Haley's arm opened and flexed, but he didn't pull away—or couldn't. Panic swelled inside her. Something was changing. She felt it—a shift of power, like electricity being rerouted to a different circuit or a drastic drop in barometric pressure. It made her want to run away and hide.

The snake, much calmer now, stretched lazily, its body rippling around the linked arms as though meaning to caress.

"Craft Fest starts tomorrow, and me and Heather want to go," Haley repeated, her voice low and even, deeper than normal. *"By ourselves."*

Papaw's chest expanded as though he were in-haling deeply, and with his gaze still sealed to hers, he nodded twice. Then his lips parted, his breath escaped, and as his chest deflated, the rest of him appeared to do the same.

As Heather noted her grandfather's consent, her heart emptied of hope. Something had indeed changed. And that change was far from good.

Haley smiled broadly, then made a clicking sound with her tongue. As if by command, the snake unfurled its body, releasing Papaw. He studied his hand, clearly perplexed.

"So whatcha want me to do with it, Papaw?" Haley held the snake up between a thumb and finger again. The cadence of her words held innocence, as if nothing had occurred between the time she'd captured the creature and this moment.

Papaw's brow furrowed deeply, and he looked about, his eyes flitting over Heather and the empty kitchen.

Haley let out an impatient sigh. "Papaw, I can't hang on to this nasty thing all day. We'll be late for school. You want me to just throw it out in the backyard?"

He swiped a hand over his face as if to clear it of cobwebs. "Yeah . . . yeah, put 'er out back."

With a nod, Haley hurried to the back door, opened it, and hurled the snake onto the lawn. Before she had time to close the door, Stump came charging into the house. He shot past Haley and ran around the table. Dog nails *tic-tic-tick*ed against linoleum as he rushed around the kitchen, nose to the floor. When he reached

Heather, he stopped abruptly, sniffed at her sneakers, then whirled about and raced straight for Haley.

Heather heard the deep, threatening growl, saw the dog and girl collide. Then the rest became a blurry, whirling nightmare. . . .

The bite.

The shout.

The yelp.

The blood.

CHAPTER SEVEN

Mark sat at his desk, shuffling paperwork, attempting to organize notes and the lesson plan for his upcoming art class. It was hard concentrating on work when his thoughts kept wandering back to earlier that morning. All those snakes. The strange haze he'd seen hovering over Buck's roof. He still couldn't figure out what might have caused either, and anomalies drove him nuts. The world always looked cleaner when he understood the why of something.

If necessary he could convince himself that the shimmering haze over the roof had been caused by pollution or certain atmospheric conditions . . . sans temperature, of course, because it simply hadn't been hot enough. The snakes, however, were a different story. Although he'd not been raised in the South, Mark had lived here long enough to know they didn't congregate en masse on front lawns. And especially not in so many different species. He regretted not thinking about grabbing his camera this morning. As an avid photographer, he'd sold several photos to various regional magazines over the years, and the snakes would have been a sure sale. The haze, too, had he captured it just as he'd seen it, all quivery and silvery white. A thought suddenly struck him, and he paused, papers frozen in midshuffle as he considered it. *Were the snakes and haze tied together somehow? Could one have caused the other?*

The clang of a bell startled him out of his musings. He glanced over at the clock perched above the marker board on the wall at the back of the room. Time for class. His questions would have to wait. Fortunately it was Friday, which meant he had only one class for the day. He planned to head home as soon as it was over and do some research on the Internet.

As his students shuffled into the room and took their seats, Mark did a mental roll call. It was something he'd done the first two weeks of every new school year since he'd started teaching. Calling roll twice, once in his head, then again on paper for school records, helped him remember the students' names, which helped him connect with them faster.

Ray Miller, Sasha Franklin, Renata Beneto, Celia Thomas, Karla Nichols, Haley Thurston, Marsha Landon, Kurt Richards, Heather Thurston—

Mark lost track of roll when he noticed the distraught look on Heather Thurston's face.

From the red splotches around her eyes, he guessed she'd been crying. He watched her slip quietly into a desk near the back of the room. Haley on the other hand, settled into a desk closer to the front, right beside Karla Nichols. It was odd seeing the twins sit apart. Since the day they moved in with Buck and Nadine, a little over a month ago, Mark had never seen one without the other. That didn't surprise him considering all they'd been through in such a short period of time. Death had not only taken Buck and Nadine's only child, it had stolen the twins' father, and its aftermath robbed them of their mother. In one fell swoop, the girls lost their parents, home, and friends. They'd lost the world as they knew it. Not many people could have survived, much less adjusted, to that kind of loss.

"Mr. Aikman, can I have a hall pass to go to the bathroom?"

Lost in thought, it took a second for Mark to realize the question had been addressed to him. Beth Windberg stood beside his desk, fidgeting.

He quickly wrote out the pass and handed it to her. "Don't be long. I've got something special planned for class today."

Beth's face lit up. "Really? What?"

He kept a grin in check. "Hurry back and you'll find out."

*Tsk*ing loudly, she rolled her eyes, then shot out of the room."

Noting that all the students were now in the room and seated, Mark got up and went over to the marker board. He wrote *Photography: The Art of Capturing a Moment* across it, then faced the class.

"A few days ago, when you first started this class, I told you that art, in its simplest definition, is the human ability to make things. Remember?"

A dozen or more heads nodded. A few glanced down at their desks.

"That definition may be simple, but it covers a *lot* of territory. In this class, we'll be covering three basic art forms—drawing, sculpting, and photography—and we're going to start with photography."

"Are we gonna need cameras?" Kurt Richards asked. "I got a Powershot, but it's like only three-point-two pixels. Will that work?"

"You can bring a camera if you want to, but it's not necessary. We have a couple here that you'll take turns using. And if you do bring a camera, no digitals. We only use film." Mark nodded to a narrow door on the other side of the room. "That's the darkroom, where you'll learn to develop film. Now since it's Friday, we'll keep things light. I'll give you a brief history and an intro to some of the topics we'll cover, like composition, lighting, and exposure. We'll start full steam on Monday, and the first subject we'll be working with will be—"

As if on cue, Beth Windberg scurried into the room and quickly slipped into a chair.

Mark gave her a little nod. "As I was saying, the first subject we'll be working with is you.

We'll take a class photo today, and then Monday we'll use it as a point of reference for the topics I mentioned earlier."

Beth gasped. "Pictures? Today? Oh—my—God, you can't, Mr. Aikman! I mean, I can't! Look at my hair!"

Sasha Franklin pumped a hand in the air to make sure he saw her. "I got to have some hair time, too, Mr. Aikman. Put on some makeup and—"

Mark held up a hand. "Ladies, you'll be fine. We're not doing glamour shots, just a class photo." And with that, he jumped into the history of photography.

An hour and a half later, long after the class had been dismissed, Mark stood in the darkroom examining the photo he'd taken of the students. He had to admit he'd done a great job at taking a crappy photo. The students as a whole were off center, which cut off Kurt Richards's left shoulder since he stood at the end of the row. There was no symmetry in height—two short boys stood in the back row, a tall girl slouched up front—and the lighting was off. Overall, the photo would provide a good contrast to better-quality work.

Satisfied, and confident the photo was dry, Mark flipped on the light in the darkroom, removed the photo from the drying clips, and jotted some notes on a tablet. He glanced back at the photo to reference color balance and spotted something he hadn't noticed before. Haley,

Karla, and Heather stood in the middle of the
front row and in that order. He thought it
strange the twins hadn't posed together, but that
wasn't what captured his eye. Haley and Karla
stood at a slight slant toward each other. Karla
had made a kissy face for the camera, but something must have distracted her at the last minute
because her eyes were cut toward Haley. And he
saw fear in them. The fear in Heather's eyes was
more blatant. She'd leaned forward a bit, and
the upper half of her body was turned slightly to
the right, so was her head. He had little doubt
she'd leaned and turned so she could see
around Karla. Heather was looking at Haley, and
her eyes were those of a deer trapped in
headlights—shocked, fearful, and seeing no way
out. Haley was the only one looking directly at
the camera. She hadn't smiled, in fact her expression appeared flat. The skin around her lips
looked darker than the rest of her face, but Mark
figured it was due to bad lighting. Something
about it, though—about her—bothered him.

He pulled a palm-size magnifying glass off an
overhead shelf and held it over the photo. The
first thing to loom larger than life was Haley's
eyes. They were huge, her pupils dark brown
and—*elliptical*? Frowning, Mark grabbed the
photo and held it up so it attracted more light.
He placed the magnifying glass over the photo
again and immediately saw what he thought he'd
seen only a moment ago. No matter which way
he turned the photo to allow for more or less
light, every angle revealed the exact same thing.

Haley's pupils were indeed elliptical—vertically elliptical, like a snake's. But that couldn't be right. He would have noticed something that extraordinary the first time he'd met her, and if not then, the next time he'd seen her, or the next. No way would he have missed that all this time.

With the sound of his heart thudding in his ears, Mark moved the glass slowly over Haley's image, pausing at her lips. He squinted, peering closely at the darker skin he'd noticed earlier. When he viewed it from certain angles, the skin appeared layered with dome-shaped ridges similar to fish scales, but he wasn't sure. There was no consistency like he'd seen with the elliptical pupils, so he marked the darkness off to shadows.

He moved the magnifying glass lower still, carefully examining the rest of Haley. Something on her right arm, just below her shirtsleeve, caught his eye. He steadied the glass over the spot. *A tattoo?* He glanced up as if to question the wall in front of him. He'd seen Haley many times out in the yard dressed in shorts and a tank top, weeding Nadine's flowerbeds. Tanks had no sleeves, which meant he would have definitely noticed a tattoo on her arm before now. And Mark knew there was no chance in hell Buck would have allowed her to get one after she'd moved in with them. He leaned over and studied her right arm again. Black—pointed tip—it looked like the end of a tail. The image of one of the rattlers he'd found in Buck's yard immediately came to mind, and it sent gooseflesh racing down Mark's arms.

"Shit," he whispered, lowering the magnifying glass. Snakes in the Thurston's yard—elliptical pupils—a snake tattoo? What the hell was all that about? Was all of it connected somehow? *Could it be?* He didn't see how that was possible. All the pieces didn't quite fit together, and the few that did appear to connect formed an image too bizarre to consider.

Thinking, thinking, chewing his bottom lip, Mark grabbed a print sleeve off the supply shelf and slipped the photograph inside. He tucked the photo under his arm, made sure he still had the magnifying glass, then hurried out of the room. He had questions that needed answers—now.

Jasmine had just bitten off part of a sandwich when Mark burst into the kitchen. Her eyes widened and sparked with surprise. She chewed quickly as she padded over to him in bare feet. "Hey, sexy, you're home early!"

He held out the print sleeve and was about to start racing off at the mouth about what he'd found when she lassoed his neck with her arms and kissed him deeply.

Despite his impatience to show her the photo, Mark eagerly returned the kiss. It reminded him once more why he'd asked Jasmine Deshotel to be his wife. No matter how many directions his head spun off in, Jasmine's kiss, her touch, just her presence, always brought him back to center. Her beauty, quick wit, and intelligence were added bonuses.

"Thought you were going to the gym after work," she said when she finally came up for air.

"I planned to, but I got hold of something pretty interesting. I want to dig into it some more."

She gave him one more kiss on the cheek, then headed back to the snack bar and her sandwich. "So the thing that came up, does it have anything to do with that envelope you're carrying?" Before he could answer, she aimed her sandwich at him. "Want one? It's ham and Swiss."

"Maybe later." He pulled the class photo out of the print sleeve, then placed it on the counter so it faced her. "Take a look at this and tell me what you think."

"Group photo, huh?" She looked up at him. "One of your classes?"

He nodded. "Art class. We started photography this morning, so I took this."

She gave him a small grimace. "I love you, babe, but I've gotta be honest. It's not your best work."

"Screwed it up a little on purpose so the kids would have something to compare it to later. But that's not what I wanted you to check out." He tapped the photo with a finger, aiming at Haley's image. "Look here. Tell me what you see."

"Haley Thurston."

"What else?"

Jasmine folded her arms on the counter and leaned over, studying the photo carefully. "I don't know about what else, but I know who else. Most of the girls in this picture are in my gym classes. The twins, Haley and Heather, then Karla, Sasha—"

"Ever notice if Haley had a tattoo on her arm?"

She frowned. "Not that I've ever seen. Why?"

Mark pulled the magnifying glass out of his back pants pocket and placed it over the photo. "Look at Haley's right arm, just below her shirt sleeve."

Jasmine took the magnifier from him and aimed it where he'd indicated. She frowned, adjusting the glass a bit higher, then lower. "Looks like it could be one. That black thing right there." She touched the spot on Haley's arm. "Kinda looks like part of a snake's tail."

Mark nodded, even though she wasn't looking at him. "That's what I thought. There's more, though. Look closer."

She cocked her head, still staring intently. "You can see Karla's better. But I already knew she had a tattoo. She flaunts it all the time in gym. Calls it a sigil, whatever the hell that means."

He leaned over and looked at the photo. "I didn't notice hers."

"See?" Jasmine pointed. "Looks like the bottom of a *U*?"

"Yeah."

"The whole thing doesn't look like much. Just squiggle lines."

"Go back to Haley. Look at her eyes."

Jasmine hunkered over the magnifier again. "I don't see—holy shit! No way!" She looked up at him, gaping. "They're friggin' elliptical!"

"I know."

"How? I mean, they can't be. We'd have noticed before now. At school, at—" She frowned. "Could the camera have done it? The lights, the way she was standing, anything like that?"

He shook his head. "Red eye maybe, but not that."

Jasmine's frown deepened, and she stared across the room for a moment.

"What're you thinking?" he asked.

Sighing, she looked down at the photo again. "About rumors I've overheard from some kids at school. I'm sure they're all nonsense, though."

"Rumors about Haley?"

"No, Karla. They say she's into black magic. It's probably just her tattoo that freaks them out, and they wound stories around it."

At the mention of black magic, some of the puzzle pieces Mark had floating around in his mind shifted, as if to make room for this particular piece. A rush of adrenaline sent him pacing the length of the snack bar. He stared at his feet, turning the pieces over and over in his mind.

"What?" Jasmine asked, watching him.

"I'm wondering if there's something to that."

"To what?"

"Black magic tied in to everything that's been happening."

"Huh?"

Mark turned to her. "Haley's been hanging around Karla at school the last couple days. Taking into account what you said about Karla and the rumors that she's involved in black magic, maybe all this weirdness is not so coincidental."

"By weirdness you mean what showed up in the photo?"

"Yeah, Haley's eyes, the sudden appearance of tattoos, the snakes in the yard, the—"

"Whoa! Snakes where?" Jasmine pulled her feet up higher on the bar stool.

Mark did a mental forehead slap when he realized she didn't know about the snakes. She went to the gym three days a week and always early in the morning. After her workout, she'd head straight to school and didn't get off until two. This morning had been one of her workout days, so she'd missed the snake invasion. And since they hadn't had the chance to talk until now, he hadn't told her about it.

"At the Thurstons'," he said, then filled her in on the morning's events.

By the time he was done, she was the one pacing. "Man, how weird is that?" she muttered.

"Yeah, I know. That's what I mean about maybe it's not so coincidental. What if—" Mark snapped his fingers. "What'd you say Karla called her tattoo?"

"A sigil . . . something like that. I don't know what it means, though."

"Bet I know where we can find out," Mark said, already heading for the bedroom and his computer.

Jasmine jumped off the barstool and followed him. "The Net."

"You got it."

Within minutes, Mark had a search engine ready, and Jasmine started prompting possible search words. Each word he typed into the engine produced tons of information, and all of that information had links that seemed to beget links times infinity. They were in information overload.

Mark popped a crick out of his neck. "We might be here for a while."

Jasmine got out of her chair, went over to him, and massaged his neck. "Maybe we should stick to keywords to start. See if a pattern shows up. A lot of links are on multiple sites, but those links and sites usually have something in common. If we keep the search tight, after a while we should start seeing the same links show up."

"Works for me." He grabbed a pen and scratch pad off the desk for their word choices. "You first. Shoot."

They quickly brainstormed a list of twenty words, then whittled that list down to four key search phrases: magic and sigils, snakes used in magic, magic and transmutation, and tattoos used in magic. More confident now that the list wasn't so unwieldy, Mark eagerly began the search again.

After a while, he *did* see a pattern emerge. Certain links started showing up repeatedly, and they all eventually led him to the same websites. Narrowing his options to what seemed and felt right in Karla and Haley's situation helped even more. He read and took notes, clicked and read, scrolled and read some more. The hair on the back of his neck stood on end as a world he never knew existed unfolded before him.

According to multiple sources, sigils were a product of Chaos magic, and Chaos was most often associated with black magic masters like Aleister Crowley. The basic purpose of Chaos was to fulfill a conjurer's wish or intent, and over seventy-five percent of its practitioners were between fifteen and nineteen years old.

For Chaos to work, a practitioner had to focus on one request, and any request was acceptable. There were no boundaries. A wish or intention could be as small as asking for rain, a new stereo, or good grades in school. Or it could be as large as killing an enemy, spreading disease over an entire state, even destroying the planet. Once the conjurer decided on a wish, he created a sigil, which was basically a symbol that represented the intent. If the wish were small, the sigil was usually small and temporary, like a drawing on a piece of paper. The larger the wish, the more permanent the sigil usually became. That's where tattoos often came into play.

After the sigil was created, it had to be charged to give it life, then fed regularly so it had strength to do the conjurer's will. To charge the sigil, the conjurer had to perform an extreme act that brought about pleasure, pain, or fear. The bigger the intent, the more extreme the act needed to be. There were no boundaries here either. Charging a small sigil might involve the conjurer masturbating in a public restroom, cutting himself, or burning himself with a lit cigarette. To charge a larger intent, like when the conjurer desires someone to die, he might be required to sacrifice a family pet and then save its blood so it can be mixed with the conjurer's semen later.

As Mark read on, he found even more disturbing information. All sigils carried the potential for payback. If not charged or fed properly, the conjurer could experience the opposite of what he'd requested. If he'd wanted good grades, he would fail. If he wanted a new stereo, his old one would break or be stolen so he'd be left with nothing. Sigils created for larger intentions were the most dangerous of all, however. If not cared for properly, one could easily manifest into a living, breathing entity, then turn on their master, take over his life, and bring destruction and death. Once manifested, only two things could destroy a sigil—death by its master—or the creation of another sigil that would battle it to the death.

Mark sat back in his chair, suddenly exhausted. He glanced at the computer clock. They'd been online for over five hours, and he still felt like he'd just scratched the surface of Chaos. What little he did know, though, suggested that if Haley Thurston was playing around with Chaos, she might have already bitten off a hell of a lot more than she could chew.

CHAPTER EIGHT

Just after lunch, Buck snatched a leash off a nail near the kitchen door. "Goin' into town to have Doc Rayburn take a look at Stump. That girl mighta gave 'im the rabies or somethin'."

Nadine wiped her hands on a faded green dish towel, then draped the towel over the edge of the sink. "*That girl* has a name . . . it's Haley. The other one's Heather, and not a one of 'em got the rabies, and you know it."

"How you know she ain't gave 'im the rabies? You ain't no vet, and you didn't see what she done." Buck shook his head, trying to shake images from this morning out of his mind. Haley hanging on to that garter snake like it was a prize, her shoving it in his face like she did. Stump running into the house like he'd lost his head, then turning on Haley, ready to attack. Then *Haley* up and taking a chunk out of Stump's right ear!

If he hadn't seen it all with his own eyes, he'd have sworn on a store full of Bibles none of it was true. And for some reason, when he tried to remember what had happened in the time between the snake and Stump, his brain went fuzzy. All that would come to mind was Haley's eyes—something about her eyes—and her talking about . . . a craft?

"I might not've seen it, but you sure told me 'nough times. And I still say you got the story back'ards."

Buck slapped the leash against his right thigh. "I ain't got *nothin'* back'ards! You seen what she did with that snake!"

Nadine huffed. "Seein' her catch a little ol' snake ain't the same as sayin' she done bit a dog."

He glared at her. "Then you're sayin' I'm lyin' 'bout what she did to Stump?"

"No, I'm sayin' you're probably just a little confused 'bout how it went is all."

Buck felt his shoulders slump as if someone had suddenly dropped bricks on them. He was more confused than ever. It was bad enough his wife thought his brain had gone soft when he told her about Haley and Stump. Now she acted like what she'd witnessed this morning had been no big deal. Yet he'd seen the fear on her face when Haley shoved the snake at him. Why was she dismissing it now? He hadn't told her about the snakes in the yard. Since they'd all been killed anyway—or so he'd thought until he came into the house and saw one slithering toward the fridge—he didn't think there was reason to worry her about it. She would've panicked and probably not set foot outside for a month. Now he wondered if he'd done the right thing by not telling her. Maybe if Nadine knew, she wouldn't think him so daft. He glanced up at his wife, at the shiny pink of her cheeks, the worry in her eyes as she looked at him, and decided to keep his mouth shut about the snakes. But he wouldn't about the girl. Something was bad wrong with her, maybe both, and he couldn't just let bad wrong go by. Not again.

He tapped his left temple with a finger. "I know you're fig'rin' my brain went sideways when I told you 'bout the girl and Stump, but—"

"Haley."

"Huh?"

Nadine propped a hand on her hip. "Your grandbabies got names, Buck. You need to be usin' 'em."

Frustrated, he rubbed the back of his head briskly. "Yeah, okay . . . Haley and . . . and the other one."

"Heather."

"Yeah."

"What about 'em?"

Buck looked at her for a moment, trying to figure out the best way to approach the issue.

"Buck?"

"Somethin' just ain't right about 'em," he blurted.

Nadine frowned. "Why would you say such a thing?"

He shook his head. "I don't know. Somethin's

jus' . . . different, 'at's all. Started 'bout the time that new girl brung 'em home yesterday. Stump acted kinda strange toward the girl—toward Haley—then, too."

"Strange how?"

"Got to growlin' real low when he got close to 'er. Then he jus' run off with his tail 'tween his legs. Ever since then, them girls been actin' funny, like possums sneakin' 'round a hen house. I'm just tellin' you, somethin' ain't right with 'em."

Nadine dropped her hand from her hip, and the furrows in her brow deepened. "They probably havin' their woman's time is all. You gotta remember they ain't babies no more."

Buck felt his face flush. "Hell, I know they ain't babies."

"You can't blame 'em if they go a bit off from time to time. 'Tween them having their woman's time and all they been through the past year, what with their mama driftin' off in the head and them losin'—"

Buck threw up a hand. "Don't say it, Nadine!"

"Buck—"

"I know what them girls lost. I already know!" He threw the leash across the kitchen. What he wanted to do was punch through a wall.

Nadine's face softened, and she walked over to him and put a hand on his arm. "How long you gonna keep doin' this to yourself?"

"I ain't doin' nothin'!"

"Buck, ain't nothin' you could've done for Justin. Ain't nothin' nobody could've done. That leukemia, it jus'—"

He pulled away from her. "Yeah, I know, ain't nothin' could've been done." *You're wrong . . . I could've done somethin' . . . jus' wasn't strong enough, didn't try hard enough . . . God, I could've done somethin'. . . .*

From the corner of his eye, he caught movement near the fridge and dipped his head to get a better look.

Nadine followed his gaze, taking a quick step back. "What's wrong?"

He scanned the bottom of the fridge and the space between it and the cabinets, but didn't see anything. "Nothin'."

"Then why you lookin' like somethin' is?"

"Ain't." Buck waved a hand dismissively. "Jus' got enough'a all this talkin' is all. You go on and tend to what you gotta tend to. I'm gonna get Stump outta whatever dang hidey-hole he's in."

Nadine sighed. "I wish you'd quit slippin' out from under me when I try talkin' to you."

When he didn't comment, she shook her head. "I swear, Buck, you're as stubborn as ten mules glued up together." She headed out of the kitchen. "I'll be out back tendin' to the laundry since it ain't gonna tend to itself."

He waited until she was out of sight, then he pulled out a kitchen chair, sat, and swiped a hand over his face. With Nadine set firmly in denial, he'd have to carry the worry he had for the girls on his own. That made him a little uncomfortable. He understood boys better than girls. Boys didn't have a 'woman's time.' They just acted weird because they were boys.

Quick footsteps sounded from the living room, and Buck cocked his head, listening. The footsteps soon faded as if heading down the hall. "Nadine?"

When she didn't answer, he got up and went into the living room. No one was there. He stood quietly, waiting to hear the footsteps again. They didn't come—but from somewhere down the hallway, a low, moaning whimper did. The sound of it sent something akin to fear zipping up Buck's spine. "Did you hear that?" he whispered, as though Nadine stood beside him.

He took a tentative step toward the hall, listening intently. He heard the whimper again, and it stopped him cold. It couldn't have been the girls. They weren't due back from school for an hour or so.

Buck forced himself forward, stepping carefully, quietly down the hall. When he heard the whimper again, it had more of a keening quality to it, and it sounded like it was coming from the bathroom. He headed in that direction. *Bet a handful of moon pies one of them girls played hooky.*

When he reached the bathroom door, he tapped a fingernail against it. "Girl?" Nadine's disapproving face came to mind. *Your grandbabies got names, Buck. You need to be usin' 'em.*

He scowled. "Haley?"

No response.

"Heather?"

Nothing.

Buck tapped on the door again, then opened it. He flipped on the light, studying the small space. Hair brush on the vanity. Toothpaste on the rim of the sink. Toilet seat down—was that blood on the floor?

He stooped to examine the four or five red droplets on the floor between the sink and the toilet. It sure looked like blood. He grimaced, remembering what Nadine had said about the girls' woman's time. Getting to his feet, he reached over and tugged at the toilet paper roll. Once he had a handful, he knelt on one knee and pressed the pad of tissue against the first drop of blood. That's when he heard the whimper again, only louder, and it held a fragile tone that could have only belonged to a little girl. A hurting little girl.

Dropping the tissue on the floor, Buck hurried out of the bathroom and toward the sound of her voice. *Hold on . . . I'm comin'.*

As he moved down the hallway, following her cry, thoughts of Justin rushed him. *I could've done somethin' . . . jus' wasn't strong enough . . . I'll damn sure do somethin' this time. Whatever it takes . . .*

Buck soon found himself at the girls' bedroom door, and fear immediately washed over him. He felt watched, like someone or something hid nearby and planned to pounce on him the second he crossed the bedroom threshold. Holding his breath, he turned the doorknob and pushed open the door.

A thousand shadows seemed to call to him from every corner of the room. "Who's . . . who's in here?"

He heard no answer, no whimpers. Rolling one hand into a fist, he stepped farther into the room. "I said who's in here?"

The shadows appeared to slither and coil, contract and lengthen as he made his way to the foot of the twin beds. He clenched his jaw, determined to check every corner of the room.

When he reached the foot of the first bed, he heard a fluttering sound near the floor. He glanced down—and a diamond-shaped head shot out from under the bed, its bowed, needle-size fangs aimed for his left calf.

"Shit!" Buck jumped back with grunt, then quickly scanned the floor to keep tabs on the snake.

It was no longer there.

What the . . . ?

He toed the bedspread hanging off the foot of the bed. Other than his foot, nothing moved. *Probably just got snakes on the brain.*

"A'ight then," he said aloud, hoping it would produce more confidence. Then he turned toward the closet.

That's when he saw her.

Buck felt his eyes grow wide as he took in the sight of the little girl huddled in the corner near the closet. Her right arm hugged her knees, which were drawn to her chest, and she held her left thumb close to her trembling lips. Tears streamed down tiny cheeks, and her eyes held more fear than Buck had ever seen in a human.

She whimpered, and he not only heard her

plea, he felt it course through his body like a lightning strike.

Please . . . Papaw, please . . . please help me. . . .

Buck gaped. She'd called him by name.

He took a step closer, then another. There was a familiarity about her that he kept trying to place but couldn't. Then something Nadine had said suddenly came to mind. *Your grandbabies got names, Buck.*

He froze. Grandbabies? The girl looked no older than three, far too small to be Haley or Heather.

Papaw, please . . .

The plea ripped through Buck's heart. "Haley?" *She's too little. She's too damn little!* "Heather?"

He was only a few steps away from her when he heard Justin's voice. It rang loud and clear and real, as if his son were standing only a foot away. *You have to help her, Dad. You're all she's got now.*

Giant waves of longing and grief washed over Buck, and he pressed a hand to his chest. "My— my boy."

Help her, Dad. Help her. . . .

Justin's voice sounded weaker, like it was fading into an eternal distance. Buck shot a hand into the air, stretching, reaching, grasping for anything that would keep his son close. "I'm— I'm so sorry, son. I know I should've done more. Justin, I should—"

Dad, help . . . just . . .

Justin's voice was soon replaced by the girl's whimper, but she sounded weaker now, too.

"Haley?" Buck reached for her, and his movements felt labored and much too slow. "Baby, c'mere. Come to Papaw."

She opened her little arms and held them out. *Papaw, please!*

The sound of her cries swirled about him, as did an urgency to pull her from danger. But what danger? She was sitting right there in front of him, seemingly safe. Still his heart hammered against his chest. "C'mere, Haley . . . Heather . . . come to Papaw."

As he called to her, he felt a wall of panic closing in on him hard and fast. He had to reach her *now,* and God how he wanted to, but no matter how much he pushed and strained, he could hardly get his legs to move. Why wouldn't she come to him?

Papaw, help me!

Buck reached out as far as his arms allowed, his body trembling as he strained. "It's a'ight, baby! It's all gonna be a'ight! You hear? You hear me, Haley? Heather?"

In that instant, her little arms shot straight up in the air as if someone were attempting to yank her upright by the hands. Raw panic hollowed out her cheeks, and she screamed. *No! Papaw! Help me! Help me! Papaw! God*—

Then she was gone.

CHAPTER NINE

"Check it," Karla said, then quickened her step and walked past the lamp booth with a heavy swing in her hips. She wore a black mini with a sheer black blouse and beneath the blouse, a bloodred bra.

The muscular blond inside the booth whistled. "Oh, yeah! You just swing that thing, girl."

Karla tossed him a smile over her shoulder, never breaking stride.

Haley felt a twinge of envy as she watched. She wished she attracted guys that way. But she didn't have the right equipment. Guys liked rounded butts that had a little push to them. Hers was small. Definitely not worth a whistle, even in the skirt Karla had loaned her. It was short, soft, and blue, her favorite color. The white blouse that went with it wasn't quite as sheer as the one Karla had on, but it was lower cut, which really didn't help because she had no cleavage. She glanced at Heather, who walked beside her, and felt a surge of anger. Her sister wore jeans and a plain brown T-shirt, definitely not a hunk magnet. Karla had offered to lend her clothes as well, but she'd staunchly refused. In fact, Heather was refusing to do just about everything, including talk to her. It had been a major ordeal getting her to come to Craft Fest, so major Haley'd had to resort to threats to get her into Karla's car.

"So?" Karla asked when they caught up to her next to a cotton candy wagon.

"You were right, girl," Haley said. "That guy was definitely hot."

Karla laughed and tossed her hair off a shoulder with a flip of her hand. "He's nothing. Wait 'til you meet my boyfriend. Now *he's* hot."

"How far before we get to his booth?"

"It's on the other end of the midway."

Haley worked at putting more swing in her hips as they walked. "Does he do booths at fairs all the time? Is that like his job?"

Karla shrugged. "I think so. Fairs and flea markets, maybe some other stuff, I'm not sure. I met him about four months ago. He had a booth in that flea market deal they do in Harris County every year. You know, the one under the big white tent?"

Haley nodded again though she didn't have a clue about any big white tent. She'd never even been to a flea market before.

Snapping her fingers to the beat of a song coming from a nearby loud speaker, Karla looked back at Heather. "What's up with you? You're quiet."

Heather didn't bother looking at her. "Nothing."

Karla rolled her eyes, then leaned into Haley and whispered, "Is your sister gonna be bummed like this the whole time we're here?"

"She'll be all right." Haley smiled, knowing she'd just lied through her teeth. Heather would not only be bummed the whole time they were there, she'd probably stay bummed for months. When she got quiet like she was now, you could bank on it; whatever she was feeling was a keeper. But Haley really didn't care what mood Heather was in. Haley was about to learn how to supercharge her sigil from Karla's boyfriend, and that was all that mattered to her.

"I still can't believe your grandfather didn't have a shit fit about y'all coming here." Karla waved to someone a few yards away.

Haley gave her a sideways glance. "Why can't you believe it?"

"Whadda ya mean, why? Isn't he strict and stuff?"

"Yeah." Haley pointed to her sigil. "But what do you think *this* is for?"

Karla's eyes grew big. "No way!"

Haley laughed. "Yeah, way."

"You mean it actually worked that fast?"

"Why? It's not supposed to?"

"Most times it takes a while. I told you that, remember? You must've really jacked up the charge on it, huh?"

Haley grinned. "You could say that." She checked to make sure Heather was still nearby. She'd fallen behind on purpose, keeping her distance.

"So what'd he say?"

"Who?"

"Your grandfather, stupid."

Haley shrugged. "He didn't really say anything. Just kinda nodded."

"You did it like this morning?"

"No, yesterday."

"And he didn't go back on it this morning or nothin'?"

"I didn't even see him this morning. I think he was still in bed when you picked us up."

"That was almost eleven. What was he still doin' in bed?"

"I don't know."

"So you just left without telling him anything?"

"Kinda. Told my grandmother we were going. She had a little hissy about it, but nothing major. She's probably gonna rip him a new one, though, for saying we could come."

Karla laughed and held out her arms. "You gotta *love* this shit, right?"

"Right!" Haley said, although she didn't quite know what 'shit' Karla referred to. If she was talking about Craft Fest, Haley wasn't sure love was the right word. Most of the booths had old-people stuff, like lamps and clocks, decorative horse blankets, handmade jewelry, cast-iron pots with fancy handles, and almost every kind of knick-knack ever made. The sound of laughter and chattering voices followed them everywhere, as did a medley of aromas—hotdogs and chili fries, popcorn and candied apples. Overall, Haley thought Craft Fest was cool, but nothing to jump up and down about. But if Karla was referring to Chaos and the power Haley had seen in it so far, then her answer was a resounding, *"Hell, yeah!"*

Karla nudged her. "There he is." With a grin that looked like it would split her face in half, she nodded to a booth up ahead. A sign that read CURIOUS GOODS hung across the front of it, and behind the selling shelf was a tall man with shoulder-length black hair. He wore jeans, a black T-shirt, and a smile as he chatted with a woman who stood nearby. To Haley, he looked a bit like Sean Penn, only taller.

As they walked up to the booth, his gaze flitted over them, then locked on to Haley's. She felt herself blush and heat spread through her body like warm milk. This close, Karla's boyfriend appeared to be much older than she was, maybe in his late twenties, early thirties. Haley had never had an older man look at her the way he just did. It made her feel uncomfortable and giddy all at once.

Karla fidgeted with a row of bracelets lying on the sales shelf while they waited for him to finish with the woman. As soon as she left, Karla all but launched herself over the booth and into his arms. Haley thought she saw disgust flicker through his eyes, but it was replaced with a smile so quickly she wasn't sure.

"Hey, Haley," Karla said, beaming. "This is the guy I told you about. This is Caster."

Haley grinned, but avoided looking him in the eyes. She was afraid if she did, she'd fall into their deep, chocolate brown centers and never get up again. "Hey."

"So, you're Haley," Caster said, and held out his hand. "Nice to finally meet you. Karla's told me a lot about you."

Haley glanced up at Karla, surprised. "You have?"

"Sure. He likes knowing about the people I hang out with."

Hang out with. Haley loved the sound of that. She 'hung out' with Karla Nichols, one of the most popular girls in school. How cool was that?

"Uh . . ." Karla pointed to Caster's extended hand.

Haley blushed again. "Sorry." She took his hand, intending to do the two pump and release bit, but he evidently didn't. His grip was soft and firm, and he shook her hand with easy, long strokes. She immediately noticed the drawing on the back of his hand. It was a bit crude, not detailed like hers, but it was a snake nonetheless. And it looked to be eating its tail, which she thought was pretty cool. When he finally did let go of her hand, she found herself wishing he hadn't.

"You must be Haley's sister," Caster said to Heather, who stood a few feet behind them.

A small scowl settled over Heather's face, and

for a moment Haley feared she'd say something mean or stupid to him. Instead, she just nodded and turned away.

Karla wiggled against him. "So what kinds of cool stuff did you bring to sell?"

He shrugged. "The usual."

"The cat too?"

"Yep."

Karla gave a little clap, then tugged on his arm. "Can I show it to them?"

Caster looked at Haley and winked. "Sure, but you can't be too long with it right now. I have some important things to take care of before we can have fun time."

"Okay." Karla motioned Haley over as she walked to the back of the booth.

Haley turned to her sister. "Coming?"

Heather gave her a look that left little doubt to her answer.

"Check this out!" Karla said as soon as Haley caught up to her. She lifted a large glass jar from a padded box and held it out. "Is this great or what?"

Haley swallowed hard. Inside the jar was a small, dead cat. It floated and bobbed around in some kind of clear liquid, its little paws folded in on themselves. Karla shook the jar slightly, causing the cat to change positions and its face to settle against the part of the jar that faced Haley. She saw that instead of having two eyes in normal cat-eye places, it had three, and they were almost vertically positioned. The eyes were open, a milky-gray color, and Haley didn't think it was great at all.

"Yeah," Haley said, then hurried back to the front of the booth. To help get her mind off the cat, she picked up a thick red candle and studied it.

"They're five-ninety-five," Caster said, suddenly standing in front of her.

"Oh." She couldn't think of what else to say, so she replaced the red candle and picked up a white one.

"Same price."

Haley grinned. "Kinda figured since they were in the same bin. Do the different colors have certain scents?" She held the white one to her nose and sniffed. The only thing she smelled was wax.

"They're not for scent," he said. "They're for spells."

Haley looked up at him, immediately intrigued. "You mean like magic spells?"

He grinned. "Yes, like magic spells. The green is for gain, like to get more money, popularity, stuff like that. The white is for love, and the red for passion."

She touched each color as he named its purpose. The only one he hadn't mentioned was black. "What about this one?" She tapped a fingertip against a short, squat, black candle.

His smile was easy, as if he'd just felt a cool breeze on a sweltering summer day. He leaned closer to her and said in a low, deep voice, "Black is used by those who search for truth and

dominance. It's used by most conjurers who
practice the dark arts."

He smelled like butter cookies and the inside
of a new car. Haley couldn't help breathing deep
while he stood close. "Truth and dominance in
what?"

"Everything." He held her gaze. "Anything."

She laughed nervously. "They're not asking
for too much, huh?"

He didn't laugh with her. He straightened and
signaled Karla to him. She scampered to his side
like a puppy, and he whispered something in her
ear. She nodded, then hurried out of the booth
and went over to Heather. Before Haley knew it,
both Karla and Heather were walking away and
leaving her behind.

"Where y'all going?" Haley called.

"I sent Karla to get me a few things, and I
asked that she bring your sister with her since
she looked so incredibly bored."

Haley watched them walk away. "I'm kinda
surprised Heather went with her."

"Why's that?"

She turned back to him. "Just a girl squabble
thing. No big deal."

He smiled. "Well, Karla has seemed to handle
the 'squabble thing' relatively well. The truth is I
sent them away because I wanted to talk to you
alone."

Haley felt her heart sputter. "About what?"

He placed a hand on her right arm, over her
sigil. "This."

She gasped involuntarily when he touched

her. His fingers felt hot through the flimsy material of the blouse, and the tightening sensation she'd had in her stomach when she'd first cut her thigh returned.

"Karla told me you had a lot of interest in the secrets and wanted to learn more. The moment I met you I knew you were serious about learning. Your dedication to the black arts will allow the secrets to serve you well."

"The secrets?" Her voice cracked, and she cleared her throat.

He glanced up as though contemplating for a moment. "Chaos, if you'd prefer." When he looked at her again, there seemed to be fire in his eyes. They shone—sparkled—danced—made her burn inside. "I can teach you a lot, Haley."

She read his lips, having barely heard him over the beat of her heart. "B-But why would you want to? You don't know me."

"Oh, I know you better than you think." He drew closer to her and leaned over until she felt his breath against her face. "And what I don't know, I trust you will tell me."

She found herself nodding without even thinking about it.

He looked steadily at her. "You share your sigil, yes?"

She frowned, not quite sure what he meant.

"With your sister?" Caster leaned closer still. "Weren't your sigils created at the same time?"

She tried to swallow but had no saliva. "Yes. But Heather didn't do anything with hers. I'm the only one who did."

He smiled. "Of course you did. I'm not surprised." His lips were so close to her left cheek she could almost feel them touch her. "But although it may look like your sister didn't do anything with her sigil, she's still drawing power from yours."

"Why? She didn't even want it in the first place."

"Because you created it together. This means that if you're interested in strengthening your sigil, your first order of business will be to reclaim the part she possesses."

"How would I do that?"

He opened his mouth as though to answer, then looked up sharply. A brief frown crossed his face, and he pulled away.

"Here ya go!" Karla came bounding up to the booth with a small brown paper bag. Heather hung back as before, only now she was eating a burger. Karla handed the bag to Caster and was about to climb over the booth again when he stopped her.

"Later," he said, a sharp edge to his voice.

Karla looked up with a puzzled, hurt expression. "Why not now? Didn't I do what you—" She cut off her words sharply and glanced at Haley. When she turned back to Caster, her eyes were filled with tears. "I can come back later, right?"

"Yes." He reached beneath the sales shelf and pulled out a pencil and a small piece of paper. He turned away, wrote something on the paper, then folded it and motioned Karla closer. She hurried to comply, and as soon as she leaned over the sales shelf, Caster grabbed the front of her blouse, pulled her to him, then kissed her full on the mouth.

Watching, unable to turn away, Haley bit back a groan. God how she wanted to kiss him like that.

When they separated, Karla looked like someone had stuck a light bulb beneath her skin. "I'll be back later then," she said, then backed away from the booth, smiling.

Caster quickly held out a hand to Haley. "It was nice meeting you. I'm sorry I had to cut our first meeting short, but duty calls. We'll see each other again soon I'm sure."

Afraid to say anything for fear she'd dribble, Haley nodded and held out her hand. When his closed over hers, she felt him press something into her palm. *Did he just give me a note?*

After they left Caster's booth, it felt like it took forever before she found a little privacy so she could open his note. When she finally did read it, Haley thought she'd have to get someone to restart her heart. The news was better than she'd hoped. Caster wanted to meet her back at the booth tonight—alone.

CHAPTER TEN

Heather watched dust billow around her sneakers as she walked. She didn't want to be at any stupid Craft Fest, and especially not with Karla Nichols and Haley. Like it or not, though, she was stuck here, and she had no one to blame but herself. She should have stood up to Haley, regardless of the threats. So what if her sister had thrown a few punches? She could've punched back.

Sighing, she kicked a small rock out of her path. *Who'm I kidding?* She knew she wouldn't be able to hit Haley even if Haley hit first. It would feel too much like punching herself, but in the heart instead of the face. That was probably why she'd caved when Haley had threatened in the first place. She wouldn't have known how to defend herself other than duck and take cover. In truth, Haley's threats alone had been painful enough.

Heather glanced up to make sure she hadn't fallen too far behind. As much as she didn't want to be here, she couldn't afford to lose track of Haley and Karla. If she did, she'd have no way to get home. She spotted them walking side by side only a few feet away, and seeing them together angered and frightened Heather at the same time.

Haley seemed to crave Karla's attention like a drug, and she always had that I'll-do-anything-for-you expression on her face when she looked at the girl. To make matters worse, whatever Karla was teaching Haley appeared to be working. What else could explain what she'd witnessed over the last day and a half? The drawing on Haley's arm moving—the way Papaw had conceded to letting them go to Craft Fest alone—and Haley's sudden weird and aggressive behavior. She'd never known her sister even to go near a snake before, much less hold one. And just thinking about what she'd done to Stump's ear made Heather nauseated. She feared what might come next.

"Hey, Jason! Ryan!" Karla did a little hop as she waved to a group of six or seven boys standing near a booth filled with duck decoys. Heather recognized a couple of the boys from school. One of the guys she didn't know motioned Karla over.

"Hold up," Karla said, grabbing Haley's arm and pulling her to a stop. She threw Heather a cursory glance, and her grin grew wider. "That's Jason Cribner, and he's always carryin'. Let's go hang with him for a while. Bet I can score us a free doobie."

Heather's body went cold. She knew Haley had never tried marijuana before, neither of them had, and it wasn't due to lack of opportunity. Even small Catholic schools in Louisiana had their share of pushers and dope heads. But they weren't back home at St. John High, and her sister's history didn't appear to be applicable anymore.

Haley frowned. "But what about Caster?"

"What about him?"

"I thought . . . well, won't he get upset if he sees you hanging out with other guys, since he's your boyfriend and everything? I mean, his booth's like just over there, not even two hundred yards away. He could easily see you."

Karla's face hardened. "I plan to razz Jason out of a little dope, not screw him."

"No, I didn't mean—"

"And even if Caster did see me and get jealous, it'd be all good anyway. Never hurts to remind a guy he's not the only bull in the pasture. Now, y'all comin' or what?" Not bothering to wait for an answer, she let go of Haley's arm and headed for the group of boys.

Haley stared after her for a moment, then shot Heather a glance.

In that brief look, Heather saw her sister, the one she used to play jacks and checkers with, the one who used to laugh at her corny knock-knock jokes and cry during sappy commercials. Something tugged hard at Heather's heart, and she wanted to run to Haley, wrap her arms around her, and never let go. This was the truth of why she was here. She hadn't come to Craft Fest because she feared Haley would beat her or that she'd have to fight back in defense. She came because they were bound by blood and love and a lifetime of memories. Even if she didn't see a way to keep Haley from slamming into disaster, Heather knew she could never stop trying. She took a step toward her sister and—

Haley immediately turned away and sprinted after Karla.

With a sharp pain replacing the tug in her heart, Heather followed as if on autopilot. She heard Karla's boisterous laughter as she welcomed Haley into the group, and Heather wanted to cram it back down the girl's throat. Just how in the hell did a pimply-faced, greasy-haired loudmouth attract so many people anyway? If the answer was really Chaos magic, then why wasn't she under Karla's spell too? What made her immune?

The group had closed into a fairly tight circle by the time Heather reached them. Knowing she'd look like a wart if she stood outside that fold, she detoured to a nearby snack kiosk and bought popcorn. After paying the vendor, she went around to the side of the narrow shed, leaned against it, then stuck a puffed kernel into her mouth. She wasn't hungry, but she needed a prop in order to watch and listen without looking too conspicuous. The burger she'd eaten earlier still sat in her stomach like a wad of Play-Doh. She hadn't been hungry then either.

When Karla had surprised her by pulling her along to tend to Caster's errand, Heather had used the burger as an escape. Feigning near starvation, she'd purposely stopped at a burger wagon that had a long waiting line. As she'd hoped, Karla soon grew antsy about keeping Caster waiting and took off on her own. It didn't require genius to see the girl's obsession with the man. He could've asked her to fetch shit-flavored Popsicles, and Karla would've found a way to do it. And Haley wouldn't have been far behind.

Heather had noticed the curiosity and hunger in her sister's eyes when she'd looked at Caster, and she didn't understand the attraction. The man was much older, on the low end of average looking, and just plain creepy. His eyes seemed to hint at a dark unpredictability, and he moved with the ease of someone used to being in control. The merchandise he sold only heightened that persona. Powders and candles, amulets and oils, all of them claiming to create or enhance magical spells.

In an odd way, it made sense that Caster and Karla were connected, only Heather didn't think it was in the romantic sense Karla imagined. It felt more like a user-used relationship, and there was no question as to who was on top. Under normal circumstances, Heather wouldn't have given two squats about who Karla dated. But this situation was far from normal. Together, Karla and Caster posed a greater threat to Haley because their combined influence would be stronger. That pushed the potential for disaster up so high it petrified her. If she couldn't keep Haley away from the weaker of the two, how would she keep her away from both?

"I said get out of my face, asshole!"

Jerked from her musings by the shout of anger, Heather looked up to see two of the boys huddled around Haley and Karla pushing against each other. One had hair dyed the color of broccoli, and the other wore a T-shirt with *Get a Grip!* printed in red across the front. Below the letters was the picture of a pistol with a hand wrapped around the grip.

"Man, fuck you!" Broccoli said, shoving the other boy hard.

The boy in the T-shirt stumbled backwards, arms flailing as he tried to regain his balance. His butt hit the ground first, gangly legs bouncing in the dust. He let out a loud *Oomph!*, then quickly scrambled to his feet and plowed headlong into Broccoli, which sent the guy flying into Haley. Both crashed into a decoy display, and plastic ducks flew from the selling shelf as though suddenly given life.

"Get off me!" Haley kicked out from under Broccoli, and her skirt hiked up over her hips. The group of boys surrounding her suddenly multiplied, most of them gawking, many shoving other boys out of their way.

Heather dropped her bag of popcorn and took off for Haley. Before she could cover the short distance between them, most of the boys began to push and shove one another. Karla stood just outside the periphery of the crowd, laughing so hard she had doubled over.

"Knock the shit out of 'im!"

"Move!"

"Damn! Get outta the way!"

"I wanna see!"

"Get off my friggin' foot!"

In an instant, arms began to swing out wildly, and fists connected to noses, jaws, someone's cheek with a loud *spack! Spack-spack!* The crowd seemed to suck in on itself, everyone pushing, shoving, pulling, kicking, and yelling in one huge heap.

Heather plowed into the crowd, screaming, "Get away from her! Move! Haley!"

Amidst the gaggle of arms and legs, Haley was curled into the fetal position on the ground, her skirt hiked up even higher. She had her hands on her head, and her arms covered her face. A thin stream of blood ran from a cut on her left leg.

"You're hurting her! Move!" Heather slammed the heel of her fist into someone's back, determined to get to Heather. The person she'd hit spun around, and she suddenly found herself nose to nose with Jason Cribner.

He bared his teeth like a rabid dog. "Back up, bitch!"

Without giving it a thought, Heather shoved hard against his chest with both hands. "*You* back up, bitch! That's my sister!"

Jason stumbled back a step, then in one fluid motion, he leaned forward and jackknifed a fist.

Another loud *spack!* rang through the crowd, and the next thing Heather knew, her jaw was on fire, and the ground was rolling up to meet her—quick.

CHAPTER ELEVEN

Mark stepped onto a thick crossbeam that jutted out from a costume jewelry booth and aimed his camera over the row of heads in front of him. He snapped three more pictures, capturing a blur of petticoats and plaid as the Magnolia Cloggers, a local square-dancing team, twirled toward their finale. He'd been roaming Craft Fest with his camera for the past hour, hoping to get a few decent shots. With any luck, he'd sell a few to some local magazines.

Leaving the Cloggers and the crossbeam, Mark headed down the midway, and it wasn't long before more photo ops appeared.

A toothless old man with a priceless smile smoking a cigar and wearing a beanie cap . . .

A heavyset woman in a flaming red moo-moo cradling a powder-white poodle . . .

Two small boys with dirt-streaked faces sitting

on their haunches, eating ice cream and sorting through a sack of marbles . . .

After taking the shots, he scanned one side of the midway all the way up to the apex—a giant CRAFT FEST sign—then back down the other side. Most of the booths looked the same, the way too many advertising signs on a short strip of highway look the same. He saw a little girl wearing a frilly yellow dress and stubby pigtails chasing a Yorkie in a circle. He trapped her in the camera's viewfinder, snapped the picture, then shifted the camera slightly to the left and zoomed in on the elderly couple sitting on lawn chairs a few feet away from her.

Mark hit the shutter button, then moved the camera again, this time settling it on a booth with an unusual sign: CURIOUS GOODS. He scanned the odd merchandise lining the selling shelf and also hanging from the canvas curtains at the back of the booth. There were pictures of werewolves and wizards, warlocks and black cats. A lot of different totems, many of them snakes. Candles, small jars filled with colored powders, and hanging pentagrams and crosses.

"Curious Goods—that's an understatement," Mark muttered, and snapped more pictures. He wondered if the owner of the booth practiced black magic, like Chaos, or if he or she only sold bum merchandise that promised to bring money and love to the naïve.

Moving the camera again, Mark refocused and suddenly Haley Thurston came into focus.

She was standing near the front of Curious Goods, talking to a black-haired man he assumed was the booth's owner. Heather stood a few feet away, eating something. Mark zoomed in on her and noticed concern on her face as she watched Haley talking to the man.

He turned his attention back to Haley and saw the guy behind the booth take her hand as if he were going to shake it. The grin on his face reminded Mark of an eel, slick and greasy looking. He did shake Haley's hand, but held on to it a little too long for social etiquette. While he held on to her, Mark noticed something on the back of his hand. He zoomed in closer to see what it was—then wished he hadn't.

Jesus, not another damn snake!

Only the one depicted on the back of the man's hand was not an ordinary snake drawing or tattoo. It was an ouroboros, the symbol of a snake with its tail in its mouth. Mark remembered reading about it while researching Chaos yesterday. The ouroboros had different meanings for various cultures, but for those involved in black magic, it was often a symbol of continuous power, constant rebirth and recreation.

"What's that sleaze bucket want with Haley?" Mark muttered. The more he watched, the more uneasy he felt about the guy. There was just something about him that set Mark's teeth on edge and made him resolute. "I've got to get the girls away from there."

He removed the telephoto lens from his camera, quickly packed it in his camera bag, then started for the girls, who were about a hundred yards away. He hadn't gotten very far when he noticed Haley, Karla, and Heather leaving the booth. The man behind it left, too, as soon as the girls walked away, but at least he was heading in the opposite direction.

Letting out a breath he didn't know he'd been holding, Mark stopped at a lemonade stand for something to drink. He kept one eye on the girls to make sure the sleaze hadn't doubled back to follow them.

After paying for his drink, Mark walked casually in their direction, hoping to have a chance to talk to Haley. He wanted to get more of the scoop on Curious Goods. More specifically, he wanted to know the extent of her involvement, if any, with the man behind the counter.

As he headed toward them, Mark noticed Heather going to a snack booth alone, while Karla and Haley headed for a group of boys standing by a decoy booth. It concerned him that as close as the twins had appeared before, they seemed just as distant toward each other now. It had to have taken a hell of an influence to cause that division, and it was hard for him to believe that Karla Nichols had accomplished that with her personality alone. Something else had to be at work here, something meant to divide and conquer. He only hoped that something didn't include destroy.

The group Karla and Haley joined held quite a few boys Mark recognized from Laidlaw High, including one he knew to be an infamous troublemaker, Jason Cribner. As bad as Jason's reputation was, though, Mark couldn't help thinking, *Better ducks than snakes* . . . At least he knew the boys near the duck decoys were controllable. He didn't know anything about the guy who sold snake totems at Curious Goods. For all he knew, the man might have been an evangelical minister who sold black-art trinkets to pay for his next missionary trip to Haiti. Then again, he might be a grand master or grand hooha or whatever they were called in some black cult and could produce a spell with the simple blink of an eye. Whatever the man's ability or purpose, Mark knew that the last thing the Thurston twins needed to be involved with was another snake charmer. *No more snakes!* Snake eyes, snake tattoos, live snakes, just way too many damn snakes.

Snippets of conversation from the boys carried over to Mark as he got closer. They were talking over one another now, trying to get Haley and Karla's attention. Their voices suddenly grew louder and more insistent, and before Mark knew it, they were pushing and shoving, kicking and swinging fists. The crowd swelled to nearly double its size with onlookers almost immediately, and he saw Haley get swallowed up in the middle of it. Mark dropped his lemonade and ran to help her.

Running at full throttle, Mark saw the pushing, hitting, and shoving increase in intensity, threatening to erupt into an all-out melee. One boy with dark green hair threw a punch that connected with the side of another's face, and the second boy went down. Another boy jumped on green-hair's back, throwing an arm around his throat. That caused a few others to jump in, and that was about the time Mark saw Heather charging into the mix. He also spotted Karla standing just outside the fight zone, watching the chaos and laughing. On either side of her, men and women were gathered in small bunches, gawking at the pit of fists, but none of them jumped in to help. Mark willed more fuel to his feet, but he still arrived too late to keep Cribner from laying Heather out with a punch.

"Cribner!" Fury pumped fire and adrenaline through Mark's body, and he grabbed two boys by the collar and yanked hard to get them out of his way so he could reach Jason. Both flew backwards, out of the tangle of fists and feet, which produced an opening just big enough for Mark to see Haley lying on the ground, exposed from the waist down. A blind fist suddenly popped Mark on the back of the head, and he spun around to face his attacker. It was Kurt Richards from his art class.

The boy's mouth dropped open when he saw him. "God, sorry, Mr. Aikman! Wow, I didn't—" Before Kurt could say any more, another boy, reeling off balance, crashed into him from the left. Both hit the dirt hard.

"Break it up!" Mark yelled so loud his throat burned. He grabbed two more boys by the collar, but before he could jerk them apart, he was shoved hard from behind and lost his balance. He stumbled headfirst into someone else's fist. The blow sent him staggering a little to the right, where he almost tripped over Heather, who was trying to get to her feet. He grabbed her left arm to pull her out of the crowd, but she immediately jerked away and plowed ahead toward Haley, who'd at least managed to roll onto her hands and knees, her skirt finally pulled down into place.

"Heather, wait!" Mark shouted. "I'll get her!" He drove his body forward through the crowd, forcing his way to the twins. Just as he reached them, he felt a tearing, searing pain in his right thigh. With a roar of agony, he crumpled to his knees, then fell on his left side as though suddenly boneless. He grabbed his leg, felt too much blood seeping through his fingers, and his eyes went in and out of focus as they swept through an ocean of legs to find his attacker. He caught the glint of a knife blade as it moved away.

As if someone had reset the world to slow-motion speed, Mark's eyes trailed the blade, following it through the crowd to a stubby-fingered hand. That hand was attached to a very short, muscular arm, which belonged to a squat, deformed torso. The head on the torso was oversized, and it sat on narrow, stooped shoulders. Its dark, broad-browed face bore small eyes, no chin, and a crooked sneer that revealed large, blunted teeth. It stood only three feet tall, and as it turned to run, it did so on . . . *cloven hooves?*

Snakes, cloven hooves, little girls in frilly yellow

dresses, old men with no teeth, elliptical eyes . . . As these images flashed through Mark's mind, he couldn't put a finger on the ones that were supposed to be real versus those imagined . . . *or do they all belong somewhere between real and imagined?*

Figuring the loss of blood was causing him to lose a grip on reality, he pressed a hand over the wound in his leg, and the pain sent shock waves to his brain, sharpening it. The world was suddenly righted to regular speed again, and it brought a rush of sight and sound, both of which told him the boys were still fighting. Gritting his teeth, he rolled from his right side to his left, searching the faces around him. He no longer saw Heather or Haley. Just a scramble of strange faces and blabbering, fighting fools.

Tired of the melee, Mark reared his head back and yelled with all the strength he could muster, "Enough!"

The scuffling sounds immediately dropped in volume by half. More than enough for him to produce emphasis with less effort.

"Dammit, I said that's *enough!*"

The world suddenly went silent, and for a moment, Mark thought he might have passed out. But then a circle of people appeared above him. Some looked concerned, a few frightened, others just wide-eyed and curious as they gawked at him. The next sound he heard was a voice saying, "Mr. Aikman's been hurt!"

The next thing Mark knew, he was looking at the back of an ambulance and being lifted onto a gurney. Most of the boys and the crowd that had gathered to see who was bleeding and how much, had dispersed. He turned his head to one side, craning his neck to look as far back as possible, hoping he might catch a glimpse of Haley or Heather so he'd know they were all right. He didn't see either. What he did see, though, was the Curious Goods booth . . . and the strange looking . . . *man?* . . . *thing?* . . . peeking at him from under the booth's selling shelf. Behind the . . . *thing*, stood Sleaze-bucket, the man Mark had seen talking with Haley earlier. He was watching Mark as well.

Raising himself up on an elbow, Mark was about to shout at the man that he was as ugly as the goon beside him, but a paramedic picked that moment to slap an oxygen mask on his face and press him back to the gurney.

As they loaded him into the ambulance, Mark thought of the sleazy grin that had appeared on the man's face when he'd talked to Haley, and the sneer on the *thing*'s face as he ran away. In his mind, their faces overlapped, then melded into one. It was then Mark knew, imagined or not, that the beast and the Curious Goods man were one and the same.

Stay away from those girls, he thought. *Both of you, stay away.* He closed his eyes against the image of man and beast, and breathed in fresh oxygen.

Before the ambulance doors shut, Mark heard a voice loud and sharp in his mind. It was so vivid, so real, it sounded as though someone had placed a bullhorn next to his left ear, then spoke through it. Although he'd never heard the man speak, Mark knew without doubt who the deep, commanding voice belonged to—the man from Curious Goods—and his message to Mark was simple.

Interfere and you die.

CHAPTER TWELVE

The afternoon was waning, and Caster knew he was running out of time. Sooner or later he'd have to allow Karla to come into the booth and drape herself all over him if that was what she wanted to do. In order to keep her focused and on task, he'd have to play along because short of picking Haley up at home himself, Karla was the only way he had to get the twin to his booth later tonight. He already knew she was going to blow a gasket as soon as he talked to her about bringing Haley to him, but he also knew what to do to keep her quiet if he had to.

Caster busied himself replenishing candles in the display bin on the selling shelf while he waited for Karla. He'd done well most of the day, which was what he'd expected with a festival this size. The best part about it, though, had been Haley. The girl was exactly right for what he wanted, and although he couldn't have both twins, she would have been the one he would have chosen if given the chance. He'd seen the curiosity in her eyes and the hunger to experience life on her own terms. That alone made her a great candidate. But add to those attributes elderly guardians who were too slow or ignorant to keep track of what Haley was into, the girl's own eagerness and her willingness to do whatever it took to gain control over her life, and he had the *perfect* candidate for answering one of his special questions.

Caster had only one concern. The photographer, and he'd had no idea the guy was even part of the equation until this afternoon. He'd noticed the man snapping photos of his booth while he was saying goodbye to Haley and passing her the note. Caster had learned a long time ago to be aware of everything going on around him. You never knew from what direction a threat might come. Initially, when he'd noticed the man adjusting his camera lens and taking pictures, he thought he was just a photographer for the local paper. But not wanting to take any chances, Caster continued to watch not only him, he'd used one of the secrets to search the photographer's thoughts and understand his intentions. It was then he realized the man had more than a passing interest in his booth and that he had an interest in Haley. He cared about her, but not like a lover would. More like a teacher or an uncle.

Wanting to keep him off center and away from Haley, Caster decided to throw out a diversion. That was when the fighting had begun, and what a sweet game plan that had been. Better than Caster hoped for. In fact, as soon as the fighting broke out, Caster had stepped out to the front of the booth so he could watch. As soon as the photographer separated one faction, he was sucked into yet another skirmish. Although great fun to watch, it got boring after a few minutes. That's when Caster came up with the idea to screw with the photographer's head and end his meddling once and for all.

The idea called for him to use one of the secrets he'd tried only once before—to create a being whose sole purpose was to do his bidding. The being had no conscience and did not understand emotions like love and compassion. All it understood were the raw basics that often controlled the human psyche—lust, greed, and anger. Although those qualities made the creature useful, it also made it dangerous. If not conjured properly or taken care of properly after conjuration, the person responsible for creating it would often be in mortal danger. The being had no conscience, did not feel love or loyalty to its master, so if absolute control was not established by the master at the time of creation, he or she often was the one being controlled . . . or killed. Many of the siblings who knew the secrets rarely, if ever, used that particular one. They figured the danger-to-benefit ratio was far too high. And it was.

Caster's first experience with it had been eight

years ago, and the results had been disastrous. Had it not been for some of his street siblings being in the right place at the right time and having the right knowledge about defeating wayward conjurations, he knew he'd be dead right now. Since then, Caster had never even considered using that secret again. But seeing the photographer, hearing his thoughts, knowing he could be a threat to Caster having his perfect candidate, had brought the secret to mind and gave him the courage to use it.

Overall, he thought he'd done well. Of course if anyone was to score on artistic value, Caster knew he'd probably bomb. The creature had come out dog-dick ugly, but Caster hadn't been concerned with aesthetics when he'd created it. He just wanted one that was strong, agile, and determined to get the job done. From that perspective, he'd made a perfect score. Not only did the creature do its job, it had created an opportunity for Caster to really screw with the photographer's head. The deep wound, loss of blood, ambulance ride, all traumatic events. But when Caster had sent his thoughts to the man in surround sound—*Interfere and you die*—the look of shock on the man's face had been worth it all.

"Can I see you now?"

Caster glanced over his shoulder and saw Karla standing with her hand on her hip at the back of the booth. He forced a smile, then turned away from the candle display and went to her.

Her eyes, large and doelike, searched his face

as he brushed a strand of hair away from her face. "How's this for seeing me?"

The smile she gave him was wide and genuine. "Perfect."

"And did my sweet one enjoy herself this afternoon?"

She gave him a questioning look.

"I saw you standing outside the crowd, watching them fight."

"Oh, that!" Karla's face brightened. "Yeah, they were really going at it."

He slowly smoothed her hair with a hand and gave her another easy smile. "I'm glad you liked it."

She gaped. "You did that?"

He shrugged slightly, feigning modesty. "I thought you might enjoy something a little more high energy."

"Wait . . . wait, are you saying you did that for me? You caused the fight just for me?" The expression on her face seesawed between incongruity and adoration.

Instead of answering, Caster tilted his head, holding her gaze. "You're surprised?" He reached for her right hand, grasped it, and before she could answer, he quickly pulled her close. He grinned at her upturned face and kissed her, his lips lingering on hers just long enough to convey his intentions.

Karla's eyes grew wide, and although smiling, she made a token effort to back away. "Caster, I don't think—"

He snaked an arm around her waist and held

her firmly, pressing himself against her provocatively. "You're mine, Karla. You know how much I want you. And you know what I can do for you." He kissed her again. "And I know what you can do for me."

Still in his grip, Karla placed her hands on his chest, holding him away from her. "I know." She glanced toward the front of the booth. "But . . . is this really okay? I mean, there are people all over the place. Someone could—"

Caster rocked his head back and laughed. It sounded harsh even to his own ears. "Not sex, Karla." His eyes softened as he fixed her in his gaze. "Not sex . . . there are many things you can do for me that have nothing to do with anything tawdry." He laughed again, a lighter sound this time, and allowed her to slip from his grasp.

She took a couple of steps back and bumped into a shelf. Caster matched her two steps and captured her waist in his hands. He drew her close, meeting her eyes with the same hypnotic gaze.

"And you'll do those things for me, won't you, Karla?" He smoothed her hair again. "You'll do anything I ask, won't you?"

Her face and eyes softened immediately. She nodded slowly, as though transfixed. "Yes . . . yes, I'll do anything for you."

Caster kissed her again, almost violently this time, nipping at her lips with his teeth. He thrust his tongue into her mouth and forced it as far back as it would go before he finally broke contact. He fixed her with an intense stare once more. *"Anything?"*

Karla nodded very slowly. "Anything. . . ."

He glanced down at her breasts. *Would you walk lopsided?* He shifted his gaze back to her eyes. *Time for that later.* His right hand lightly brushed against her breast as he reached up to stroke her hair again. "Good. That's very good, my sweet Karla. Because there's something I need . . . desperately." He barely breathed the last word.

Her breathing grew rapid, and he felt it hot against his face. "Anything," she repeated.

He laughed softly. "You're a very bad girl. We're going to have such fun together."

She trembled visibly.

"We'll start small for now . . . see what you're willing to do for me." He tapped a finger against his lips, as though thinking up a test. "I know . . . remember the girls you brought here earlier today, the twins?"

She kept her eyes steady on his. "The twins, Haley and Heather Thurston."

"That's right. The ones I had you introduce to Chaos magic."

"Yes."

"Yes . . . that's exactly the right answer every time, sweet Karla. Always remember that. Otherwise you might have to spend some time with my little friend."

"Your friend?"

He stared at her, his grin widening. "I . . . *created* a friend, someone who will do my bidding without question. Look, Karla . . . look deeply into my eyes. Do you see my friend? Can you see my power?"

As he spoke, he felt Karla's gaze falling deeper into his eyes. She drew a little closer, then jerked her head back, her eyes wide and filled with fear.

Having little doubt she'd seen the image of the creature, Caster blinked and dismissed the vision.

Karla took a step backwards, fear still solid on her face.

Caster matched her steps once more, drawing close. "Would you care to meet my friend in person?"

"No!" She threw frantic glances around the booth as if expecting the creature to appear at any moment. "What—what do you want with the twins?"

Caster held up a hand and shook his head. "No, no. No questions. You will bring Haley to me tonight."

"But what if she won't—"

He caressed her cheek with a finger. "She will come, Karla. You will see to it." He kissed her again. "Understand?"

She nodded quickly, as though petrified that if she didn't, the creature she'd seen in his eyes would suddenly materialize. "Yes . . . yes, I understand."

"Good." He held her chin firmly between his forefinger and thumb. "Either you bring Haley to me tonight, or . . . well, let's just say you'll have a date with my little friend. And he isn't as nice as I am."

When he released her chin, Karla opened her mouth as though to say something, then snapped it shut and ran out of the booth.

Caster walked calmly to the front of the booth and looked out. Karla was still running. *Nice ass,* he thought. *I wonder if she'd run lopsided?* He laughed at the thought, then sighed.

"It'll be a perfect night for a game," he said softly. "Perhaps a little Russian roulette, only with a slight variance. One twin lives, the other dies—or both die." Either way, someone would die—and Caster knew he'd have a great time playing.

CHAPTER THIRTEEN

It was almost nine-thirty and had been dark for some time when Karla dropped them off at the house. Besides leaving Craft Fest late, they'd had to make another stop at a fast-food place so Haley could change into jeans and give the borrowed clothes back to Karla. The car was still rolling to a stop when Heather opened the back passenger door and jumped out. From the front seat, Haley watched her sister storm toward the house. She wondered how they were going to explain the swelling and new bruises on Heather's jaw to their grandparents. It was only a minor worry, though. Haley's biggest concern was how she was going to get out of the house undetected later so she could get a ride with Karla back to Craft Fest and Caster.

When the car came to a complete stop at the end of the drive, Haley glanced over at Karla. The girl's jaw muscles were working overtime, and she stared straight ahead, unblinking. After announcing to Haley that she'd drive her back to Caster later that night, Karla hadn't spoken a word to her, which confused Haley even more. What kind of guy sends his girlfriend to pick up another girl? And what girlfriend would actually be stupid enough to do it? If Caster really wanted to see her tonight, he could have picked her up himself after Craft Fest closed. Why did he involve Karla? Judging by the pain and anger that flashed intermittently in Karla's eyes, she was probably wondering the very same thing and getting pissed about it.

"Thanks for the ride," Haley said, and opened her door.

Karla continued to stare straight ahead.

Haley got out of the car, then held the door open and leaned in so Karla could see her. "So I'll see you around eleven?"

Cutting her a look that would have chewed her in half if it'd had teeth, Karla nodded curtly, then turned away.

"All—all right . . . well, I guess I'll see you then." Haley waited a moment, and when Karla didn't respond, she closed the car door, and the girl immediately peeled out of the driveway, gravel and dust spraying everywhere.

Heather was standing next to the front door when Haley climbed onto the porch. "Why'd she take off like that?" Heather asked.

Surprised that her sister was even talking to her, Haley shrugged. "Who knows? Maybe she got into a fight with Caster."

"Wouldn't blame her," Heather said. "The guy's a creep."

Haley bit back a response as they went into the house. She didn't want to argue with Heather about Caster. She just wanted to see him later that night.

They crossed into the living room and saw Meemaw sitting on the couch with a pile of mending. She worked a needle through the toe of a sock and glanced up only briefly when they walked in. "Have a good time?"

"Not bad." Haley signaled for Heather to walk beside her on the right so Meemaw wouldn't see her bruised jaw.

Having finished the sock, Nadine picked up a shirt with a torn pocket. "Dark outside, ain't it?"

Heather sidled up to Haley's right side and ducked her head. "Sorry, Meemaw. We didn't mean to be late. There was a lot to see. More than we thought."

"Papaw go to bed?" Haley asked, glancing toward the kitchen.

Nadine laid the shirt on her lap, her face pensive, her voice calm. "Reckon he was tired. He had a long day." She picked up the shirt again and turned her attention back to the torn pocket.

"Okay, well . . ." Haley motioned for Heather to hurry past her and go down the hall. "Guess we'll see you in the morning."

Nadine looked over at her, smiled, and rested the shirt in her lap again. "Somethin' botherin' you, child?"

Haley grinned. "No . . . everything's fine. 'Night."

"Okay then. Sleep tight."

Haley turned on her heels and headed for the bedroom. Despite the scare they'd had at Craft Fest, getting trapped in the middle of all those boys, excitement fluttered in her stomach like a riled hive of bees. In an hour and a half, she'd be heading to Caster to learn some of the biggest secrets in Chaos magic. And all those secrets would be hers to use as she chose. Maybe then Heather would stop treating her like she was five years old and give her the respect and attention she deserved as an older sister, even if she was only older by six minutes.

Crossing into the bedroom, Haley closed the door quietly behind her. Heather was at the dresser, pulling out pajamas.

"Okay, what's going on with you?" Heather asked.

Haley sat hard on the foot of the bed and bounced once, grinning. "What do you mean?"

"You know what I mean. What's going on? You've been acting all funny and giddy since this afternoon, even after that awful thing that happened with those boys. I mean, God, Haley, half the school saw your underwear, but you're acting like it was no big deal. Why?"

Haley couldn't get her grin to recede. "I don't know what you're talking about. I'm just happy. Is that all right with you?"

Heather frowned.

Haley got off the bed and went over to put a

hand on Heather's arm. "Look, we went to the fair all by ourselves and had a good time—no, a great time . . . well, except for the fight—and . . ." She felt the grin on her face broaden. She couldn't hold back any longer. "I'm going back. Caster wants me to meet him there later! Can you believe it?"

Heather's mouth dropped open. "You can't do that! How are you gonna get there? You can't walk to Craft Fest, and I'm sure not going back!"

"Shhh! Not so loud! Karla's gonna come get me in a little while. God, was she ever pissed!"

"Why? What was she upset about?"

Haley walked back to the bed, flopped onto her back, and stretched her arms out above her head. " 'Cause she wasn't invited. She's jealous because she thought Caster was her man." She turned on her side, propping herself up on an elbow. "For that matter, you weren't invited either."

Heather frowned. "Caster invited you? *Caster?*"

"Yes, Caster invited me." Haley sat up. "That's what I just said. He wants me to meet him." She jumped off the bed and twirled in place. "And you'll never guess what else . . ."

"What?"

"He kissed me on the cheek, and he gave me a note asking me to meet him tonight." She arched a brow. "And he's gonna teach me things . . . secrets."

Heather paled. "Haley, you can't go! I mean, if Papaw and Meemaw catch you—"

"They won't!" Haley glowered at her. "Understand?" She turned away and walked over to the closet, hating that her good mood had been ruined. "They'll be asleep before too long anyway. Papaw's already gone to bed, and Meemaw will be going soon. Besides, Papaw said we could go by ourselves . . . he didn't say how many times."

"You can't, Haley, please!" Heather said, shaking her head. "And Papaw *didn't* say we could go either. You did something . . . said something . . . He never said we could go. He just stopped saying no."

Haley narrowed her eyes and took a step toward her sister. "That's right. You're absolutely right. And he stopped saying no because *I'm* in control of my life now. Got it?" She pointed at her. "When Meemaw and Papaw are both asleep, I'm going . . . and if they find out, I'll know who told them."

Heather stared at her, gaping. "Haley, this has got to stop. Don't you understand? This whole Chaos magic thing is getting out of control. It has to stop. I'm worried about you."

"You don't tell me what to do, you hear? I'm in control!" Haley glanced at the bed, then back at Heather. "In fact, why don't you just go to bed? You can have both to yourself tonight. When I get back, I'll sleep in the living room." She headed for the bedroom door.

"Haley, don't—"

"Stop it! You had your chance to be supportive, to be a sister. Just leave me alone!" Haley stomped out, closing the door softly only to avoid waking her grandparents.

Tiptoeing into the living room, Haley saw that

Meemaw had already packed it in for the night and gone to bed. Relieved, she went to the kitchen and glanced at the clock on the stove. *Ten. An hour to go.*

Haley went back to the living room and peeked out one of the windows. Night had a full moon stuck in her bellybutton, and it cast a white, gauzy light over the yard. Although she technically still had an hour to wait, Haley started to worry that Karla might not pick her up. She'd been so angry when she left. *She'd better pick me up, or Caster'll have her ass,* Haley thought. She went over to the couch and sat, throwing a glance at the window every few minutes.

Papaw's voice startled her as he shuffled past the back of the couch in his socked feet and blue cotton pajamas. "Gotta get a drink of water. What you doin' up, girl? An' why you still dressed?"

She smiled at him. "Just didn't feel like sleeping yet. I'm fine. Everything's fine. You should go back to bed, Papaw."

He nodded and headed for the kitchen. A few minutes later he reappeared with a glass of water and made his way around the couch again. He stopped behind the sofa and laid a hand on top of it. "What you still doin' up, girl?"

"I said I'm not sleepy." Haley turned around to meet his gaze. "I know you had a long day, Papaw, and must be tired." She placed a hand on his forearm and squeezed lightly, thinking of the snake that had bound their arms together. "You should go back to bed. Get some rest. Don't worry about me. I'm fine."

Papaw looked at her for a long moment, then shook his head slightly before turning toward the hallway. " 'Night then. Get some rest."

Haley watched him enter the hallway, then listened for his bedroom door to close. She glanced at the clock again. *Ten thirty-five.* She turned toward the window. *Bitch better get here.*

When she looked at the clock again several minutes later, Haley heard a soft noise, like the smooth side of sandpaper being dragged lightly and erratically across a wooden table top. But no . . . Now it felt more like a sense than a sound—a sense of something slithering. The moment she came to that realization, something moved in her stomach. A kind of wriggling, writhing, twisting . . . then an exciting warmth spread from her stomach downward.

It's him, Haley thought. She placed her hand on her stomach. Her legs trembled. *It's Caster.* She smiled. *Something big's going to happen tonight. Something really big. . . .*

CHAPTER FOURTEEN

Back in bed after drinking his water, Buck tossed and turned, restless, shivering, his hands clutching his stomach and chest protectively. Shadows writhed and slithered through his uneasy dreams. Faces and whispered fears teetered on the edge of silence, then fell into his mind, filtering through his subconscious.

Them girls got names, Buck Thurston. . . .

Dad, you're all she's got now. Help her.

Man, look at all them snakes! What'd you do, Buck?

The baby in the corner . . . Please, Papaw! Please . . . !

Haley . . . Heather . . .

Whimpering . . . choking . . .

Haley . . . Heather . . . Heather . . .

Shadows weaved through the faces, through the whispered pleas. *Cat's eyes . . .* An evil, elliptical head shot out of the darkness, fangs flashing.

Buck sat bolt upright in bed. *"Heather!"*

Nadine made a hard, snuffling sound in her throat, her breath catching, releasing, then catching again as she snored on her pillow. She opened one eye, her voice quiet, scratchy. "Buck? You all right?"

Moonlight filtered in through the bedroom window, casting an eerie glow throughout the room. Buck's attention shifted from one corner of the room to the next, from the floor to the ceiling, back to the floor. Shadows were moving, coiling, writhing. Eyes peered at him, grinning, threatening. A cold sweat glistened on his forehead. *What the hell? Somebody there? Somebody—*

"Buck?"

He shot Nadine a quick glance. "I'm a'ight." Then he turned his attention back to the corners, the shadows.

She eyed him suspiciously. "Well, be still then. Both of us're needin' some rest. I worried half to death over them girls 'til they came home."

He shook his head as if trying to clear his mind. "The fair . . ."

The fair had been last night, right? Must be gettin' near dawn . . . .

What had Haley said? Ever'thin's fine . . . fine . . . .

He glanced at Nadine again. "Maybe you can put on some coffee?" *Water. . . .* "Maybe put on some water, an' . . . put in some grounds. . . ." *Snakes're on the ground . . . snakes in the water . . . snakes . . .*

"Buck Thurston, what're you gabbin' about? I

know full well how to make a pot of coffee. It ain't time yet. Now go on and get some sleep." She huffed onto her side, turning her back to him. Her soft snoring soon resumed.

Buck continued to study the corners, the shadows writhing there. *Flowing . . . like liquid . . . like water . . .* He reached over and patted Nadine's hip. "I know . . . I know . . . you go make coffee . . ." He watched the corners, the shadows, his eyelids heavy, heavier.

Finally his eyes closed, and he slumped back to his pillow. He reached for Nadine's shoulder again, missed. "Careful . . . snakes . . ."

She didn't respond.

In his dream, her soft snoring became her rising from the bed—slipping into her house slippers—pulling on her house coat—leaving the room to make coffee.

He nodded weakly. "A'ight . . . I'm a'ight . . . water . . ." *Water . . . What about water? Las' night . . . water . . . Haley . . .* Snippets of the previous night's events and conversation slipped through his consciousness.

Water . . . need a glass of water . . . Haley . . . Haley, why you sleepin' on the couch, girl? Git on back to bed.

I'm fine, Papaw . . . everything's fine . . . sideways with Heather . . . big day at the fair tomorrow . . . big day . . . everything's fine. . . .

Smilin' at me . . . up to somethin' . . . grinnin' . . . her eyes . . . cat eyes . . . cat's eyes . . . shinin' . . . sharp . . . sharp. . . .

Everything's fine, Papaw . . . fine, Papaw . . . fine. . . .

Fear reared up in his mind. *The fair? What's there? Who's there?*

Everything's fine, Papaw. . . .

No, . . . girl . . . Haley . . . you need to git back to bed . . . you need to . . .

Back to bed . . . everything's fine, Papaw . . . bed . . . you need to get back to bed . . . back to bed . . . bed . . .

And he'd returned to bed.

An hour after he'd lapsed back into a trembling sleep, Buck stirred again, imagined reaching for Nadine. *Where is she?* Again, fear momentarily flashed through him. *Coffee . . . she went to make coffee. . . .*

The soft sound of her snoring washed over him, warm, like coffee. *Making coffee . . . careful . . . be careful . . . snakes . . . water. . . .*

Suddenly his eyes flew open, and he immediately started searching for the shadows in the corners near the ceiling, near the floor. They were still there, interlocked, flowing over and through each other like liquid . . . *like water* . . . coiling, writhing, hissing, larger now than before, more defined, their eyes staring at him, focusing on him, calling to him.

Instinctively, Buck pulled the covers up to his chin and squeezed his eyelids shut. He trembled. *Snakes . . . 'em damn snakes're still in my head . . . damn snakes. . . .* Even with his eyes closed, he could still hear the shadows calling to him, speaking to him, hissing at him, taunting him.

Hayyy . . . leee . . . Heath . . . errr. . . . Hayyy . . . leeee . . . sssss. . . .

Buck forced his heavy eyelids open. There was something else, something more. Something—*someone*—in the room. He could smell it, feel it, almost taste it. But he couldn't see it.

For the first time in his life, fear completely engulfed him, and he tugged with gnarled fists at the covers again, snugging them tightly against his chin. He concentrated on the corners, the shadows. *Snakes . . . they jus' snakes . . . .* But they were talking to him. Drawing his attention. Diverting his attention . . . *from what?*

He forced himself to look away from the corners, to look for something—someone—larger. A larger shadow. Someone. A shape.

There!

His eyes wide, he gaped at the wall near the door, then tore his gaze away momentarily as the writhing shadows in the corner grew more frantic, the hissing more insistent.

Hayyyy . . . leeeee . . . sssss. . . . Heath . . . therrr. . . . Heath . . . therrr . . . sssss. . . .

His heart slammed against the inside of his chest as the undulating shapes began to shift, moving from the corners toward the larger shadow, flowing into the larger shadow, bleeding into it, congealing there. And the larger shadow growing denser, fuller.

Buck gaped, wide eyed as the larger shadow shifted and moved. The corners of the room remained full of sinuous, writhing forms, hissing, speaking to him, beckoning him. He shivered,

tried to call Nadine, to yell at the snakes, to
scream.

But no sound came out of his mouth.

The snakes beckoned him, hissing. Some of
them began to separate from the corners, creeping across the floor, slithering over the foot of
the bed.

*No . . . ! No escape . . . ! Snakes . . . ! This can't
be! No . . . !*

He struggled to throw off the covers, to scramble from the bed, sprint from the room.

But his arms wouldn't move.

His muscles wouldn't obey.

The larger shadow shifted, shrugged as if tearing its shoulders from the wall.

Buck could only stare, unable to move, unable
to scream, unable to breathe. *Careful . . . keep
watch! Snakes! Got to keep watch!*

But his final defense, his eyes, failed him, too.

His eyelids felt sodden, weighted.

His breathing became labored, heavy, deep.

He struggled to stare through his slitted eyes,
watching in horror as the snakes converged,
slithering up over the covers, nearing his motionless head.

He focused on the larger shadow, watched as
it shrugged again, harder, then tore itself away
from the wall and into the room, one arm rising
stiffly, as if from the grave, gesturing . . . reaching . . . straining . . . straining toward Buck.

As a scream ricocheted off the inside of his
consciousness, a great fluid weight slithered
across his eyelids, forcing them closed.

Even with his eyes shut, Buck could see the larger shadow nearing the bed, could sense the tread of sodden, shadowy feet in hard-soled boots.

Boots . . . where I seen them boots?

His fevered mind raced back to visions of boots. His own rough work boots as he slammed snakes with his shovel in the yard. His daddy's old black boots he used to wear to work in the fields. Then there were the nice dress boots he'd seen. *Them boots down to the Boots & More. Tony Lama . . . Laredo . . . Justin . . . an' 'em good workboots . . . RedWing . . .*

Justin boots! Justin's boots! No, Justin! Oh my boy! Justin!

The larger shadow neared the bed. Justin neared the bed.

Dad . . . Dad, help me . . . please . . . help me . . . help the girls . . . you can save them . . . please, Dad . . . please . . . .

But I can't move! I can't move. Oh my boy, my baby boy! I can't . . . I'm so sorry . . . I can't . . . Justin, I couldn't . . . I can't . . . .

A strong wave of helplessness washed over him, and Buck sank into a deep sleep, one from which he was sure he would never escape, would never awaken. His eyelids seemed to grow together. His breathing deepened. His muscles relaxed.

No more . . . I can't . . . I just can't . . . .

As the darkness sucked him into oblivion, his son's face—sorrowful, ravaged by the grave—faded back into the shadows.

And Buck's mind clicked off.

CHAPTER FIFTEEN

The writhing in Haley's stomach induced a strange but welcome sensation—a smooth, evocative tingling—that spread down her thighs and up into her chest. Her stomach felt like it was on fire, but in a warm, glowing way.

She struggled to sit calmly on the couch, alternating between glancing at the clock and out the window as she waited for Karla. Her head soon felt like a metronome, swinging one way towards the clock—*ten forty-two*—then over toward the window, then back to the clock. *Damn! Still ten forty-two. Is the damn thing busted?*

Haley got up from the couch and went over to the clock. She stared at it closely. Even though she expected to see the long, thin second hand hanging useless and immobile, she heard the steady *tick, tick, tick* as the needle dragged itself around the clock face. Anger flashed through her. If she could make the hands on the clock move faster, maybe Karla would get here sooner.

She stared at the clock, trying to make the second hand get on about its business, but the relentless *tick, tick, tick* remained steady, as if time itself had staunchly folded its arms and refused to advance any faster.

Balling her right hand into a fist, she pounded it against her left palm. "Move dammit!" She could've sworn the clock face smiled smugly at her just as she turned away.

She went back to the couch and plopped down on the cushions, then reached behind her to adjust the throw pillow nestled in the corner of the couch. She glanced out the window again, the soft, taunting *tick, tick, tick* of the clock echoing in her mind, relentless in its stifled regularity. The writhing, twisting in her stomach seemed to grow stronger and more intense as the clock ticked off milliseconds.

She looked back at the clock. *Ten forty-three . . . dammit!* She placed her palms on her stomach and pressed down hard, not so much to still the stirring there as to bring it more deeply into her, to make it as much a part of her soul as it was a part of her body. She sighed. She thought of Caster. . . .

She and Karla would drive up and Caster would open the door for her. He would pull her tenderly into his arms, his chest pressed firmly against her breasts, crushing them just enough. He would kiss her, deeply but gently. And when the kiss was over, he would keep hold of her hand and lean over to look at Karla through the passenger side window. *You can go now, and don't come back,* he would say. Then he'd smile at her, then look back at Karla again while gently squeezing Haley's hand. *This is the love of my life. We need to be alone.* And Karla would cry. Tears would stream down her cheeks as she shifted the car into drive. She would glance longingly a final time at the man she'd dared to love, then drive away, relegated to a life of emptiness.

Haley was startled from her reverie by the crunch of gravel. She glanced at the clock—*ten forty-four*—as she got up from the couch, straightened her blouse, then walked around the couch to the front door. Despite the nervous anticipation that made her want to rip the door off the hinges and burst out into the world, she gripped the doorknob deliberately and turned it with great care, making sure to avoid the click she'd heard it make before.

Still holding the doorknob firmly in her right hand, she glanced down at the threshold as she pressed the screen door open with her left palm. *This is the gateway to my new life . . . my new love.* The writhing in her stomach intensified for a moment, then calmed. She pulled the door closed carefully, again applying pressure to the doorknob to keep it from clicking as the latch went home. She closed the screen door with the same great care, then hurried to the passenger side of Karla's car, opened the door, and slipped into the seat.

"God, I thought you'd *never* get here!"

Karla looked at her.

Haley thought she saw a smirk just before Karla turned away and shifted the car into drive. She smoothed a hand over her blouse again. "What was the hold up? You know Caster wants to see me tonight." She glanced at Karla, who seemed more like a distant silhouette than a real person. "You know, he's not a guy you want upset with you. I bet he can get pretty mean if he wanted to. He's a *real* man."

Karla kept her eyes on the road, seemingly oblivious to Haley's presence.

Haley reached over and touched her arm. "You've been a good friend, Karla. I know Caster was your boyfriend and . . . well, I just want to say there are no hard feelings. I can only imagine how hard it must be to lose him." She glanced out the passenger window at the dark trees standing sentry along the side of the road. "Of course, you'd know more about that than I would." The stirring in her stomach increased, then waned. She felt her face flush. "I mean, I don't mean that in a bad way. It's just . . . you know . . . the guy's incredible." She looked back at Karla again. "Don't you think?"

Karla kept her eyes on the windshield, her attention apparently fixed on the road.

The writhing in Haley's stomach surged again, sending a warm shiver through her body. She lowered her head and laced her fingers together, rubbing one against the other, working her fingers in and out and around each other as she stared at her lap. She glanced up at Karla again and chuckled. "So you watching for deer or what?"

Karla didn't answer.

The stirrings in Haley's stomach surged yet again, and a warm kind of rage flooded through her. "Hey, you ain't pissed at me, are you? I mean, I didn't do anything but be myself." She ran her fingers through her hair, then cocked her head to one side. *My beautiful, beautiful self.* Her body was lean and trim and young. Was it any wonder Caster wanted her? "Look, it isn't my fault you introduced us. And you can hardly hold me responsible for the man's feelings, you know? He just wants what he wants, that's all. Guys are just like that."

Karla steered the car around a curve then onto the road that led to Craft Fest, and the commotion in Haley's stomach swelled again.

She *tsk*ed at Karla. "Okay, look . . . you can be pissed at me if you have to. Whatever. Just drop me off at the booth, and then you can leave." She laughed. "You've taught me all you can anyway. I'm sure Caster will want to continue my lessons in private anyway."

Karla turned into the Craft Fest lot, parked the car, then killed the engine. She turned to Haley. "I'll be here when you're ready."

Haley gave her a half smile. "I'm sure." She opened her door, got out of the car, then slammed the door shut and hurried off toward the Curious Goods booth.

Had it not been for the full moon, Haley might have been searching for Caster's booth forever. Most of the other booths were closed for the night, and the only light she had to work with other than the moon was a camper parked a few hundred yards away.

When she found the Curious Goods booth, Haley also found Caster waiting.

She rushed up to him. "God, Caster, I'm sorry! I thought she was *never* going to show up!"

He grinned, then gently stroked a palm over her hair. "It's okay. I've got nothing but time."

Haley stared at him, awestruck. *God, he's even more beautiful than I remembered.* Something writhed furiously in her stomach, and a warm surge washed through her. "But it's late. I know you need your sleep and—"

He put a finger to her lips, his eyes locking onto hers. "Shhh. It's all right." He squeezed her hand. "Everything's all right now."

She smiled, feeling her eyes grow wide and expectant.

"Come on." He squeezed her hand again. "We have a lot to talk about."

Haley smiled again and breathed, "Okay." She followed him into the booth.

As soon as they were inside, Caster pulled Haley into his arms and kissed her gently, then longingly. When he finally broke the kiss, he gestured toward his cot. "Here. Let's sit down."

Haley's stomach fluttered with anticipation. She was certain her thighs and abdomen would burst into flames at any moment. *God! God, it's going to happen!*

"Haley, you've learned quite a bit about magic—Chaos magic, right?"

She nodded, rapt in his beautiful eyes. *The most beautiful eyes I've ever seen on a man,* she thought.

He lightly stroked her thigh through her jeans, and she shivered. "But I can teach you more . . . so much more." He got up from the cot and turned to her, his pelvis only a foot away from her face.

Desire surged through her body, and it was all she could do to remain upright on the cot.

He turned his right hand so the ouroboros was only inches from her nose. "You see this symbol? The serpent eating its own tail. It's the ultimate symbol of control . . . of life creating itself, devouring itself, and re-creating itself all in one smooth motion."

Haley's gaze fixed on the beautiful tattoo, but her mind was focused on other parts of his anatomy.

"Haley, I've never met anyone who has so much potential, who would make such a perfect student." He stroked her hair, then pinched her chin lightly between his thumb and forefinger. "Look . . . look at me." He leaned forward as she looked up into his eyes. "I can teach you the magic, Haley. I can take you the rest of the way." He kissed her tenderly. "I am the master of Chaos magic. And you—*you*—will sit at my right hand, my special love." He sat next to her on the cot and took her hands in his. "There's just one thing. . . ."

This is it! she thought. *He's going to make love to me! Oh, God! Right here! Right now!* Nothing had ever felt so right. She sighed deeply and fairly breathed the words as she surrendered to his eyes. "What? What's the one thing?"

"Together we can bring you so much more than you've ever known . . . but first there is the one thing. You have to take back the power from the sigil your sister carries." He gazed at her, pulling her firmly into the universe in his eyes. He nodded slowly. "Understand?"

She nodded, feeling utterly lost to him. The stirring in her stomach waned, then stilled. "The power . . . take back the power."

He grinned. "That's right. Being a twin is problematic. It means sharing power with your sister."

"But I thought sharing the sigil would double our power since we're twins."

He shook his head. "No. It dilutes your power. Karla should have taught only you . . . either that or she should have taught you separately. If your sister were as strong as you in this, your power would be cut in half. That's why you have to take back the power she now wields." He kissed her gently but quickly, then stood and reached into his jacket pocket. "But it's all right. I have something here that will help." He sat back down on the cot, then took her hand and pressed a small clear vial into her palm.

Haley studied it carefully. It was filled with a clear liquid.

Caster smiled. "That's a very special potion. I mixed it myself." He stood, turning to her. "I have people who usually mix things like this for me, of course—after all, I'm the master—but in this very special case, I wanted to prepare it myself." He smoothed her hair gently. "You're just too special to me to leave anything to chance. You understand that, don't you?"

She nodded tentatively. "Yes . . . I guess so."

"Okay . . ." He touched the vial in her hand. "So all you have to do is take this home and make sure your sister drinks it."

She looked up at him quickly.

He held up a hand. "All it will do is counteract the power of her sigil. You have to do this to take back the power."

Haley chewed her bottom lip for a moment. "How will it counteract her sigil?"

Caster sighed, then moved away from her a little, clearly disappointed. He stared at her, locking her eyes in his gaze. "First, you have to trust me. Do you trust me, Haley?"

"Yes," she said quietly.

"Okay then. You know your sigil is just a symbol of your intention, right?"

"Yes, but—"

Caster put a finger to her lips. "And your intention comes from your mind, right?" He didn't give her a chance to answer. "Well, the sigil actually acts on your spirit, your soul. That's the only way you can affect what's going on around you, is through your soul. Understand?"

"I think so."

"Okay." He tapped a finger against the vial. "This potion disrupts the connection between the mind and the soul. Her intention might still be there, but her sigil will no longer be able to make that connection . . . that transition. She won't be able to put her intention into practice." He snapped his fingers. "And just like that! No more power. See?"

Realization zapped Haley between the eyes, and she blinked. "Oh! Okay . . ." She peered at the vial. "So this will keep the sigil from building a bridge from her mind . . . her intention . . . to having the power of her soul to put her intention into practice. Is that it? Will it hurt her?"

He cocked his head, studying her. "It might."

Haley frowned, then chewed her lip again. "A lot?"

"You have to decide, Haley. You have to choose whether your sister is more important to you than the power to have everything your heart desires."

"But—"

"Give her the potion, Haley. Take back the power."

She sighed, turned the vial over in her hand, then slowly nodded. "Take back the power—it's what I have to do."

Caster smiled, then leaned forward and kissed her lightly on the forehead. "That's exactly it. I knew you'd be an excellent student." He took her hands and helped her from the cot. "And when it's finished, my sweet love, you will have united the power your sister now has with your own. Just think of it, Haley. Everything you've ever wanted—everything you seek, including me—will be yours. All yours."

As she looked into his beautiful eyes, he kissed her. His lips were tender, gentle at first, but they soon grew hungry and more passionate.

And for a moment, Haley could have sworn his tongue felt flat—and forked.

CHAPTER SIXTEEN

Heather had slept fitfully at best ever since Haley had stormed out of the bedroom to go back to Craft Fest. *Back to meet that damned Caster,* she thought. *What a creep.* She'd seriously considered telling her grandparents what had been going on—in fact, she'd actually gotten out of bed at one point to do just that—but something had stopped her. She'd returned to bed, but had lain awake for what seemed like hours, dozing in and out, waiting for Haley to return.

Sometime during the night, she sat bolt upright in bed, angry with herself for having fallen asleep. She peered across the room in the darkness toward her sister's bed. "Haley? You there?"

Getting no response, Heather got up and felt her way to Haley's bed. When her knees touched the side of the mattress, she'd reached out to touch what she thought was her sister, but only found a pillow.

Then she remembered Haley, angry at the time, telling her she was going to sleep on the couch. *But wouldn't she want to tell me what happened after she got back?* Heather shook her head and whispered quietly in the dark. "Need to go see if she made it back."

After grabbing her robe off the end of her bed, Heather draped it over her pajamas, then hurried out of the bedroom. It wasn't fair that her sister had changed so much in such a short time. Heather felt anger bite at her insides. Haley shouldn't have gone out there at all, and even if she'd felt like she had to go, at least she should have had the decency to come back to the room to let Heather know she was all right.

Heather crept quietly down the dimly lit hallway and into the living room. From here, she noticed that someone had left the kitchen light on. She tiptoed toward the couch. "Haley?" she whispered. "You there? You home yet?"

Nothing on the couch but couch.

Thinking she should turn off the kitchen light, then come back to the couch and wait for Haley to get back, Heather headed out of the living room. She'd had enough. When Haley got back, everything was going to come out. And if she refused to talk with her about it, Heather planned to get loud enough to wake their grandparents. Then they could all discuss the odd goings-on of the past few days.

As soon as she walked into the kitchen, Heather froze midstep. Haley was standing near the refrigerator, drinking a glass of Meemaw's sweet tea.

Haley smiled at her. "What's up?"

"How come you didn't let me know you'd made it back?"

"I was gonna. After I drank this." Haley tilted the glass of tea toward her.

Heather pulled out a chair and sat down. She wanted to drill her sister with questions but was afraid she'd get angry and storm out of the house again. Propping her elbows on the table, she cupped her chin in her hands. "Coming to bed anytime soon?"

Haley shook her head, then sipped more tea. "Don't think so." Her eyes were shining. "You can go on back to bed though, sheriff. I'll just sack out on the couch when I get tired."

Angry that Haley was treating her trip back to Craft Fest so nonchalantly, Heather slapped the table lightly, remembering at the last second how late it was. She didn't want to wake her grandparents. "Dammit, Haley, don't you know I'm *worried* about you? Ever since we were kids— probably ever since we were born—we've been tight, stuck together all the time like two wads of chewing gum. But the last few days, ever since that friggin' Karla came into our lives, you've been slipping farther and farther away." She felt a sob about to slip from her mouth and bit it back. "And I don't know what to do about it." Sighing, she studied the table for a moment, then glanced up at her sister. "Is there anything I can do about it? Isn't there something I can do to help?"

A fleeting sadness fell over Haley's face. For a moment her eyes softened. "I'm sorry, Heather. You're right." She shook her head slightly. "Maybe it's time to call it a day on all this stuff. It's probably just a bunch of crap anyway." She smiled, and Heather laughed softly.

Haley took another sip of tea, then reached across the table and gently squeezed her sister's arm. "Hey, you want some water? Your voice sounds kinda scratchy." She held up a hand. "Yeah, I know. Probably my fault for worrying you so much, but I'll make it up to you. I promise."

Heather grinned. "Sure." As Haley got up to get a glass, Heather eyed her sister's tea glass and changed her mind. "Nah, make it tea. Won't help me sleep, but it sure tastes good."

"Yeah, for real. Meemaw makes the best," Haley said.

Heather watched her collect a glass from a cupboard, then set the glass on the counter. "So how'd it go tonight? Everything go all right at Craft Fest?"

Haley went over to the refrigerator and pulled out the pitcher of tea. She gently kicked the door closed, then turned to Heather and nodded. "Went all right, I guess. Karla was a little weird during—"

Heather laughed. "Karla's weird even on her good days."

"That's the truth. But I mean she wouldn't even talk to me all the way out there and back."

"Well from what I picked up when we were out

there earlier, she's pretty sure that Caster guy is *her* boyfriend, not yours."

Haley turned away. "Yeah, I guess so. It's just . . ."

"Just what?"

"It's just that Caster is so . . . powerful. There's something about him. . . ." She turned to look at Heather. "And he's willing to *teach* me, Heather. He can teach me a lot more than Karla can."

Heather arched a brow. "I'll bet. Question is, what he's gonna teach you?"

"No, I'm serious. Really, it isn't like that."

"Hmm," Heather smirked. "Really?"

Haley bit her bottom lip, then smiled. "Well . . . okay, maybe it's a little bit like that . . . but oh, my God, Heather, he's just such a hunk!"

"I'll have to pass on agreeing with that one, but in your support—and *only* because you're my sister—I'll say to each her own." Then she remembered what Haley had said only moments earlier: *Maybe it's time to call it a day on all this stuff. It's probably just a bunch of crap anyway.* She almost mentioned it, but something warned her to keep it to herself. "You said Caster was teaching you something. What's he supposed to teach you? Seriously I mean."

Haley blushed. "I don't want you laughing at me."

"No way I'm going to laugh."

Haley shrugged. "You know . . . just more stuff about Chaos magic." She looked at Heather, and her eyes seemed to glow for a second. "He's a master, you know?"

"I didn't know that."

"He is . . . and before you ask, yeah, he's the one who told me that. But he seems to know an awful lot about it, so . . . well, I believe him." She shrugged. "That's about it. So you ready for that tea?"

"Sure."

Haley filled Heather's glass with tea, then stirred it lightly. "There," she said, smiling sweetly as she handed her sister the drink. "Even stirred it with my finger. Put some sister cooties in it for you."

Heather laughed and took a small sip of tea. "Sister cooties, huh?" She sipped again, then set the glass to the table. "Whew, man that *is* sweet." She glanced up in time to see a frown leaving Haley's face. "Something wrong?"

"No. Nothing at all. What could be wrong?"

"I don't know. It's just . . . you sure you're all right?"

"I'm fine. Hey, know what? Remember those chugging contests we used to have when we were kids?"

"Yeah, the milk-chugging thing, I remember. You know, I bet Mom made up that game just to get us to drink our milk." Heather smiled, but felt it quickly fade. "You ever wonder about her?"

"Who?"

"Mom. I mean, you ever wonder how she's doing? Where she is? We're sixteen. Won't be long before we'll be able to go see her whenever we want."

Haley smiled wistfully. "I'd like that . . . I

think." She shrugged. "Yeah, I think about her sometimes. To be honest, though, I think about Dad more than her. Maybe because she could probably call us if she wanted to. She could stay in touch, I'll bet."

Heather shook her head. "I don't know. She might be in a place where she can't call. Or maybe she forgot the number or something. It's not like she called here all the time, you know. Meemaw and Papaw were Dad's parents, not hers."

"Yeah, she might be in a place in her head where she can't call. That's what I'd bet on if I was gonna bet."

"I know . . . I know, but there were some good memories. Just like that silly chugging contest you were talking about."

Haley picked up her glass. "So . . . you wanna?"

"What?"

Haley grinned. "Chug."

"Okay . . . but we're a lot older now. Let's make it interesting."

"What?"

"You know . . . let's bet something."

"Like what? A quarter or something?"

"No, it's gotta be something big. Let's see. . . ." Heather snapped her fingers, then picked up her glass. "Tell you what . . . if you win, I'll jump all into that Chaos magic thing with you or whatever else you want to do. But if I win, we're out of it."

Haley nodded. "As Papaw would say, a'ight then!"

Heather laughed and raised her glass to her lips. "Ready?"

"On three. One . . . two . . . *three!*"

Both girls lifted their glasses at the same time.

Sweet, Heather thought. *Very sweet tea.* As she drank, she had a weird feeling that she was falling. It reminded her of the flight she'd taken out of the loft when Haley'd pushed her. The falling sensation got stronger, though. And stronger.

As she swallowed the last drop, she glanced at Haley, who had already set her glass on the table. Haley's lips had curved into a strange smile, and her eyes looked darker than usual, almost evil. Heather glanced at her sister's glass and noticed it was half full.

Heather set her empty glass down on the table hard. "Did you . . . ?" She got so dizzy she had to grab the edge of the table. Tears stung her eyes as the room seemed to tilt. "Haley?"

"Huh?" Haley walked over and helped her up, then put her hands on Heather's shoulders and turned her in the direction of the hallway. "Here, let's get you to bed. Everything's gonna be fine, I promise." She giggled. "Caster said so."

As Haley guided her out of the kitchen, through the living room, and down the hallway to their bedroom door, Heather felt like she'd been falling forever. The sensation grew stronger with each passing moment, and so did the sense that this was one fall she might not survive.

CHAPTER SEVENTEEN

Mark had returned home Saturday evening, after they'd stitched up his thigh at the hospital, then released him. The doctors might have fixed that problem, but they weren't aware of the bigger one—the new one—the one that tortured his mind.

He'd been tossing and turning since midnight, trying to sleep. Every time he closed his eyes, though, he saw the thing—the creature that had attacked him. Over and over again, he felt the knife rip through his jeans and sink deep and cold into the flesh of his right thigh. And as the scene replayed, he imagined the hilt of the knife turning into a snake's head, its blade transforming into a long, curved, venomous fang.

He was drenched in sweat as he nestled into his pillow and looked over at his fiancée. Jasmine lay quietly on her back on the other side of the bed, her breathing regular, the covers rising and falling steadily, rhythmically with each soft inhalation, each smooth exhalation. *So easy for you to sleep,* he thought, then immediately wondered where the thought had come from.

Mark closed his eyes, and the scene immediately started playing in his head again, this time in still frames. . . .

Sleaze-bucket holding Haley's hand, knowing he was up to no good . . .

The fearful, nervous look on Heather's face as she watched her sister with the man. In contrast, Haley seemed enraptured.

The tattoo on the back of the man's right hand—the snake with its tail in its mouth . . .

Boys shouting, pushing, shoving. The cloud of dust that hovered at shoulder height—him hit on the back of the head—fists flying, cursing, screaming, punching, kicking.

And the ugly, squat creature running through a cloud of dust right after it plunged the knife into his thigh.

The same sneer on its face that he'd seen on the man from Curious Goods. The two were connected.

The two were one.

I interrupted something, Mark thought. *I interrupted something, and the guy wanted me out of the way. Somehow . . . somehow he sent that thing to hurt me.*

Mark played the scene over in his mind again and again, looking for a common thread. The thoughts tumbled over and over until it finally occurred to him: *The guy wants the twins. He wants the girls. He wants the girls. . . .*

That thought caused him to sit bolt upright in bed, sweat dripping down his face and bare chest. "No!"

Jasmine jerked awake. "Baby, you okay?"

He stared at her for a moment, blinked. "I'm all right. Go back to sleep."

She snuggled deeper under the covers. "You sure? Your leg okay?"

"I'm all right. Just go to sleep."

She sighed, untangled herself from the blanket and moved up beside him. She put her hands on his shoulders and began massaging them lightly.

He shrugged her off, hard. "Dammit, Jasmine, what're you doing? You can't fix my leg by massaging my shoulders. What the hell's wrong with you? Go back to sleep."

"But, baby, I just wanted to—"

Mark glared at her. "I *know* what you want. I know *damn well* what you want." He rose to his knees and swung around to face her. "Here, you want me to *show* you what you want?" He grabbed her shoulders and shoved her hard against the headboard, then pulled her to him and twisted her onto her back on the bed.

"Mark, stop! Stop it!"

He saw the girls—the creature—the fight—the man—the girls—the creature—the girls. *What am I doing?* But he couldn't stop.

He grabbed Jasmine's negligee at the shoulder and ripped it from her body. "You want me to show you?" He held her down, his left hand on her throat.

Jasmine fought him, kicking and slapping, but it only made him more determined. "Mark, stop!"

Maintaining his grip on her throat, he reached for the waistband of her panties, twisted it in his fist and ripped downward, tearing them, tugging them over her hips.

"Mark, no! Stop, please stop!"

But he didn't stop, nor did he stop thinking. The pictures kept running through his mind. *The sleazy man . . . the creature . . . Haley . . . Heather . . . the fight . . . the creature . . . Haley . . . Haley . . . Haley . . .*

And here she was—Haley, her lucious lips curled into a sensual smile, flashing those beautiful, slitted eyes as she moved beneath him. *Finding anything you like, Mr. Aikman?* He redoubled his efforts. Her arms stretched over his shoulders, loving, caressing, sinuous, sensual. The snake on her arm moved slowly, fluidly, coiling, then stretching. It moved slowly . . . fluidly . . . up around her shoulder, over her neck, up over his head and neck and shoulders. Her arms and the snake slithered down along his back, down over and around his legs, feeding his rhythm, *informing* his rhythm. The snake twisted and writhed, its rhythm—his rhythm—building to a fevered pitch, a smile on its face. *Do snakes smile?*

As if seeing the scene from outside his body, Mark watched the snake raise its head behind him, the smile broadening into fully gaping jaws. Haley's eyes flashed again, this time right *through* his rhythm, this time becoming evil. *You're my teacher, Mr. Aikman! Finding anything you like?* The snake's eyes flashed again. *Interfere and you die!* The snake's head flashed downward, and its fangs sank deep into his right thigh.

Mark screamed and pushed himself violently away from Haley . . . *Haley? No! Jasmine! Oh, God, Jasmine!* The snake still clinging, unbearable pain shooting up through his right thigh. The leg throbbed, throbbed, throbbed, pushing waves of pain up his thigh and into his torso.

He bent to grip his thigh with both hands and saw his fiancée, the lovely creature who loved him, who allowed him to love her. It was all he could do to breathe. "Oh, baby . . . baby, I'm sorry. God, I'm sorry!"

Jasmine slipped out of bed and moved quietly to the bathroom.

As the pain in his leg began to abate, tears ran down Mark's cheeks. *Why did I attack her? Why?* He knew one thing for certain: His mind had not been on her. He'd been thinking of Haley Thurston and didn't have the slightest notion why. It was as though all that had happened to-day had planted itself in his mind and was taking root. He'd never before treated Jasmine the way he had just now. He'd be lucky if she ever spoke to him again, much less married him.

The creature—the man—they were screwing with his head. Or maybe it was his wound—the pain. What if the creature had put something on the knife, a chemical of some sort that would cause his mind to slip? Make him see things that weren't there, hear things. He couldn't believe he'd just attacked Jasmine! God, he needed answers. And he needed them quick.

CHAPTER EIGHTEEN

When Karla had dropped Haley off in front of her house, she hadn't pulled away quietly. She'd peeled out, like before. Karla hadn't talked to her all the way back, either, not that it really mattered. Haley hadn't wanted to talk. In fact, she'd actually hoped Karla wouldn't suddenly snap out of her hissy fit and decide to start yammering. She had too much to think about.

During most of the ride home, Haley had considered what Caster said she had to do. *It does make perfect sense that the power of Heather's sigil would dilute the power of mine,* she thought. *Caster would know. After all, he's a master at Chaos magic. And he didn't say the potion would actually harm Heather, only that there might be a chance.*

After she'd crept back into the house, she went over to the couch and sat, thinking about Caster's request. *No, his demand,* she thought. He had given her a choice: She could be loyal to him—prove her loyalty and dedication to him with this act—or she could be loyal to her sister. *But it's the power. The power is what really matters.* She cocked her head, resolute. *And if I want the power, I have to take it back from Heather. I have no choice.*

But the whole loyalty issue still bothered her. Sure, she wanted Caster, wanted to be his student, his confidant, his lover. She wanted to be his partner. On the other hand, Heather was her twin sister. Loyalty was more than just a word between sisters, and even more so between twin sisters. She and Heather had been through a lot during the past few months, and they'd gotten each other through it all. Sure, there were adults around, and they were supposed to be the responsible people in their lives. *What a damn joke that is!* Fleeting glimpses of those adults passed through her mind.

She and Heather had idolized their father, and he'd left them in death. Everyone else had said all that generic, greeting-card crap—like he was a good man and that he was *taken* from them—and in reality she knew it wasn't his fault, but fault didn't matter in the real world. He wasn't around anymore, and that was all that really mattered. Haley *tsk*ed and forced a bitter smile as she remembered one of his favorite sayings when things didn't work out the way he'd hoped. *It just is what it is. . . .*

And their mother. She'd left them as surely as their father had left them, and it was even worse in a way. She was still alive, but she was so wrapped up in her own misery that she couldn't even see theirs. She was so selfish that she'd become trapped in her own mind. *Hell, she probably wouldn't know us if she passed us on the street . . . like I give a crap.*

Then there was Meemaw and Papaw, whom she secretly thought of as Nadine and Buck. Nadine was all right, but she was almost too understanding, always clucking around them like an old mama hen. Haley had actually overheard her telling Buck that she and Haley sometimes had their "woman time." *Good God,* she thought. *The woman can't even bring herself to say the word period!* She'd also heard her reminding Buck that they had names. *How messed up is that? Our loving, condescending meemaw has to tell the old fart we're human. Give me a friggin' break!*

And Buck, the man in their lives. The one who had been tasked with taking care of them after their father had died. The man they'd been raised to believe was a true Man, with a capital M—and Haley had controlled him as easily as if he'd been nothing more than a bothersome gnat. She'd told him they were going to Craft Fest alone, and she'd told him to go back to bed. *I sent him to his room!* She smirked at the memory.

The fact was she and her sister had been alone ever since their father and mother had abandoned them. And now her sister—whom she loved more than anyone on earth, on whom she'd depended her entire life, and even more

so these past few horrible months—was stealing
from her. She was stealing the little bit of power
Haley needed to be complete. *How could she turn
on me like that?* Caster, the most beautiful man
she'd ever met, filled her mind for a moment.
She thought of his awkward, boyish grin and
smiled. *I'll do it . . . I have no choice.*

Feeling more confident but still antsy, Haley
had gone into the kitchen, thinking a cold glass
of Nadine's sweet tea would go down perfectly.
As she sat at the kitchen table sipping her tea,
she heard Heather come into the living room,
calling for her. *Little twit— why do you care whether
I'm home?*

Not long after that, Heather had come into
the kitchen. And the first thing she'd asked was
when Haley was coming to bed. What was that
about? *You aren't my mother,* she thought, but
she'd said something else, something smart-
assed and noncommittal. Then Heather had gotten upset and had gone on for what seemed like
an eternity with all the sisterly crap she could
muster. *Telling me she's worried about me . . .* Haley
snorted.

After that tirade, Haley had decided to change
her approach. She'd smiled and fawned and practically groveled. She'd done her best to look tired,
as if fatigue were the root of what she was sure
Heather thought was her attitude problem. She'd
even told her she would drop Chaos magic.

It hadn't taken long for Heather to warm up
to her again, and Haley had put a cap on the

deal by offering Heather a drink. But while she was getting Heather's tea, the brat had almost derailed her by bringing up their mother. How was that fair? *She knows all my soft spots, that's all. She just knows how to push my buttons.*

But soon afterward, Haley had turned it around on Heather. She continued to feign sisterly love, telling Heather she'd stirred the tea with her finger to add sister-cooties or some crap like that. Then she'd remembered the milk-guzzling game they used to play and managed to use her sister's sick interest in nostalgia to get her to gulp her tea . . . and the potion.

But she got sick, Haley thought. *That wasn't supposed to happen.* Caster had said the potion *might* make her sick. He didn't say that it definitely would. She knew he loved her and couldn't believe he'd ever do anything to really harm her or her sister.

Still, Heather had been woozy, so she'd guided her to their room and gotten her into bed, then tucked her in snug and warm, like a good sister. Afterward she'd gone back to the kitchen to turn off the light and put away the tea. Then she went into the living room and curled up on the couch for a while, thinking . . . just thinking. Caster had been right. Heather was siphoning her power and had to be stopped. But he wouldn't have given Haley a potion that would harm her sister.

Still, Heather had seemed so out of it. A little later, Haley decided to honor her promise to

Heather and sleep in her own bed in their room instead of on the couch. And she did.

On Sunday morning, not long before sunup, Haley woke with a start. She stared at the ceiling for a moment, getting her bearings. The events of the previous evening and early morning played in her mind like a choppy movie, one of those old black-and-whites she and Heather had seen in school. The ones that would skip frames occasionally.

She remembered seeing Caster, the ride home with Karla, Heather coming into the kitchen to find her, their conversation about their mother. She smiled. Mom . . . *God, how I'd like to see Mom.* . . . She remembered the milk-gulping game they used to play, Mom's way of getting them to drink their milk. She remembered—Wait!

She sat up in bed, her eyes wide, and pivoted toward her sister's bed. *The potion!* The potion had hurt Heather; she was sure of it. It wasn't supposed to—Caster had promised—but something had gone wrong. It had hurt her. *God! Heather!*

Haley frantically kicked the covers off her legs and sprang from the bed. She practically flew to Heather's bed, and her worst fears were confirmed.

Heather's head lay on the pillow just where it had lain when Haley had put her to bed, but now the pillow and the sheet beneath it were covered with vomit.

YES! ☐

Sign me up for the Leisure Horror Book Club and send my TWO FREE BOOKS! If I choose to stay in the club, I will pay only $8.50* each month, a savings of $5.48!

YES! ☐

Sign me up for the Leisure Thriller Book Club and send my TWO FREE BOOKS! If I choose to stay in the club, I will pay only $8.50* each month, a savings of $5.48!

NAME: _____

ADDRESS: _____

_____

TELEPHONE: _____

E-MAIL: _____

☐ **I WANT TO PAY BY CREDIT CARD.**

☐ VISA ☐ MasterCard ☐ DISCOVER

ACCOUNT #: _____

EXPIRATION DATE: _____

SIGNATURE: _____

Send this card along with $2.00 shipping & handling for each club you wish to join, to:

Horror/Thriller Book Clubs
1 Mechanic Street
Norwalk, CT 06850-3431

Or fax (must include credit card information!) to: 610.995.9274. You can also sign up online at www.dorchesterpub.com.

*Plus $2.00 for shipping. Offer open to residents of the U.S. and Canada only. Canadian residents please call 1.800.481.9191 for pricing information.
If under 18, a parent or guardian must sign. Terms, prices and conditions subject to change. Subscription subject to acceptance. Dorchester Publishing reserves the right to reject any order or cancel any subscription.

JOIN NOW!

Clapping her hands over her mouth to keep from screaming, Haley tried to think. What could she do? If she woke the old folks, they'd surely blame her. But if she didn't, they'd find out soon enough anyway.

Tentatively, she reached a trembling hand to touch her sister's face. It felt cold.

She remembered a scene from a medical show and used her thumb to pry one eyelid open. The white of Heather's eye stared out at her. She reached almost frantically for her sister's carotid artery, but felt no pulse. She grabbed Heather's wrist but couldn't find a pulse there either. *Do you put your fingers on the wrist or your thumb? If Caster were here he'd know what to do.*

The thought of Caster stopped her cold, and Haley took a step backward. As she looked at her sister, an eerie calm settled over her, and she felt a smile crease her face. Heather deserved this. *She shouldn't have tried taking my power.* A wave of delight rushed through her, but it was almost immediately followed by revulsion—not with her sister, but with herself. *How could I feel good about this?* She grabbed her sister's shoulders and shook hard. "Oh my God, Heather! *Heather!*"

When Heather still didn't respond, Haley raced out of the room and pounded on her grandparents' bedroom door. "Papaw! Meemaw! Help! You've gotta help! Something's wrong with—"

The door flew open, and Buck stood gaping. "Haley? What's wrong, girl?"

"Heather . . . I . . . I think she's *dead!* Please help her! *Please!*"

Papaw shoved past her and raced to Heather's bedside. Nadine followed on his heels, still tying her robe.

Haley stood at the bedroom door, watching them, her hands pressed against her face as she sobbed loudly, tears streaming down her cheeks. *God oh God oh God! What did I do?*

Papaw stared at Heather for only a second, then bent to shake her. "Heather! Wake up, girl!"

One quick look was enough for Meemaw. "I'm goin' t'call the ambulance! They'll be here in a minute." And she was gone.

Papaw yelled after her, "Don't call no damn ambulance! Hell, they won't get here for a week! I'll take her m'self." He bent over the bed, slipping one arm under Heather's knees and the other under her shoulders. As he straightened up with Heather in his arms, Stump came racing through the door, barking wildly.

"Stump, get out the damn way!"

Just as he got to the door, Meemaw came hustling up the hallway. "Buck, put that baby on the couch! The ambulance'll be here soon!"

He brushed past her, turning sideways to get Heather down the hallway. "I ain't puttin' her down. I'm takin' her to the hospital." He turned into the living room and yelled over his shoulder, "Nadine! Get the damn door!"

Stump raced past him, barking around his feet. Meemaw passed him and turned the doorknob. "Buck, I told you I was callin' the ambu—"

Again Papaw brushed past her, kicking the screen door open so hard that it slapped against the wall. "*Dammit,* woman! They get here 'fore I get her to the truck, they can take 'er!"

Stump followed him out the door, still running in circles and barking.

Haley stood by the couch, staring through the window as Papaw stormed across the yard carrying her sister's lifeless form to his pickup. Her sobbing had calmed, but terror had iced her heart, and she was trembling all over.

Meemaw followed Papaw all the way to the truck, wringing her hands at her waist. "Buck, listen . . . you can't jus'—"

As Papaw loaded Heather into the pickup, he yelled, "Don't tell me what I can't do! Dammit, Nadine! Jus' call the damn hospital an' tell 'em we're comin'. Either that or jus' get in the damn truck." He quickly slipped in behind the steering wheel, and before he could start the pickup, Meemaw jumped into the truck with them. Papaw waited for her to close her door, then popped the clutch and took off.

Stump raced after the pickup, frenzied and barking.

As soon as they left, Haley got up from the couch and ran to her room. She pulled on a pair of jeans, tugged a sweater over her head, then put on a pair of socks and her running shoes. *Goddamn Caster! Son of a bitch! I'll kill that bastard! I swear I'll kill him!*

She ran through the house and out the front
door. She would hitchhike to Craft Fest or walk
there if she had to. Caster had lied to her, and
her sister was dead. The man was going to pay.

CHAPTER NINETEEN

Well after midnight, Caster drifted in and out of sleep as he lay on his sleeping bag in the back of the booth. His little meeting with Haley had gone well. He'd explained the ouroboros on the back of his hand, implying that it meant he was a master of Chaos magic. *You're special,* he'd told her. *You will go far.* It had taken all he had to keep a straight face. What a naïve little brat she was.

She'd even fallen for his explanation that being a twin meant sharing power with her sister, and that was problematic. *Karla should have taught only you, or she should have taught you separately,* he'd explained.

She'd told him she thought sharing the sigil would double their power since they were twins, but he'd explained that the opposite was true. *Because you're twins, creating a sigil together halves the power of it instead of doubling it,* he'd said. *To be truly powerful, you must retrieve the power of the sigil your sister carries and unite it with your own.*

Her eyes had grown wide with surprise, but she didn't question his authority in the matter. The look in her eyes was one of pure admiration. He'd thought she was going to kneel and kiss his tattoo. Afterward, he'd really piled it on by stroking her hair and adding, *Do that and you will reign with me.*

Then he'd produced a small vial of liquid from his jacket pocket. *This is a very special potion that I created just for you. When your sister drinks this, you will have all the power of both sigils. Everything you seek, sweet Haley—myself included—will be yours.* Then he'd bent to kiss her, softly at first, then more passionately, then hungrily, his tongue snaking into her mouth.

She was almost gasping with pleasure by the time they'd parted.

The intense pleasure of the memory awoke him. The level of control he'd levied over Haley was satisfactory. She would kill her sister for him. And then she would give herself to him, body, mind, and soul. He was sure of it, and that certainty made him grin.

Caster glanced across the room at the tarpaulin, behind which crouched the creature. He peered up at the stars overhead and spoke quietly. "At least she will give herself to me if she knows what's good for her." He felt a stirring somewhere below his stomach, and he wondered what she would feel like writhing beneath him.

While enjoying his ruminations, Caster suddenly sensed a presence and sat up. The moon was full and huge and provided plenty of light. Not seeing anything or anyone in the booth, he got up, went over to the side of the booth, and peered out into the dark. He saw Haley headed toward him. *Sooner than I expected,* he thought. As she drew nearer, he stepped out of the shadows.

Haley raised both fists and ran at him. "You bastard! You killed my sister! You *killed* her!"

Caster put his hands up to ward off her blows. "Wait! What happened?"

She continued to flail at him but was doing minimal damage. "You rotten bastard!" Tears ran down her cheeks. "How could you do that? How could you kill her?"

"Haley, I was right here all night, you know that. I don't even know where you live. Calm down."

"That stuff you gave me . . . that liquid . . . you said she had to drink it! It *killed* her, Caster! She's dead!"

He feigned surprise. "But that was a harmless potion. Wait . . . you didn't mix it with anything did you?"

Haley dropped her arms. "What?"

"The potion is harmless. It was meant to drain the power from her sigil, but nothing else. But it had to be taken in its pure form."

"You didn't say anything about that!"

He held back a grin and shrugged. "Must've forgot."

Haley renewed her attack, but Caster caught her wrists and held them tightly.

Still she struggled to hit him. "Forgot? *You* told me to give it to her! *You* told me it wouldn't hurt her! She's *dead*, Caster! Dead!"

Suddenly she stopped fighting and sagged.

He released her wrists and let her drop to the ground in front of the booth. "Look, it's going to be okay. I'll just mix up another potion . . . an antidote. We can give it to her, and she'll be better." He offered her his hand. "Come on, it's in my van, which is good because it's getting a little chilly out here."

Haley looked up at him, but didn't take his hand. Instead she pushed herself up from the ground and took a step toward the booth.

When he tried to slip an arm around her, she stopped walking and shrugged it off. "I can't believe you killed her. I thought you loved me."

"Let's talk about it in the van. It's two rows back behind the booth. I can mix the potion right there while you watch."

Haley followed him quietly, staring at the ground as she walked.

When they reached the van, he opened the cargo doors in the back. "Go on and get in."

Haley stood with her arms crossed over her chest and looked him dead in the eye. "That second potion had better work." Her tone conveyed an unconcealed threat.

Caster chuckled. "Or what?"

Still meeting his gaze head on, Haley poked him in the chest with a finger, her eyes ablaze. "Or else your ass is going to jail!"

Caster studied her for a moment and felt his

power wane slightly. *I'm losing it. Her sister can't be dead or she wouldn't be this strong*. He put his hands up. "Okay, okay! I told you it's gonna be all right. Just give me a minute." He leaned into the cargo area of the van and pretended to search for a vial.

"Just get the damned potion!" she screamed.

The next thing Caster knew, she was pummeling his head and back. He spun around, enraged. "Damn, Haley!" He shoved her hard, and she stumbled backward and dropped onto the ground. He advanced on her, his right fist raised and his index finger extended. "You will sit there and keep your mouth shut! Do you understand? I will *not* take any more of your crap! You *belong* to me! I control you! I *own* you! If your damn sister dies, she dies! Nothing changes! You . . . are . . . *mine!* Got it?"

Haley sprang up from the ground, swinging wildly at him and screaming loud enough to wake the dead and half of Jackson.

Caster fended off her blows and mentally called to his creature, who sprang from behind the stack of tarpaulins in the booth. When it reached them, the creature grabbed Haley around the thighs, and Caster wrestled her to the ground again. He straddled her, then pulled a bandanna from his hip pocket and used it as a gag, tying it tightly behind her head. He stood Haley up, roughly snaked his left arm around her stomach from behind, then leaned in close to her. "I have a knife right here," he whispered, making sure the tip of the dagger poked her in the rib cage so she'd know he was telling the truth. "I'll shove it right through your damn lung if you make another sound, I swear." He jerked on her to make his point. "Now keep your mouth shut, you understand?"

She nodded frantically.

"Now, we're going take a little trip." He nodded at the creature, who scrambled into the back of the van. As soon as it was inside, he pushed Haley toward the cargo doors hard. "Get in, and don't forget what I told you!"

Whimpering, Haley clambered into the van behind the creature, and Caster slammed the doors shut behind her and locked them. Then he hurried over to the front of the van, opened the door, and slid behind the wheel. After slamming his door shut, he whirled around in his seat so he faced her. "You are *mine,* you got that? *Mine! I* control you. Your stupid bitch sister means nothing to me! You are mine forever!"

With that, he turned back sharply, started the van and pulled out of the fairgrounds and onto a paved road, occasionally glancing in the rearview mirror. *Stupid bitch. What'd she expect? Did she really think she was going to screw with me and get away with it?*

Caster scanned the sides of the road, looking for a particular place. *There!* He turned left onto a dirt road, then drove another two miles before turning off again, this time onto a side road, the opening of which was all but concealed with overgrown brush.

He parked the van where it would least likely

be seen, then killed the engine, got out of the van, and headed for the cargo doors.

As soon as the doors swung open, he yelled at Haley, "Get out!" Then he gave the creature a mental command to stay put.

She scrambled out of the cargo area, and when her feet hit the ground, Caster shoved her toward an old barn. "In there." He grinned. "Like I said, I own you."

Once inside the barn, Caster dragged her to a back corner, then chained her ankles to anchors set in the dirt floor. He then tied her hands together above her head with the same bandanna he'd used earlier as a gag. "Scream all you want. Nobody's around to hear you." He sneered and spat on the floor. "You're miles from anything here. And like I said, you're mine." He grinned, then leaned close and licked her cheek. "All mine."

He would use her body and torture her mind until he grew tired of her. *Or until she dies,* he thought, then shrugged. *Whichever comes first. . . .*

CHAPTER TWENTY

Buck stormed into the house and plowed his way through the kitchen and living room. "Haley! C'mere, girl! We gotta talk!"

No one answered.

"Haley?" He stood by the couch, listening. "Haley, c'mon out here!"

Nothing.

He stepped into the hallway and looked at the girls' open bedroom door. The image of the three-year-old girl crouched in the corner of the room from two nights ago crossed his mind, and he shivered. "Haley?" he called quietly. "This . . . this is Papaw. . . . C'mon out here now. Come on. . . ."

Buck raked his fingers through his hair and moved slowly down the hall. *I'll search the house from back to front. If she's hidin', she'll move out ahead of me.* He reached his bedroom. "Haley, if you're in there, this ain't the time for jokin' 'round."

He poked his head into the closet. "C'mon out, now. I need to find out what happened to your sister."

After looking between the bed and the wall, he left his bedroom, closing the door behind him, then moved to the bathroom.

The door creaked when he pushed it open. *Gotta oil that hinge.* "Haley?" He pulled the shower curtain aside and breathed a sigh of relief at the empty tub. *Too many odd things happenin' 'round here.*

He walked out of the bathroom, pulled the door shut, then glanced toward the girls' bedroom again. He thought about crossing the hallway, but his feet wouldn't move. "Haley? You in bed?"

No answer.

Forcing his feet forward, managing one labored step at a time, he made it to their bedroom door, then leaned against the doorframe and peered into the semi-darkness. "Haley? Haley, you in there?"

The image of the little girl flashed in his mind's eye again, and he audibly gasped and released the doorframe as if it had suddenly grown hot. "Haley, c'mon out!" He listened for any sound but heard nothing. "Haley?"

Well, I know she ain't in the kitchen. He left the bedroom, walked quickly down the hallway to the kitchen, where he grabbed his cap and slapped it on his head. He went outside, into the backyard, and stopped on the back stoop as Stump came loping around the corner.

"Hey, dog." He scratched Stump behind the ears while scanning the yard. "Wanna help me find that girl?" Stump yawned. Buck straightened and cupped his hands around his mouth. "Hay . . . lee . . . !" He repeated the call twice more, and when he got no response, he crossed the backyard to the barn lot, Stump trailing behind him.

Tugging the left bay door open on the barn, he cupped his hands again and repeated the call. When he heard no answer, Buck took a step to enter the barn and nearly tripped when Stump hurried inside, crossing directly over his feet.

Buck scowled at him. "Gonna get stepped on if you keep that up." He glanced around the bay. *I know that girl's gotta be 'round here somewhere. She wouldn't jus' take off.*

Confident he'd find Haley, Buck went through the barn, peering into the feed stalls, looking under every nook and cranny. Stump explored each corner of the stalls, nosing through the straw before tail-wagging an all-clear to Buck. They went through the tack room and the shop, even checking the bottom cabinets. But found nothing.

Well, I'll be. . . .

Beginning to think their search futile, Buck moved into the smaller bay and took a token look around the tractor. *Nope. . . .* Stump looked up at him and Buck reached to scratch his ears again. "We'll find 'er. Takes time, 'at's all."

On his way out of the barn, Buck stopped at the base of the ladder to the loft. He looked up into the darkness, listening intently. He peered down at Stump. "Whaddya think? Should we go up there?"

Stump's droopy, bloodshot eyes agreed with Buck's aching knees. They wouldn't climb. They'd listen.

Buck turned his attention back to the ladder and gazed up at the hole in the floor of the loft. Dust particles sifted through the plank floors and glimmered in the scant rays of sunlight that forced themselves through a small, dirty window. He listened again, carefully judging each silence against the next. Soon he heard a mouse scurrying across the floor of the loft, then a heavier tread, but still much too light for a teenage girl. *Coons makin'a racket.*

He shook his head at Stump. "Guess 'at's it then." He went to the front of the barn and waited for Stump to move past him before shoving the big bay door closed.

His hand lingered on the door latch while he scanned the yard again. He squinted, making sure he covered every inch of ground. After going over it a fourth, then fifth time, Buck swiped a hand over his face.

Haley was gone.

Where could she've got off to?

With a shake of his head, he dropped the

latch into the eyelet on the barn door. "Where you reckon she went, Stump?" He scanned the yard again, then mumbled, "Guess we jus' soon check the front porch, too."

With Stump following closely at his heels, Buck trudged through the barn lot and past the south side of the house. When he reached the porch, he dropped slowly to his hands and knees, then peered under the broad porch. "Haley?"

Nah, she ain't in there.

Before he could get to his feet, Stump shot past him and onto the porch.

"What's got into you, dog?"

Stump ignored him, sniffing almost frantically along the base of the front door. Then he began to whine and paw at it. When the door didn't move, he growled, then looked over his shoulder at Buck and barked.

Grasping the railing at the south end of the porch, Buck pulled himself up, bumping his right knee on the corner post in the process. He slapped the post with the heel of his hand. "Damn!" Rubbing his knee, he looked over at his dog. "What's wrong with you? You smellin' somethin'? Is there—"

A low, moaning wail echoed from inside the house, then another came, similar to the whimpering sound the little girl had made the other day. This one was louder, though, and much more insistent.

Forgetting about the pain in his knee, Buck felt the hair on the back of his neck stand on end. He grabbed the screen door handle, but

Stump leapt against the door, pushing it away from him and slapping it hard against the frame.

The dog looked up and growled, then leapt at the door again, digging hard at the threshold, the screen door repeatedly slamming against the frame. He barked again and again, circling tight, his hackles standing stiff on his neck between repeated, vicious attacks on the door. Soon he'd torn a wide gash in the bottom of the screen.

The sound came again, and Stump attacked the door with renewed vigor.

Buck kicked at him. "Git back, dog! Git! *Git*, I said!"

Stump backed away, but his attention stayed riveted to the screen door. Saliva dripped from his jowls as he watched Buck pull the screen door open, then turn the doorknob on the front door.

No sooner had he turned the knob than Stump rushed past him, grazing Buck's right knee with his shoulder and nearly knocking him over. The living room door slammed hard against the wall, and Stump tore past it, barking frantically as he sped across the living room and into the hall.

"What the hell's got into you, dog?" Buck followed as quickly as he could, practically hobbling across the living room. "Dog's gone nuts, 'at's what." But somehow he knew he'd find Stump in the girls' bedroom. He took a breath, then turned the corner into the hallway.

Buck's assumption had been right. Stump stood in the middle of the girls' bedroom, yelping and barking as if possessed. He raced from the side of the bed to the foot, frenzied, barking all the while, then back to the side, then around to the other side, then back to the foot. His bark grew high pitched, as if his throat had been strained.

Buck stood at the threshold to the girls' room, staring at Stump. *Never seen 'at dog so messed up.* "Stump? C'mon, boy. C'mere."

The dog continued to bark and race back and forth around the bed, as if keeping a ghost at bay.

Nothin' for me to do but go in an' git 'im. "A'ight Stump. 'At's enough."

But when Buck flipped the light switch on, his attention was immediately ripped from Stump. He grasped the doorframe and sagged.

The bed was covered with vomit, and a partial outline of the girl's head, torso, and one arm was plainly visible in the still-foamy, greenish and meat-pink ooze. *Oh, God . . . Heather . . .*

Buck looked at the floor for a long moment, then collected himself and moved into the room. His heart froze when he saw the comforter piled up at the foot of the bed. *Haley?* He thought about the little girl he'd seen near the closet. How she'd whimpered, pleaded for him to do something—anything . . . pleaded with him to help her.

Stump continued to bark, racing back and forth on each side of the beds.

Buck couldn't take his eyes off the comforter as scenes unfolded in his mind. He began to tremble, and a tear traced a hot path from his

eye to the dimple in his cheek. It pooled there
for a second before slipping down to his chin.

*Damn! Dammit! Dammit! Why'd I have to let 'em
go to that craft thing?*

Stump's barking grew more frenzied by the
moment.

Buck glanced back at the corner by the door,
but the little girl wasn't there. *I couldn't do
nothin'. I couldn't, jus' wasn't nothin' I could do. . . .*

He turned back to the bed, and Stump suddenly bolted and sped past him, again almost
knocking him down.

"Stump! Stop it! *Stop*, dammit!" He wiped a
tear off his right cheek. *Why'd I have to let 'em go to
that fair? Wasn't no call for that. Wasn't no call.
Justin wouldn't've ever let 'em go off by theirselves like
that. The boy was a good daddy to them girls.*

Nadine's face pushed its way into his mind.
Them girls got names. . . .

Buck batted the air with a hand as if to swat
away her words. *No matter . . . ain't the point . . . 'at
boy, he was a good daddy. He'd never let 'em go off like
'at by theirselves. Lot better daddy'n I'll ever be, an'*—

His gaze suddenly settled on a blouse lying on
the floor near the foot of the bed. "Stump!" Buck
picked it up. "Stump, c'mere boy." *Maybe 'at dog's
got enough hound left in 'im to help. We can still find her.*
"Stump, dammit, c'mere! We can still find her!"

Stump raced back and forth at the foot of the
bed, first one side, then the other, barking viciously all the while, his attention constantly riveted on the comforter.

"Dammit, Stump, c'mere. Let's find Haley!"

As the dog ran past him again, Buck reached for his collar and missed. On the next try, his fingers caught, and Stump nearly pulled him off his feet.

"Settle down. Settle down, now!" He proffered the blouse. "Look here, we can find her. Track her, Stump. We can track her!"

Stump tore free from Buck's grasp and raced around to the other side of the bed, still barking frantically. As he passed again, Buck grabbed his collar once more, then tugged Stump away from his well-worn path.

But the dog turned, his eyes vicious, and snapped at Buck, his canines grazing the knuckles of his right hand and leaving an instant bruise.

Buck yelped and jerked his hand away, then stared as Stump raced back around the bed, still barking at the comforter. *Ain't never tried to bite me b'fore . . . never.* He watched for a long moment and finally realized it was the comforter, not the bed, that had captured the dog's attention.

He nodded. "A'ight then. Let's see what's got you so riled."

The thought crossed his mind again that he might find Haley under the comforter, perhaps a victim of her guilt over her sister. His hand trembled as he reached for the thick cover.

He shook his head, his voice quiet. "Naw . . . can't do it. I couldn't bear it. Never should've let 'em go to that fair. Never should've let 'em go alone. I can't do it."

But Justin had spoken with him, begged him to help them—had begged him to help his girls.

Still trembling, Buck grabbed the edge of the comforter with both hands, hoping both hands wouldn't be necessary, hoping he wouldn't feel the weight of a little girl tumbling out of it when he pulled. He gripped the comforter tightly. This time tears streamed down his face. *So sorry, Justin. I wanted to be strong . . . wanted to help 'em . . . God, I wanted to save 'em . . . I jus' couldn't . . . .*

Resolved to get it over with, Buck tugged with all his strength. Light in his grip, the comforter fairly flew from the bed, slapping against the wall. He watched with an overwhelming sense of relief as it parachuted into a heap on the floor.

Nothin' there. Haley wasn't there.

Stump's barking became nonstop.

In an instant, Buck's gaze shifted back to the bed. He broke into a cold sweat and gooseflesh raced across his arms.

Heather's bed was covered with snakes. Rattlers, milk snakes, garters, king, moccasins, corals, just about every type and color snake ever cataloged—and at least as many, if not more, than Buck had killed in his front yard.

Buck's mind went numb, and for an instant he couldn't move. Memories flashed in rapid succession. . . .

Snakes . . . snakes in the yard . . .

Haley . . . those eyes . . .

Haley's gone!

Dad, please . . . help my girls. . . .

The little girl . . . the corner . . .
Heather . . .
Heather!

Emerging from his mental fog, Buck gaped at the bed again, as if seeing Heather's partial outline for the first time. The numbness drained and noises began to filter in from outside himself.

The snakes writhing and hissing across and through the outline of his granddaughter.

Stump barking relentlessly.

The snakes coiled, writhed, hissed . . . looked at him.

Those eyes!

A calm settled over Buck, and as Stump passed him again, still barking and yelping, he caught his collar and twisted it. " 'At's *enough!* No more!" He half lifted, half dragged Stump out of the room and tossed him into the hallway. Then he slammed the door and turned back to the bed.

"A'ight then." He slapped his hands together in brushing motion, then approached the bed. "Gotta finish this."

He found the seam of the fitted sheet at the bottom of the mattress and tugged it out and up. Pulling it to his chest, he watched as some of the snakes writhed and rolled toward the center of the bed.

After flopping the end of the sheet over the snakes, Buck reached for both sides of the bed and flipped the fitted sheet out along the mattress and over the bundle of snakes until he came to the head of the bed. Freeing the sheet from one corner, then another, he folded each corner tightly over the snakes, effectively wrapping the whole thing in a ball.

He went to the bedroom window, shoved it open, then turned back to the bed.

The sinewy forms writhed beneath his knuckles as he wrapped part of the sheet tightly in his fists and lifted it off the end of the bed and onto the comforter. *Been needin' new bedclothes for a while anyhow.*

He quickly brought the four corners of the comforter together, then removed his belt and wrapped it tightly around the gathered corners. In one smooth motion, he picked up the bundle and shoved it through the window.

Buck drew in a deep breath, closed the window, then went over and opened the bedroom door. Stump raced into the room, his voice breaking in midbark.

" 'At's right. They gone."

Ten minutes later, Buck was returning from the barn with a gallon of gasoline, a much calmer Stump trotting alongside him.

After dragging the comforter a safe distance from the house, Buck retrieved his belt, then soaked the comforter, the sheets, and the snakes in gas.

He fished a box of matches out of his pants pocket, then removed one of the matches, struck it on the box, glared at the comforter and tossed the burning stick onto it. *Damn snakes.*

CHAPTER TWENTY-ONE

Mark was surprised to hear the tentative knock on his door, and even more surprised when he opened it and saw Buck standing on his porch.

"Hey, Buck. Come on in."

Buck shook his head. "Ain't necessary."

"Oh . . . okay . . . well, what's going on?" Mark's mind flashed back to a scene with him and Buck battling snakes in his yard, and it made him want to ask whether Buck needed his help again. But something in the man's eyes kept him from asking.

"Nadine . . ." Buck fidgeted with a side seam on his overalls and looked down at his work boots.

Mark frowned. "Is something wrong with Nadine?"

"She's still down at the hospital—"

"Nadine's in the hospital?"

"No, ain't her." Buck glanced at him, then

studied the molding surrounding the door jamb. "Got that girl down there . . . got that Heather girl down there an'—" '

"Oh my God, Heather's in the hospital? What happened?"

Buck eyed him. "Nothin' . . . nothin' too much. She was throwin' up, 'at's all." He looked down again, continuing to finger the side seam on his pants. "Only she's in a coma now . . . somethin' like that. Doc . . . Doc said she got into some ethyl . . . ethylene . . ." He shook his head. "Aw hell . . . ethylene somethin'r other."

"Ethylene? Ethylene alcohol? Glycol?"

Buck nodded. "Glycol . . .'at's it. Ethylene glycol."

"That's antifreeze! Where'd she get hold of antifreeze?"

Buck shot him a hard look. "How'm I s'posed to know?"

"Buck, I didn't mean—"

" 'At's a'ight. I know." Buck grimaced. "Anyhow . . . thing is, Haley's gone missin' now."

"What?" Mark felt like someone had just given him a one-two punch in the gut.

Buck nodded. " 'Fraid so. I come home from the hospital an' I wanted to find out what that girl . . . what Haley might know 'bout what happened to Heather. An' well, me an' Stump, we looked all over the place." His eyes flashed. "All through the house, ever' room, an' all through the yard an' the barn an' cver'thin', but she jus' ain't over there nowhere." He turned his hat in his hands. "An' well . . . I was sorta hopin'—"

"You want me to help you find her?"

Buck looked down and nodded.

"Just let me change clothes." He was about to swing away from the door but stopped and motioned to Buck. "Come in for a minute. I'll just be a sec."

"Well . . . if it ain't no bother." Buck stepped across the threshold.

"Of course not. It won't take me long."

"I got snakes again, too."

Mark stopped short and turned around. "What?"

Buck nodded again. "Yep, 'em snakes is back. Ol' Stump was goin' crazy in the girls' bedroom an' I pulled the comforter back an' there was snakes all over the bed."

"Damn!"

"Yeah."

"Buck, I was just wondering . . . I mean, have you thought about maybe calling the police . . . maybe let them know what's going on? I'm just thinking, what with the snakes in your yard a couple days ago and then Heather being in the hospital for drinking antifreeze and now Haley suddenly missing . . . well, it seems to me all of that adds up to something they might need to be involved in. Have you called them?"

Buck stared at him for a long moment, his right hand rolling into a fist then unrolling. He glanced back at the floor. "Thinkin' maybe this was a mistake." He turned to leave. " 'Sides, I can always—"

"No, no . . . I didn't mean to pry or anything. I just thought—"

"Don't want the whole town knowin' 'bout this. An' them cops don't know what they're doin' half the time, an' the other half they're eatin' donuts an' drinkin' coffee." He hooked a thumb in his pants pocket. "I always took care of my own. Reckon I can do the same now."

"Wait!" Mark grabbed his arm, then immediately released it. "I agree. It *would* be better if we do it ourselves and . . . well, I want to help, Buck. Just give me a minute to get changed." He motioned toward the couch. "Have a seat . . . please. It'll only take me a minute."

Buck looked at the couch and nodded, but remained standing. "I got a minute. 'Preciate your help."

Mark found his jeans on the back of the chair in the bedroom. *What the hell is going on over there? Snakes in the yard . . . Heather drinking antifreeze . . . snakes on the bed . . . and Haley . . . just what the hell is going on?*

He quickly peeled off his sweat pants. Momentarily forgetting the wound in his thigh, he reached for his jeans and hurriedly tugged them up over his legs. A searing pain shot up through his thigh into his hip. "Shit!"

He yanked the jeans down again and saw blood seeping through the bandage. "Oh, man!" The immediate, throbbing ache was almost unbearable.

Jasmine came into the room, frowning. "What's the matter?"

"Nothing. This damn leg. It's bleeding again."

She seemed uncertain of what to say. "Oh . . . well. . . ." A look of distrust crossed her face. "You're changing clothes? You aren't getting into something you shouldn't be involved in again, are you?"

He limped toward the bed, then sat on the edge of the mattress. "Dammit, Jasmine, what's your problem?"

She gaped at him, then shifted her gaze to the floor. "Mark, I . . . nothing." She shook her head. "Never mind. No problem . . . no problem at all." She turned as if to leave the room, then stopped. "It's just that . . . you know, last night I was trying to help and . . . well, you know what happened." Her frown deepened, and fear flickered in her eyes. "I'm not sure . . . I mean, it's like I didn't even know who you were."

"I was just me!" he snapped. "You . . . look, I'm sorry. You just surprised me last night, that's all."

She seemed disappointed with his response. "Mark, I . . ." Sorrow filled her eyes. "I don't even know what to do with that." She went over to the dresser and grabbed her purse from the top of it. "I have to run into town. I'll be back a little later."

He glared at her back as she left, and his thoughts wandered to the previous night. She'd tried to tend to his wound, and he'd viciously turned on her, attacked her . . . practically raped her . . . and he hadn't even recognized Jasmine for who she was. He'd seen Haley.

Was she trying to tend to my wound? Really? Or was she trying to make it worse, keep me out of com-

mission? He glanced at the still-seeping bandage, and an odd feeling came over him, a sense of being drawn deeper into a dark, forbidding room. *Damn woman's in league with the creature that did this to me. She's just trying to keep me away from Haley . . . helping the bastard keep her all to himself. Well, it won't work!*

He sat for a moment, drawn back to reality by the throbbing in his legs. *Damn . . . what the hell's wrong with me? Jasmine wouldn't do anything to hurt me.*

Mark got up from the bed, stepped out of his jeans, then hobbled into the bathroom and searched through the medicine cabinet for fresh bandages. Not finding any, he shut the medicine cabinet and opened the door to the shallow linen closet wedged between the bathtub and bathroom door. His gaze fell on a roll of elastic fabric. *Ace bandage . . . that'll do it.*

Sitting on the closed toilet lid, he began wrapping the Ace bandage tightly over the original bandage. *Not too tight. Don't want to cut off circulation.* Finally he set the metal prongs into place, then got up and tested his leg by walking back to the bedroom. Each time he put weight on it, the same searing pain shot up through his thigh. He thought about the creature at Craft Fest that had come out of nowhere to stab him in the leg. Still, the pain seemed distant somehow . . . conjured.

Back in the bedroom, Mark retrieved his jeans, then winced as he slowly tugged them on. He thought about Buck and grinned, glad for the opportunity to help. *Hope the hard-nosed old guy's still out there.*

He grabbed a T-shirt from the dresser, pulled it over his head, then tugged on his boots. As he limped down the hall toward the living room, he heard Jasmine's voice.

"So what are you and Mark up to today?"

When he came out of the hallway, he saw Buck was still standing where he'd left him, fidgeting nervously.

Buck shifted from foot to foot, and his eyes volleyed between Jasmine and the floor. "Oh, uh . . . nothin' much. Think he's gonna help me look for—"

"Look for what? Or is it whom?"

Mark walked past her. "I'm going to help him look for Haley. She's missing."

Jasmine glared at him. "You're going to . . ." She went over to him and spoke in a loud whisper. "You're going to look for *that girl?*"

Mark stepped away from her and nodded. "That's right." Thoughts of Haley filled his mind as if he had no control over his own brain. Again he replayed the previous night, what he'd done to Jasmine. He struggled with the thought, with the guilt, wondering whether he should even feel guilt. He was only vaguely aware that Jasmine had turned away. As if from a great distance, he heard her telling Buck she hoped they'd find Haley soon.

Unbidden, thoughts of the creature visited him again. It grinned, sneered at him . . . spoke to him. *Leave her alone . . . she's mine now!*

"Yes'm," Buck said, still talking with Jasmine. He turned to Mark "Uh, we ready?"

Mark felt hatred fill his chest when he looked at Jasmine. *Always acting so caring. Just wants to keep me all to herself. Keep me from the girl. She's working with that creature, I just know it. She's keeping me away from Haley.*

Buck cleared his throat. "Uh, I think maybe—"

Mark tore his gaze away from Jasmine. "Sure . . . sure, let's go. I'll get my hat." He turned to head for the door, then suddenly turned back. His shoulders slumped, and his hands trembled as he reached for Jasmine. He gently placed a hand on each of her shoulders and looked at her as softly as he could. "Look, I . . . it's all right. We'll be back as soon as we can. I'm sure everything will be okay . . . *every* thing." He kissed her on the cheek, then grabbed his ball cap and headed out the door after Buck.

Buck led the way out of the yard, and as they crossed the road, Mark pulled up alongside him. "Got any idea where to start looking?"

"No . . . not really."

Mark thought back to his brief conversation with Karla at school. "For starters, why don't we search the old barns around here? Be a good place to stay if she's running away for some reason."

The creature flashed through his mind's eye again—evil incarnate, sneering at him. He winced as he felt the knife stab deep into his thigh again, the pain just as real, just as strong as when it first happened. Visions of a creeping, velvet darkness spread from the wound throughout his body. Mark's next thought came without prompting and made him grin for reasons he didn't know. *Old barns are good for lots of things. . . .*

He couldn't be sure whether the thought came from the creature or directly from his own brain, but it really didn't matter. What mattered was that old barns were good. What mattered was that old barns were good for *lots* of things. Especially Haley things . . .

CHAPTER TWENTY-TWO

Haley's feet were bound to the floor with heavy chains, and her wrists were tied with rope. She strained against her bonds, knowing full well she couldn't break them.

Caster watched her, grinning, then leaned over and brushed hair from her brow. Haley jerked her head up as far as she could and tried to bite him. He laughed, bobbing his hand up and down, just keeping it out of her reach.

Unable to get to Caster with her teeth, Haley thrashed from side to side, whipping her head about in a futile attempt to avoid his touch. "Bastard!" she screamed. "You lousy, crap-head bastard!" She spat at him. "Liar! You're a goddamn liar!"

As Haley struggled against her bonds, Caster went about setting up an altar, of which she was the centerpiece. He knelt near her as he placed a thick, fat black candle on the floor above her right shoulder. "How am I a liar? Because of that stupid little bitch of a sister of yours?" He placed another, identical candle above her left shoulder, then rocked back on his haunches. He grinned and nodded. "If that's what you're talking about, then yep, you're right. I *am* a liar."

Haley struggled against the rope and chains again. She growled at him, a guttural sound that belied her craving for his blood. "If I could just reach you . . . just *once!*"

Caster rocked back on his heels, laughing, and as he rolled forward to the balls of his feet, he swung out and slapped her hard and without warning. Then he reached down and gripped her chin firmly so she couldn't turn her head away. "If you could reach me, what? You think you can hurt me? Let me tell you something: I've been targeted by the best. You can't do shit to me."

As he got to his feet, Haley screamed, "You had no *right* to hurt Heather! Dammit, you had no *right!* You goddamn liar!" She spat straight up at him, narrowly missing his face.

"I don't know what you're bitching about. Sure, I wanted the little slut to die, but I'm the unlucky one here. At least you got to see it." He sighed. "My only regret is that I couldn't be there to watch with my own eyes as the bitch choked and gagged. Tell you what—you should've seen that idiot twelve-year-old down in New Orleans. Now that was funny! *Damn* he suffered beautifully."

He casually walked over to the wall nearest him and retrieved the long poker leaning against it. Caster touched the tip of the poker to her right ankle, then dragged it slowly up her leg as he walked and talked. "You know that little rounded tip on a potato peeler? That part you use to pop the eyes out of a potato? It works to pop the eyes out of a human, too . . . well, part of the eyes. I gave him a potion that zombified his ass, then braced his eyes open and dug his corneas out. I always wondered how thick those were and whether there was color behind them." He shook his head, a faraway look in his eyes. "And all the little bastard could do was leak a tear or two. Couldn't talk. Couldn't move." He snapped his fingers. "And you know, I also used to wonder how it would feel and how long it would take to squash a human-size bug with my feet. I couldn't get the little bastard to snap out of it—and you know, I'm way too much of a humanitarian to watch people suffer—so that stupid little shithead answered two questions for me that day. I only had to stomp on him five times as it turned out." A wistful look crossed his face, and he shook his head. "It should've taken longer."

Haley gaped at him, horrified. How had she not seen this part of him until now? What could have possibly made her so blind to Caster's bullshit?

Caster chuckled, apparently over his temporary sadness at having ended the boy's suffering too soon. "But he *did* answer those questions for me. That he definitely did." He cocked his head and leered at her. "And now you and that stupid sister of yours are going to answer my twins question."

Haley's heart skittered to a stop. "Twins question?"

"Of course. Life is a *series* of questions." He dragged the tip of the poker up her left thigh. "Do you really think so much of yourself? Do you really think I'd give a rat's ass about you or your sister if you weren't twins?"

Heather strained against the rope, strained harder. "Let me go! Dammit, Caster, let me go!"

"But you want to know the question, don't you?" The tip of the poker traversed her hip and abdomen. It was nearing her throat. "I have to know . . . are twins really joined at the soul? Hmm?"

Haley just stared at him.

He pressed the poker against her throat. "I'm asking. Are twins joined at the soul? You're a twin. What do you think?"

"Yes . . . yes, twins are joined at the soul. My sister and I are joined at the soul."

"And yet you gave her the potion." He grinned. "You *knew* it would kill her, but you gave her the potion."

"No! I didn't know!"

He laughed. "Sure you did. You asked me whether it would hurt her. And I just said you'd have to choose: your sister or the power. And you chose, didn't you, Haley?" He lifted the poker and brought it down hard beside her head. "Didn't you?"

Haley burst into tears. "Yes! Yes, you son of a bitch! I knew! And, yes, I gave her the potion—I killed my sister!"

Caster threw his head back and laughed. "You should be proud of yourself, you stupid little bitch. You've answered the greatest question I've had so far. Whether one twin would dump all that bullshit loyalty to the other to get what she wants." He laughed again. "And I didn't even have to make you do it. I just mentioned it almost in passing, and you jumped at the chance to kill her. It's my greatest feat by far. Like I said earlier, I just wish I'd been able to watch. I *like* to watch . . . but you'll find out about that soon enough." He disappeared from her field of vision for a while, which made Haley nervous. God only knew what he was capable of.

When Caster came back, he carried an assortment of small knives and a few things that looked like skewers. He placed them around her just so, then grew quiet and knelt alongside her again. He stroked Haley's cheek with the back of his hand, and when he spoke again it was barely above a whisper. "Ready to take a little trip, sister killer?"

She glared at him. "You won't get away with this. My papaw is already looking for me—and when he finds you, you sorry—"

Caster slapped her again, hard. "Shut . . . your . . . *mouth!*" He got up and loomed over her. "You are *mine,* Haley. You *belong* to me. I *own* you." Then he whirled about and stumbled toward the barn door.

Haley thought she heard car doors slamming, and for a moment she allowed herself to hope Buck and Nadine had found her. Tears stung her eyes. "I mean Papaw and Meemaw," she whispered to the barn roof.

But she soon realized that what she'd heard were the cargo doors on Caster's van. When the barn door crashed open again, Caster stormed in and grabbed some sort of stick that leaned against the wall near the door. As she watched him draw nearer, her hatred for him caused her to shiver uncontrollably. *God I wish I could get my hands on him! Just for one minute!*

Caster knelt alongside her again and opened his right fist to reveal the blood smeared in his palm. Then he swiped his palm across her forehead. "Look." He held up what looked like a Magic Marker. "This is going to start you on that little trip I mentioned."

Despite her fear, the horror that would always mark this day as life altering, a bubble of laughter rolled all the way up Haley's chest and burst through her lips. "*That's* your magic? *That's* it?"

"It's just as magical as the one Karla used to draw the snake sigil on you and your sister." Caster's mood changed abruptly, and he flushed with anger. "And you're going to be scared. I guarantee it!" He lowered his face to hers, his tongue protruding from between his lips.

Haley jerked her head from side to side in an

effort to keep him away, but she couldn't. Caster ran his tongue from the tip of her nose to her forehead. Then he sat back, took the cap off the marker, and drew what felt like a squiggly line down the bridge of her nose, over her face and chin, and onto her throat.

Every patch of skin he'd touched with ink tingled, and she soon felt light-headed and dizzy. Someone else seemed to take control of the images and thoughts inside her head. They were wild, extreme, and unwanted, but Haley had no idea how to make it stop. She saw Heather lying in the pool of vomit, then Buck, with an evil grin on his face, sticking his finger into what she'd hurled and licking his finger clean while Stump raced around in the corners of her mind, his mouth moving as if he were barking, but what she heard was the voice of Charlie Brown's teacher on his Christmas special: *whon whon whon.* . . . Nadine—Meemaw—flew past her head on great patchwork bat wings that appeared to be made out of Buck's shirt material and coveralls. And Heather sat up, her eyelids open but only the whites of her eyes showing, and she crooked a finger in her direction. *Want some tea, Sister Haley? Care for some extra-sweet tea?*

Haley thought she screamed, but she wasn't sure. Her hearing seemed to be off, too. Caster leaned over her, and she saw his lips move, his mouth gaping wider and wider until eventually his top lip curled up to the top of his head. Despite his apparent desire to swallow himself, Haley still heard noises coming from him, but they sounded farther away than he was, and the words were skewed. She thought he said, *What's the matter? Trip? Mind slipping sideways?*

When his lips fell back into place and had shrunk to form a mouth again, Caster produced another marker and drew more squiggly lines, one on each side of her head. To Haley, they felt as if they'd eventually circle back on themselves. She heard more of his silly, seemingly made-up quasi-words: *Get there fast . . .*

Haley giggled. *Get where fast? Must be losing his mind.*

She felt a tug on her blouse, then a light tickle as another squiggly line made its way down her body. She tried to lift her head to see what was causing it, but found it easier to lie back and let the squiggle come to her. When she summoned it, the little garter snake crawled out from under the refrigerator at her feet, went up over the chains that bound her ankles, up along her legs, over her stomach and chest, and up her nose, then into her mind. The delightful sensation of its soft belly scales moving over her skin tickled her the entire way.

Soon it started raining, but it was an odd rain. She felt only a drop every few inches, and the drops seemed to fall in a regular pattern, something she knew was impossible for rain. Having learned from her experience with the snake that she could see things without looking, she concentrated on the drops as they hit her forehead, cheeks, chin, throat, chest, abdomen, hips, legs, and feet. As she watched a drop hit and splatter, water cascaded all around like a beautiful fountain, and her mother splashed out of it. When the next drop hit, Heather splashed out. The next drop carried her father. Then Papaw. Then Meemaw. Then Stump. Then her art teacher . . .

Just before Haley lost her frail mental tie to the normal world, she saw Caster move a few feet away. He picked up a knife and plunged it into his right palm, then muttered something that sounded like a mixture of unintelligible words and howls.

Through the brilliant colors flashing in her mind, Haley thought she heard sounds . . . something ancient stirring somewhere far away. She couldn't tell whether the short, squat creature slithering on the floor was real or a product of her hallucinogen-warped mind—but it looked like the same one she'd seen in the Curious Goods booth—and it was now headed for her.

CHAPTER TWENTY-THREE

From a million miles away, as if in a dream, Heather overheard someone who spoke like a doctor. He was assuring someone else that everything would be all right eventually. *Wonder what they're talking about?* She kept trying to open her eyes, but they felt nailed shut.

She heard her meemaw's voice, and it made her homesick. "Thank almighty God! You know, I believe it'd kill my husband if . . ." Either Meemaw paused or Heather's mind paused, she couldn't tell which. Then the voice returned. "Y'all fig're out what's wrong with her? Why's she on that breathin' machine? Why's it makin' that god-awful noise?"

The doctor's voice came through a little more clearly. "Ethylene glycol poisoning. I know the respirator looks bad, but it's just a precaution. It breathes for her, so her body can use what energy it has to clear the toxins. And that little hissing sound it makes might even help keep her relaxed, if she can hear it at all. It's almost like a mother's heartbeat in its regularity. Anyway, we'll keep a close eye on her. If there's any change at all for the worse, we'll administer hemodialysis to remove the poisons from her blood directly."

Silence for a moment; then Meemaw's voice again. "What's glycol? Where would she get that?"

"It's basically antifreeze. Any idea where she might've gotten hold of antifreeze, or why she might have ingested it?"

Nadine's voice came through again, but was muffled. Heather imagined her hand was over her mouth. "No! She couldn't've . . . Heather would never—"

Heather was shocked to hear her name. *Me? They're talking about me?*

"No, no . . . I just meant maybe she sat a glass of something she was drinking too close to a jar that maybe held drained antifreeze. Then she might have confused the two when she reached for her glass again. You'd be surprised how often that happens. I'm sure it's just something like that. Anyway, nothing to worry about. We have it under control." The doctor's voice faded for a moment. Heather imagined he was patting her grandmother on the shoulder, comforting her.

Then his voice grew in volume again, still comforting Meemaw as he tried to explain the process. "Since we weren't sure when she ingested it, we tried pumping her stomach, but

there wasn't much there. It was already in her
system. So we gave her activated charcoal to help
absorb the poisons. We also gave her fomepi-
zole, a medicine that inhibits the formation of
toxins from the glycol. Kidney failure was our
biggest concern at first, but we administered a
kidney-function test, and it's all right so far. Always amazes me how resilient young people are."

Meemaw's voice again. "So you're sure she's
gonna be all right?"

"We'll keep a close eye on her, but yes, I think
so, and . . ."

As the doctor's voice faded, Heather wandered back into a darker place. *I drank antifreeze?
How?* This was just another in a series of odd
events lately. She thought about how simple her
life had been before Karla had approached her
and Haley. *Must have something to do with her. . . .*

She tried to concentrate, tried to think back
over the events of the past few days. She and Haley had gone to Karla's trailer. She'd introduced
them to something called Chaos magic. *Intention . . . decide on an intention. . . .* The first real
disagreement she and Haley had encountered
was over that intention. Haley had seemed more
insistent on her own way than usual.

Once she and Haley had agreed—or rather,
once Haley had decided and Heather had
relented—Karla had drawn a symbol of their intent directly on their skin. What had she called
it? *Sigil . . . it's a sigil. . . .* And later, she'd seen
Haley's sigil actually move, like it was alive, part
of her but separate too.

The barn . . . They'd gone to a barn with Karla, and Haley had done horrible things to herself. *And mean things to me . . . shoved me out of the loft . . . mean things . . . not like the old regular Haley . . .* And Haley hadn't been like herself ever since. Dressing like Karla, teasing Heather about being a prude, coming on to boys. *Flirting with that awful man . . . Caster . . .*

But even as she investigated and indicted her sister in her mind, Heather acted as Haley's defense attorney as well. Haley had drifted, she argued with herself, but she had come back, too. In the house, in the kitchen, she'd said Chaos magic was all nonsense, that she was dropping it. She'd even laughed like the old Haley, making fun, but not being mean.

Then again, although she'd talked about dropping Chaos magic, she'd also mentioned Caster again, saying that he still had a lot to teach her. It had put Heather back on her guard.

She tried to focus on that conversation. It seemed like their last conversation, but she couldn't find anything in it that would help her understand what had happened to her, why she was in the hospital. The doctor was wrong. She hadn't mistaken a glass of antifreeze for a glass of something else. *The only thing I drank was some of Meemaw's sweet tea . . . no other glass close except Haley's. . . .* She thought again of her sister's desire to drop Chaos magic and become her old self again. She smiled in her mind and thought if she could feel her eyes she might have felt tears

welling up there. *Even brought me my tea . . . sweet,
like old Haley . . . sweet Haley, sweet tea . . . even
made a game of it . . . laughed . . . a chugging contest
like when we were little. . . .*

In fact, Haley had been even sweeter than
she'd been before all the Chaos magic nonsense. *Even stirred my tea with her finger . . . must've
been why it tasted so sweet. . . .* Haley was sweeter
than before, and so was the tea. *Sweetest tea I've
ever tasted . . . sweetest tea ever. . . .*

The chugging contest began to play through
her mind again: Haley smiling, taunting, turning up her glass. Heather turning hers up as
well, seeing Haley looking at her over the top of
her glass, watching her. Slapping her glass on the
table, done. *I won!* Feeling a little dizzy, like she
was falling. Grabbing at the table, seeing Haley's
glass. How odd that Haley hadn't finished hers.
It was still half full.

Half full? Why? Suddenly the realization that
Haley had poured her tea seemed a bad thing.
The defense attorney stepped to the forefront
again. After all, Haley had been sweet, stirring it
with her finger and bringing it— Another realization caused horror to wash over her. *She stirred
it! Why? It was already sweetened. Everything was already mixed. Why stir it?*

And suddenly she knew why. Her body jerked
with the realization that her sister had poisoned
her.

Heather knew Haley never would have
harmed her on her own. If she'd poisoned her, it

had something to do with that man. *She must be going back to him,* she thought, and an urgent sense of alarm swept through her body.

From a great distance, she heard Meemaw's voice again. *No . . . no words . . . humming . . . songs . . . gospel songs . . .* She'd heard the sound before in the living room after supper. When the house was quiet, Meemaw would sit on the couch and mend clothes and hum gospel songs. She was humming *The Old Rugged Cross* now, but slowly. The tune saturated Heather's mind, seemed to fill the corners of the darkness. For some reason, it was both comforting and troubling. *Old rugged cross . . . lots of old, rugged things . . .* Papaw came to mind. *Old, rugged men . . . build old, rugged crosses . . . and old, rugged barns . . . they drive on old, rugged roads . . . roads that lead to the old, rugged barns . . . old, rugged barns. . . .*

She thought about Haley again, about going to the barn with her and Karla, Haley shoving her out of that old, rugged barn. A brilliant, bright image of her sister flashed through her mind. *Haley's in danger! Bad danger! Save her!*

She tried to fight the panic, tried to go back, tried to listen to the comforting gospel tune her grandmother was humming, but she found herself screaming to her grandmother instead: *Save her! Save Haley! Save her!* No sound came out, but another sound came in, and it seemed to mimic her. *Sssave . . . sssave . . . sssave . . .*

Hissing like a snake. Karla had used a snake for their sigil. But why a snake? The intention

was that everyone would be well and happy. The
thought about the intention made her feel better, softer, and she began to focus on it.

Haley came to mind again, and now she could
see her more plainly. *Chained to the floor . . . a fat
snake close to her . . . a fat, dangerous snake . . .*
The respirator continued to hiss and the fat
snake drew nearer. Heather watched as it slithered over her sister, watched as she writhed, trying to defend herself.

The respirator hissed. Their sigil was a snake.
But their intention was more important than the
symbol itself. The symbol is fearful; the intention
is pure. The intention tied her to Haley, allowed
her to remain with Haley, allowed her to protect
her. She pushed her fears down and concentrated on the intention. It repeated over and over
in her mind. *Everyone will be well . . . everyone will
be happy . . . everyone will be well . . . everyone will be
happy. . . .*

As Heather concentrated, the connection to
her sister grew stronger, almost physical. She
could see her more plainly now, as though just
beyond a membrane. It reminded her of a thick,
fluid sheet of plastic. She sensed that it was protecting her, letting her protect her sister while
remaining safe, separate. She continued to repeat the intention and watched as the fat snake-
thing slithered away. She saw Papaw and Mr.
Aikman come into the barn. Stump was nestled
against Haley as if to protect her.

Heather settled into a steady repetition of the
intention, and the scene grew more and more

clear. The membrane remained, but it seemed to pulsate. She was pressing against it, being drawn into it, being drawn through it. *I want to go through. . . . I have to help Haley. . . .*

But she knew the membrane was protecting her. She sensed that if she seeped completely through it, she would die. *But I want to go through. . . . Haley . . . Haley . . .* With that thought, she consciously reached out with her arms and legs, intentionally pushing through the membrane. *Everyone will be well . . . everyone will be happy. . . .*

CHAPTER TWENTY-FOUR

Dust whirled into a cloud behind Buck's pickup as he turned onto a side road. He hit the brakes, slowing the pickup just before the right front tire slammed into what would have been a bone-jarring hole in the road. The springs on the old truck creaked as the tire dropped into the hole, then bounced out on the other side.

Despite the pickup being eased into the impact, the motion unseated Mark, and he grabbed the dashboard as he momentarily lost contact with the bench seat. The button on top of his ball cap brushed the ceiling of the cab; then he slammed back to the seat. He grasped his thigh with both hands, teeth clenched. "Damn!"

"Sorry. Road's a might rough." Buck glanced in the rearview mirror, checking to see whether Stump was all right.

"It's all right. Leg's just tender."

Buck gave a short nod, then aimed a finger at

the windshield. "Guess this'n's as good a place to start as any."

He pulled to a stop in front of a dilapidated barn. What was left of the sideboards was weathered, almost white along the center and dark brown down both edges. Broad splinters curled away from the wood like thick, twisted fingernails. Wild roses, thistles, and blackberries grew in thick patches all around the barn, and blankets of ivy clung to its sides as if commissioned to guard the building.

Buck opened his door and got out of the truck. "Think I'll let ol' Stump run for a minute . . . maybe sniff around a bit." He went to the back of the truck, lowered the tailgate, then lifted Stump out of the bed and set him on the ground. "Ol' boy don't get 'round like he used to."

Mark winced as he climbed down from the passenger seat, then slammed his door shut. "Guess none of us do."

Buck leaned over to scratch Stump's ears, giving Mark a sideways glance. "You a'ight?"

"Yeah, fine."

The deep wrinkles in Mark's brow and the glaze of pain in his eyes told Buck he was anything but fine, but he decided to leave well enough alone. A man had the right to keep misery to himself if he wanted to. He went back to the cab of the truck, retrieved Haley's blouse, then brought it to Stump.

Grimacing, Buck lowered himself to one knee and held the blouse to the dog's snout. "Here, boy. Find 'at girl . . . find 'er."

In a matter of seconds, Stump was traversing the brush alongside the road, nose to the ground, methodically searching for Haley's scent as he worked his way toward the barn.

Mark scanned the woods, his body stiff and turning ever so slowly as though to take in the whole of the land. When he faced the barn again, the furrows lining his brow deepened, and he folded his arms across his chest, then unfolded them, and folded them again. "What do you think?" His voice held the tone of a man facing a worry he wished belonged to somebody else.

Watching Stump work and fearing they might be searching for a needle in a pin factory, Buck shook his head. "Don't know. Jus' have to see what turns up."

Stump trotted back and forth along the road, his nose sweeping through bluebells, dandelions, and other wild flowers. As he neared the barn, the fur on the nape of his neck bristled and his blunt tail froze ramrod straight. He gave two sharp barks, then ran up to a narrow door that stood to the left of the barn's large bay doors. He sniffed hard along its base and let out a long, low growl.

Buck took off for the barn in a stiff-kneed lope, hoping and dreading they'd found Haley all at the same time. Suppose she was in there, but they'd reached her too late? He couldn't handle another failure, another fault that would stare him down like a bully in a schoolyard. *You're a pathetic, worthless old man. Justin died because of you, because you could've done something, anything, when those doctors said there was no hope. Now look at you with your gimp leg, moving slower than a turtle on the tonic, just gettin' nowhere fast. She's gonna be dead when you find her, you know. She's gonna be dead because you were too damn slow, old man. Just too damn slow.*

"Ol' man my ass," Buck mumbled and doubled his efforts, pushing past the arthritis biting at his knees. His skin tingled with gooseflesh as he neared Stump. He glanced back at Mark, who stood in the same place he'd left him, staring off at the barn as though mesmerized. "You comin'?"

Mark snapped to attention. "Huh? Oh . . . yeah." He took a step, flinched, then hobbled over to Buck, favoring his right leg, which had swelled noticeably. "Damn leg's giving me fits."

"Take you home after this'n."

"No . . . no, I'm all right."

With Stump still standing at attention, nose twitching, Buck placed a hand against the narrow door and pushed gently, cautiously. It moved less than an inch before he felt resistance. "Think somethin's wedged against it." Pressing an ear to the door, he listened for movement inside, but all he heard was Stump snuffling and growling below him. Placing both hands against the door, he shoved a bit harder. It creaked open a few more inches, and something slid across the dirt floor on the other side. He paused, his heart thudding an irregular beat, then pushed even harder. As soon as the door widened to a dog's width, Stump leaped into the barn with a vicious snarl.

"See anything?" Mark asked, sidling up to Buck.

"Ain't looked yet."

Slipping his head through the opening, Buck peered into the semi-darkness. He spotted Stump sniffing around a coil of rusted chain a few feet ahead. Suddenly the dog's head jerked up, and he bolted toward the deeper recesses of the barn.

Quickly shouldering the door open wider, Buck stepped into the barn. From out of the shadows, a rabbit suddenly zipped past him, grazing the inside of his left ankle. His heart rate blasted toward the ozone layer, and he slapped a hand to his chest. "Damn!"

"What?" Mark asked, pressing in from behind him.

"Nothing. Rabbit. Stump must've flushed it out. If it had been a man, he would've run right over me."

Buck inched farther into the barn, then paused, setting a hand on his hip, letting his eyes adjust to the dim light filtering in through the few broken windows. He heard Stump snuffling and snorting off to his right and the sound of Mark breathing behind him, but little more. An old tractor layered with years of dust sat in an open bay straight ahead. Aside from that, the place held a whole lot of empty. "Ol' dog's a little off I think. Prob'ly picked up on that rabbit's all. 'Fraid there ain't nothin' else here."

Mark pulled up alongside him, peering up and around. "Place doesn't even have a loft. Really no place for her to hide—or for somebody to hide her."

Letting out a heavy sigh, Buck clapped his hands together once. "Stump, c'mon! C'mere, boy!" Instead of waiting for a response, he left the barn, not wanting to think about a *somebody*, and that *somebody* holding his granddaughter against her will. Mark followed silently behind him.

No sooner had they sidled out the doorway that had given them access into the barn, then Stump stuck his head through the opening. Then he trotted out of the barn, head held high, tongue lolling, as if he expected to be rewarded for a job well done.

Buck leaned over and lightly scratched the top of Stump's head. "C'mon, boy, back in the truck. Looks like it's gonna be a long day." He glanced over at Mark. The man looked exceptionally pale, and sweat lined his upper lip and forehead. "I can bring you back to the house. You ain't gotta—"

"I'm sticking with you," Mark said, his expression pained but determined. "We've got to find her, that's all there is to it."

Buck nodded curtly. "A'ight then." He helped Stump into the bed of the pickup, then went around the truck, opened the driver's side door and climbed in. He waited for Mark to settle into the passenger seat, then started the truck. "How many of these ol' barns you reckon there are?"

"I don't know . . . If I had to guess, I'd say probably fifteen, twenty."

Shifting the pickup into gear, Buck nodded. "Best get on with it then." He edged the truck out to the road, remembering to avoid the pothole. One road at a time—one barn at a time.

He had to stay focused on the simplicity of one. Otherwise he'd get so weighted down by the size of the task ahead he wouldn't be able to move.

Two hours and five barns later, they came away with the same results—nothing. Stump would nose around the grounds and inside each barn, occasionally flushing out a rabbit or a family of mice or rats or a raccoon, but little more. They'd approached each new location with a thread of hope, only to leave it under a blanket of dejection.

After they'd hunted through yet another dilapidated hay house and were on their way to the next, Buck sighed heavily. "Well, 'at's number seven . . . an' you said there's what, prob'bly twenty?"

"Something like that."

Buck squeezed the steering wheel tighter as he approached a graveled side road. *Damn, twenty—an' what if she ain't in none of 'em? What if all we been doin' is chasin' our tails?* He squinted over at the old barn nestled in a grove of oak and sugar gum trees some forty yards away. He didn't know if he could handle another dose of nothing. "I'm hopin' this ain't a los' cause."

"It's not like we've got a choice." Mark stared out the windshield for a moment. "Thing is, I'm pretty sure both girls are in serious trouble, and I don't mean because one of them's in the hospital."

Buck shot him a look. "Whadda you mean?"

Mark hesitated. "I teach an art class in school,

and a couple days ago I took a group picture of the class. Haley and Heather were in that picture. When I developed it, I noticed something sort of different . . . odd, you might say." He eyed Buck. "I saw some strange things in that picture . . . not sure how to explain it. Anyway, it got me to thinking about how the girls have been acting lately and about some of the other things that are going on."

Mark held up an index finger. "For one thing, the snakes in your yard that time. That was just a day or two after they spent time with that new girl, right? Supposedly at the cheerleading tryouts or something?"

Buck nodded.

He raised another finger. "Then the craft fair. I have a feeling you didn't want to let them go there by themselves, but you did. And there was a fight near Haley. . . ." His mind seemed to drift for a moment. "Or maybe it was *about* Haley. . . ." His ring finger joined the others. "And that's when I got stabbed by . . . well, that's when I got stabbed."

Finally, Mark raised his little finger. "Now Heather's in the hospital because she drank antifreeze . . . *antifreeze*, of all things, and Haley turns up missing right afterward."

Frowning, Buck turned the truck down the side road. "I didn't hear nothin' about no fight. Didn't know—"

"Some boys got carried away, big fistfight," Mark said, lowering his hand. "But the point's not about the fight. It's about it being just another odd thing that happened after the girls started hanging around together." He swiped a hand over his mouth, then blew out a breath. "After seeing what I saw in that picture, all the odd goings-on, I decided to do some research. And well . . . thing is, I think the girls are mixed up in something called Chaos magic. It's based on the idea that the user can change the laws of probability and directly affect certain realities."

Buck looked at him blankly.

"I mean, it's based on making a wish—something important, most often—then turning the wish into reality by using something called a *sigil* . . . that's like a magical mark or image. In most cases the sigil is represented by a crude tattoo, one that's drawn with a pen or a permanent marker, usually where it can't be seen easily."

"A'ight, I'm with you so far. But what's got you thinkin' the girls is into that nonsense?"

Mark looked away, shaking his head. "Well . . . in that picture I saw a tattoo on Karla's arm—that's the girl they were with the afternoon just before all this started—and I saw part of a tattoo on Haley's arm, too. Not only that, her eyes—Haley's eyes, they looked . . . well, strange. Sort of like a cat's eyes. Or a snake's."

Buck glared at him. "How come you spillin' all this now? Might've helped to know 'fore we started."

"Because I wasn't really sure what there was to know. I've been collecting a piece here, a piece there, and even those pieces by themselves didn't make sense or lead to anything concrete. Like what I said about Haley's eyes—I mean, that might be faulty film for all I know. I wanted to be sure before I said anything."

"So you sayin' you're sure now?"

Mark shook his head.

"Then what?"

"Even though I'm not sure, I figured I should say something because of what might lay ahead."

Buck's shoulders slumped with exhaustion. "You 'bout to make my brain bust with all this talk. Just spit out what you gotta say."

Mark eyed him. "Jasmine told me she heard from other kids at school that Karla's into black magic."

Pursing his lips, Buck parked the truck about twenty feet from the barn, then killed the engine. "So you sayin' that 'cause them two girls is friends with her they into that black magic, too?"

Mark shrugged. "Can't say for certain but . . . thought you ought to know in case. I'm not sure of what we might be facing if . . . when we find Haley."

Buck nodded curtly. " 'Preciate you lettin' me know." He grabbed Haley's shirt which he'd placed on the seat beside him, then got out of the truck and slammed the door shut. Mark's news hadn't upset him so much as how well the news fit with everything else Mark didn't know. The snake under the fridge, the little girl near the closet . . .

Mark scrambled after him, grimacing. "Buck, even if you'd known earlier, there's still nothing you could've done until some of this played out. You couldn't have known the girls were in trouble until they started showing the signs."

Buck nodded. " 'Preciate that, too. But we know *now*." He headed for the back of the truck. "Ain't nothin' left but to find her."

"Of course."

"I gotta find her," Buck mumbled as he dropped the tailgate. "Can't jus' let 'er go."

"I know," Mark said quietly.

Buck shoved Haley's blouse under Stump's nose, then set the dog on the ground.

Stump began searching the road behind the truck, then abruptly backtracked and headed for the barn, nose to the ground, zigzagging in short, quick steps.

Buck watched intently as Stump methodically worked his way to the barn. Something about the dog's manner made him feel jittery, more anxious. *Ain't gonna flush no rabbits'r coons this time, are you, boy? This time . . . this time you'll find the girl.*

In that moment, as though hearing his thoughts, someone—or something—shouted from inside the barn, startling both men. The words, if they were words, were indecipherable.

With a sharp yap, Stump took off for the barn. He disappeared through a foot-wide hole in the base of the right bay door, his barks ricocheting off the rotted wood.

Buck raced after him, his arthritic knees screaming in protest.

"Wait!" Mark shouted, hobbling along, his

pace a little better than a walk "Don't go in by yourself!"

Although he'd heard him, Buck didn't wait for Mark to catch up. He already knew the hole Stump had slipped through would be too narrow for them, so as soon as he reached the bay doors, Buck jerked on one of the looping handles. Only then did he notice the thick-linked chain and padlock binding the doors together. He yanked on the padlock, but it held fast.

Spotting a single, narrow door a few feet to the left, Buck hurried over to it. The door hung on one rusty hinge, had no knob, but had a crack wide enough between it and the outside wall for Buck to slip all of his fingers through. He grabbed onto the lip of the door with both hands and yanked hard, then nearly whooped with joy when the damn thing flew open.

Quickly squaring his shoulders, Buck sucked in a breath, then stepped inside—ready for war.

CHAPTER TWENTY-FIVE

Caster still had Haley shackled to the barn floor. It was critical that she be there—and stay there. She was the centerpiece, the meena-meena, of his altar, and he'd already surrounded her with candles.

He was proud of his quarry and wanted to prove to her that he was worthy of the name master. Kneeling near Haley, Caster spat on both his palms, then rubbed his hands together before leaning over her and using his palms to smooth the hair on either side of her face.

She jerked her head side to side in an effort to avoid his touch.

Caster tsked. "Don't be such a brat. You can't get away, and you know it, so why put so much energy into a struggle? You know, my other playmates weren't bratty. In fact, they were pretty good considering, and they were both boys and girls. They were all so beautiful—suffered so beautifully. They brought me *such* pleasure."

Haley glared up at him defiantly. "You won't get away with this. My grandfather is already looking for me—and when he finds you—"

Caster let out a loud grunt and slapped her. "Shut . . . your . . . *mouth!*" He turned away for a moment to compose himself, then looked back at her, forcing a smile. "You really don't under-stand, do you?" He reached over and caressed her cheek with a finger. "You are *mine*, Haley. You *belong* to me. I *own* you."

"Fuck you!"

With a laugh, he got to his feet. "You just might get that wish, bitch." With that, he pivoted on his heels and headed out of the barn.

As soon as he got outside where she couldn't see or hear him, Caster balled his hands into fists and punched the air, grunting loudly. God how he wanted to pulverize that smart mouth of hers!

He stormed towards the back of the van. "Stu-pid little bitch. Must actually think her warnings about some old man coming to rescue her will scare me. Must actually believe the old fart can save her." He jerked the cargo doors open, then reached inside. "Whole damn family must be made of fools."

After pulling a box up close, Caster rummaged through it, then shoved it away and pulled up another. As he opened the second box, a sharp edge on the folded cardboard sliced a thin gash in his right palm. He jerked his hand away.

"Shit!" He examined the cut, then closed his fist and slammed it against the door of the van. "That bitch won't escape—she's mine!"

He growled, leaned into the van again and tore open the top of another box. After scrounging through it for a moment, he finally found what he was looking for. A small black cloth bag, the top wrinkled shut with a leather drawstring. He stuffed the bag into his jacket pocket, then shoved the box deeper into the van and slammed the cargo doors shut.

"I'll show that little slut what true power is," he muttered, heading back for the barn. "If she thinks she can screw with me, she's gonna need to think again."

Caster was about to pull the barn door open when he spotted a branch about the size and length of a walking stick lying on the ground. He grinned, scooped the stick up off the ground, then went into the barn.

Whistling a mindless tune, he carried the stick over to Haley and placed it on the floor near her feet. The girl trembled visibly as she watched him. *That's more like it,* he thought.

He stuck his hand in his right jacket pocket to collect the black bag, then winced when his hand curled around it. He'd forgotten about the cut on his palm. The nagging pain fueled his anger. "Now, you stupid little bitch, now you're going to learn some secrets!"

Kneeling beside Haley's head, Caster brushed her hair away from her face. He made sure to smear the blood from his palm on her cheeks, her forehead. *Blood's not the only thing she's gonna get from me*, he thought with a sneer.

Taking the bag from his pocket, he opened it and removed three more markers, these smaller than the ones he'd used earlier, the ink tainted with a stranger hallucinogen. He removed the cap from one, then held it up so she could see it. "This will begin your journey into the secrets of your mind." Before she could respond, he leaned over and licked the bridge of her nose, then quickly ran his tongue up to her forehead, being careful not to disturb any of the smeared blood.

Haley jerked her head from side to side. "Get off me! Stay away from me!"

Sitting back on his haunches, Caster grinned. "You'll never be rid of me, Haley. Never." He leaned over and started drawing again, this time sketching a crude black snake between her eyes with the marker. He made the tail weave down her nose, over one cheek, then back and across her upper lip. From there, he made it wiggle down the length of her throat.

Haley's eyelids began to flutter, and her eyes jittered in their sockets as though she was trying to see everything in every direction at once. He chuckled. "What's the matter, Haley? Your mind slipping sideways on you?"

To make sure she wouldn't snap back to reality too soon, Caster drew two more snakes, one on each temple. He used a design similar to the ouroboros he carried on the back of his hand.

Then he kissed her on the cheek. "These will speed the process, but not too much. Don't want to get there too fast," he said quietly.

After capping the marker, Caster picked up a knife and reached for the neckline of Haley's blouse. He ripped downward again and again, effectively shredding it. Then he sat back and removed the cap from another marker, this one red.

Placing the broad felt tip of the marker near the base of her throat, he drew a squiggly line down half her body, moving it over and around her shoulders and breasts and across her stomach. In some places the lines crossed the remaining fabric of her blouse, and in others it applied directly to her skin.

After Caster repeated the process a few times, he sat back and examined his work. She looked like she'd been slashed with a knife. Her eyes rolled to white while her head lolled from side to side. Then her nostrils flared, and she blinked rapidly.

Wasting no time, Caster tossed aside the second marker and opened the last one. This one looked like the others, but it was actually a vial that held a clear liquid. He began at her hairline on her forehead and worked his way down to her hands and feet, squeezing a drop or two of the liquid every few inches along the way.

Haley moaned and mumbled something incoherent.

"This should seal that smart mouth of yours," he said, then held the vial up where she could see it if she was able to focus at all. "You'll live, but only within yourself." He studied her slack face and laughed. "You won't be able to shake that ugly head of yours anymore. And soon you won't be able to flap those pudgy lips."

Her eyelids began to flutter uncontrollably. "P-Papaw . . . find you." A smile seemed to flit across her lips. "Gonna . . . hurt you . . ."

Caster leapt to his feet and threw the vial across the barn. "Shut the fuck up! You really think an old man can touch me? You really think he can do *anything* to me? Nothing can harm me, you understand? *Nothing!* Here, you want to see power?" He picked up the knife, plunged it into his right palm, then let out a high-pitched howl.

Something stirred deeper in the barn, and soon a short, squat creature came slithering out of the dark on its stomach toward Caster.

Caster glanced at Haley, whose eyelids appeared pinned open now, her head immobile, then pointed at the creature. "Just watch." He laughed. "As if you have a choice."

Feeling power swell inside his chest like lava ready to burst from a volcano, Caster faced the creature. "Stand!"

The creature rose and faced him, throwing furtive glances at the girl bound to the floor. Its hands, curled into fists, unfurled, revealing thick, black talons where fingernails should have been.

Noting the creature's interest, Caster chuckled. "You like that, huh? Then go on—touch her." He motioned toward Haley. "Go on! *Touch her!*"

The creature stared at him, seemingly puzzled. It took a step backwards, then turned and shuffled up alongside Haley. It knelt and tentatively touched her cheek with the back of a gnarled hand. It cooed, as though enraptured by the smoothness of her skin. The creature touched her again, poking one cheek, her chin, the base of her throat.

When the creature reached to touch Haley's breast, Caster threw up a hand and shouted, "Enough!"

The creature quickly backed away a few feet.

Caster straddled Haley, settling one foot on either side of her. "You liked it touching you, I'll bet. But did you notice what happened? It can touch you only when I give it permission to touch you."

Stepping over her, Caster picked up the walking stick he'd found earlier, thinking he'd show Haley more of his power. He circled the creature, prodding it. "And *only* when I give you permission, got it?"

The creature glared at him, then moved toward Haley, its tongue flicking over thick, cracked lips. It dropped to one knee and reached for her again.

Caster struck it hard across the right shoulder with the stick. "Only when I give you permission!" He jabbed the creature in the side. "You will obey me!" Staring the beast down, he brought the stick down hard across its back. "Get away from her!"

The beast stood, fixing Caster with a fierce, piercing gaze.

Caster struck it again. "I said kneel! Kneel before me!"

The creature dropped to one knee again, casting a sidelong glance at Haley. It licked its lips.

Caster brought the stick down hard on the creature's head. "All the way down!" He hit it again. "I said all the way!"

The creature squinted and rolled its head from left to right, glancing toward Haley, then to him, to Haley, to him. It trembled slightly as though preparing to fall prone in supplication.

Caster widened his stance, the stick still raised over his head, ready to deliver yet another blow to the creature. "This ugly, hideous beast is *my* creation! I hold complete control over—"

The creature suddenly jumped to its feet, scurried toward Haley and reached for her.

"Stay away!" Caster landed a hard blow across the back of its neck, this time wielding the stick with both hands. "Stay away from her, I said!"

As though it had gone deaf, the creature touched Haley's ankle. Caster struck it again, even harder than before.

The beast roared and launched, its large head striking Caster in the solar plexus and bowling him over. The force of the impact sent the stick flying, and it came to rest several feet away. The creature growled as it landed on Caster. "The girl . . . is now . . . mine!" it said, its voice a thunderous threat.

Caster punched the beast in the face, then struggled to draw up his knees so he could kick it. He managed to sink his teeth into the creature's right arm when it reached for his throat.

The beast screamed, then stood over Caster, straddling his waist. With a long, drawn-out howl, it descended on him again, its talons ripping at his face and throat, its teeth ripping at his ears and cheeks and neck.

When he felt his attacker draw back for the coup de grâce, Caster forced his eyes open. He saw the beast, the barn, the blood, everything now freeze-framed, all stuttering images he could no longer control. The creature bent over him, talons fully extended, and Caster watched it reach down, down, down.

As the talons made contact, Caster thought hell itself had suddenly taken up residence in his chest. He felt skin and muscles ripping open, shredding, then the horrific, indescribable pressure and pain as his ribs were torn from his sternum. The creature's talons sank deeper into his body. That's when the world began to disconnect permanently, leaving only two fluttering images behind: his heart, its hands.

The creature reared its head, howled, and with one final roar of victory, it shoved the heart into Caster's mouth.

CHAPTER TWENTY-SIX

Haley wished her mind back into the fog, into the whirling colors and impossible images that even combined and at their worst, couldn't compare to what she'd just witnessed. To what she saw now.

Her head had started to clear soon after Caster summoned the creature. The hallucinogenic haze had lifted slowly at first, the bright colors and surrealistic images clinging to her synapses as if they'd planned to hang around forever. But gradually she remembered where she was, who she was with. What she had done.

In an effort to either reward the beast or to further torture her—or maybe both—Caster had encouraged the creature to touch her, and it had . . . intimately, with a kind of gentle groping that had made her skin crawl. Then, each time it did touch her or even reach for her, Caster would poke it or slap at it with a stick.

In what seemed to be a blatant effort to impress her with his power, Caster had continued to poke and aggravate the beast mercilessly. When the creature finally turned on him, engaging Caster directly, she'd said a silent prayer, hoping, wishing they'd kill each other. Maybe then she could escape. And even if she couldn't find a way to break free from the chains that bound her to the floor, dying of thirst or hunger seemed a hell of a lot better than what she had been facing.

Half of her prayer was answered when the creature ripped Caster's heart from his chest. She'd watched, paralyzed with shock as the beast attempted to shove the bloody organ into Caster's mouth. Only the bottom third of the heart would fit, and the sight of it now poking out of his mouth reminded Haley of the mark on Caster's hand. A snake devouring its own tail—Caster with his own heart in his mouth—coincidence or providence?

Still dizzy and frozen with shock and disbelief, she could only gape as the creature licked its lips then began to slither towards her on its belly. When Caster had first summoned it, the creature had come to him in much the same way, creeping along on its stomach, hands at its sides, head lifted slightly, eyelids lowered to half-mast. At the time, even with her brain refried, she'd thought it offered this approach as a sign of submission to its new master. But now, as it drew closer, Haley knew submission was the last thing on its mind. The creature wanted her, and the wild, hungry look in its eye clearly said the beast meant to get what it wanted. Terror rode through her high and hard, and she wanted to tear out her own heart so she'd be done with death. Done waiting for it, done fearing it, done hoping for it to happen quickly.

In the only defensive move available to her, Haley turned her head, looking away from the creature. She focused on the darkness that devoured the far corners of the barn. The dark and all the uncertainties that lurked in its depths had frightened her when she was a child. Now those black obscurities seemed comforting when compared to the inescapable horror that was creeping towards her and the nightmare that lay bloody and dead only a few feet away.

Her mind struggled to fill the black emptiness of the barn and the gritty scratching sounds of flesh sliding across dirt. She tried to think of happier times—birthdays, Christmases, Mardi Gras, Easter—but all she could access were the bad days: the day her dad died; the day her mom had been diagnosed and committed; the day she and Heather were forced to leave their home. So she tried concentrating on the people she loved, the people who'd held her, comforted her: Mama, before they took her away—Daddy, so strong and loving—friends at St. John High— Heather—even Papaw and Meemaw. But the only images that would come to mind were Caster's leering grin and Heather's lifeless body.

A long, lascivious hiss pulled Haley from her thoughts and sent a fierce shiver through her body. A wave of nausea followed, creeping up and settling in her stomach like day-old regret. Something slithered down her right arm, like someone pulling a wide, wet ribbon quickly along her skin. It settled around her wrist, a heavy, writhing bracelet that threatened to cut off circulation to her hand. Haley didn't have to look to know what it was. She simply—knew. Her sigil was changing again. Only this time it was changing because *it* wanted to.

The hiss came again, longer and louder as though the creature knew her attention had been diverted. She knew she should look at it, should gather up all her courage and face what came head on. Instead, she willed her eyes closed, choosing to shut out the darkness of the barn. As her lids narrowed into slits, Haley saw the tip of her nose. *Needs powder*, she thought, grasping for even the smallest bit of normalcy. Then she noticed the underside of her upper eyelashes. She had never seen them this clearly before, and the two, thread-thin, black fans suddenly gave her a modicum of hope. She imagined them to be a collection of stainless steel bars, an impenetrable barrier that would protect her from any and all harm. As long as she stayed behind them, she'd be safe. *Nothing's here. It's gone away. Nothing's here. It's gone—*

"Hayyyleee." The whisper gurgled in her left ear. "Hayyleee. . . ."

Oh, God, it's still here! Without waiting for permission, her eyelids flew open, and in that moment a horrendous, heart-rending scream blasted through the barn—a scream so loud and powerful she couldn't imagine it ever coming from a human—much less from her own mouth.

The creature lay just beyond her splayed feet, its hideous face, still splattered with Caster's blood, only inches from the floor. It seemed to watch her every move, its flat, forked tongue flicking over its lower lip. "Hayyyleee. . . ."

Feeling her mind ready to collapse in on itself, Haley threw her head back and another monstrous scream rent the still, stale air. Glaring at the darkness between her and the roof of the barn, she gasped for another breath and heard the creature draw closer.

A heavy, slimy weight moved over her right foot, past her ankle, up her calf. "Hayyyleee. . . ."

She felt hot breath soaking through the fabric of her pants as the creature pressed its mouth against the inside of her knee, her lower thigh. Her own breath stolen now, Haley stared, stared up into the darkness, silently begging for it to come to her, cover her. Take her away. But the dark refused to listen, and she became all too aware of material whispering across her bare stomach, the feel of something rough and thick inching its way to her left breast. It was then Haley understood the fullness of the creature's intent, and that terrifying realization tore another scream from deep within her lungs. And this one didn't stop.

Haley wanted, *needed* to get away, but one kick of her legs as the creature's weight settled between her knees reminded her of the chains binding her ankles. Hopelessness and exhaustion seemed to saturate her every pore, and she fell limp as though suddenly freed of blood and bone and muscle. Only the violent beating of her heart attested to her still being alive. And not for the first time that day, Haley wished she weren't.

From what sounded like a great distance away, she heard the rip of heavy fabric. Seconds later, she felt the whisper of air and breath and the world gone wrong on her bare thighs, her hips, and reality immediately zoomed back into focus.

Oh God! Please let this be a bad dream! Please! But she knew all the prayers in the universe wouldn't allow her to wake in the comfort of her own bed. The creature was real, not a figment of her imagination. She could smell its acrid, vinegary scent, feel its hairy, stunted body settling over hers.

"No!" Haley arched her back, writhing and bucking to get the creature off her.

It nestled closer, grunting, trying to force itself between her thighs.

"Get off! No! Get off!" She twisted and jerked, bucked and arched, but nothing she did threw the creature off balance. It seemed glued to her, a grotesque growth that needed to be amputated.

The beast shifted its weight as though seeking more leverage, and Haley thrashed even harder, adrenaline fueling her every movement.

Seemingly undeterred by her efforts, the creature lowered its head toward hers, and its thick lips parted.

"God!" Haley cried, thrashing her head about. "Stop! God—"

White-hot pain seared her shoulder, then her neck as the creature bit into her flesh with its jagged, blunt teeth. She meant to scream, but barely managed a whimper. Tears dribbled along the sides of her face and pooled in her hair and the cup of her ears. The futility of her recent struggles seemed to smother what little will she had left. What good did it do her to fight anyway? There was no way for her to win. Not alone. Not chained to a floor.

The most Haley could hope for was that it would be over quickly. But how quick was quick? A minute? This very second? Even that wasn't soon enough for her. With no one left to control the creature, how long would she be able to last? How long *could* she last?

Judging from the hungry look in the dark, elliptical eyes staring down at her . . . not long at all.

CHAPTER TWENTY-SEVEN

When Buck yanked the narrow door open, it slammed against the barn, then seemed to teeter on an unseen precipice before snapping free of its only hinge and whumping to the ground in a cloud of dust.

Waving dust away from his eyes with a hand, Mark limped toward the opening and peered inside. "Buck?" He heard movement to his right, and his pulse galloped. A large, dark form stood in the shadows about forty feet ahead. *Was that Buck?*

As if to answer, Stump appeared seemingly out of nowhere and began to race frantically around the figure, barking ceaselessly.

Only when the figure leaned over and pushed the dog away, subsequently pulling its head out of the deepest shadows, did Mark recognize Buck. He spoke, and at first Mark thought the words were directed at Stump, then he saw something

else move, something shorter, smaller, just behind Buck.

"It's a'ight now Ain't nobody gonna hurt you."

Mark felt hope slam into his chest, and he
stumbled forward. *Haley?* He barely recognized
his own voice when he spoke. "You've got her?
Haley? Is she all right?"

Before he reached them, Buck turned to face
him and shook his head. "Naw . . . jus' this ol'
man. Sleepin' here to get in out of the weather
or somethin'." Disappointment sat heavily in his
eyes. "Poor ol' soul, Stump liked to've scared
him to death."

Buck put a fist on his hip, looked around the
barn, then back at the man who Mark now saw
half-lying, half-sitting on the dirt floor. He looked
two meals away from scrawny and had shoulder-
length, scraggly white hair. "You ain't seen a girl
'round here, have you?" Buck raised a hand in
the dim light, holding it parallel to the floor.
"Sixteen years old, 'bout this tall?"

"Naw, Mister, I ain't seen nothing like 'at.
Ain't seen no peoples at all, girls'r otherwise."
The old man clicked his tongue against the roof
of his mouth. "Fact is, I ain't seen no critters neither 'til 'at dog of yours come hollerin' 'cross
here. 'Sides 'at, ain't seen nary so much as a rabbit."

Buck sighed loudly. "A'ight then. Jus' another
damn dead end . . . jus' another waste of time."
He turned and headed toward the door they'd
entered, brushing past Mark. Stump stayed
close, matching Buck's dejected gait.

Knowing no amount of words would offer consolation, Mark simply followed him out.

Two hours later, after they'd searched through three more barns and still found nothing, Mark was ready to cry uncle. He was past tired and his leg was killing him. Buck looked exhausted, too, his face pale, with deep, dark circles under his eyes.

Evidently sensing that he was being watched, Buck glanced over at him. "You doin' a'ight?"

Mark nodded. "You?"

Buck faced the windshield again. "Makin' it."

A strange sensation suddenly went through Mark, a vibrating pulse that seemed to emanate from the wound in his thigh. He knew it didn't have anything to do with the wound, though, because the sensation immediately settled in the center of his chest and identified itself.

Just call me All-This-Is-Fucking-Hopeless.

Mark hated having to utter the words he knew that needed to be said. To Buck's ear, they would undoubtedly sound like the rattle of defeat. He turned toward the windshield, but kept a peripheral eye on Buck. "You know, I don't think there're any more barns out this way. Might want to head back to town, maybe grab a bite to eat. We can pick up again afterwards if you want. Head in another direction maybe."

Buck shook his head, stubbornness settling over his lined face. "I can drop you off at your place right quick if you wanna eat, but I'm gonna keep lookin'." He voice softened. "Can't let 'em down again. Justin's needin' . . ." He paused, shook his head as if to clear it. "Haley . . . Haley needs me. Can't let 'em down again." He glanced up at Mark. "You good with that?"

Knowing he couldn't just desert Buck, Mark nodded, then leaned his head against the seat, holding back a sigh. "I'm good."

Except for the hum and clicks coming from the truck's engine, they rode in silence. Hours seemed to pass as Mark gazed out the passenger window at the pasture land, red-dirt fields, and piney woods rolling by. He fought sleep while he watched the sun float its way down to the horizon, where it sat now, looking like a giant, orange jawbreaker. If life could only be as simple as piney woods and jawbreakers . . . .When Buck finally spoke, he started.

"I'm supposin' you was prob'bly right 'bout there not bein' no more barns out here."

Respecting the crackle of heartache in Buck's voice, Mark continued to stare out the window, listening.

"Dark's 'bout settin' in on us now anyways, so—"

"Stop!"

Buck slammed on the brakes. "What?"

Mark sat bolt upright in his seat, praying the fresh tire tracks he'd just seen running through a patch of short brush hadn't been an illusion. He jabbed the window with a finger. "Tracks—tire tracks, back up."

Without further prompting, Buck worked the gearshift into reverse and slowly backed the truck. "Where? 'Bout how far?"

Mark twisted around in the seat, peering intently through the back window. "A little farther . . . a little more . . ." He could hardly breathe. Somehow, he knew Haley was nearby. He knew it, felt her as surely as he did the pain in his leg. "There! Tracks." he said, spotting the clearly lined trail again. It seemed to run straight toward a tangle of trees a few yards away. He glanced over at Buck. "Pretty fresh, too. Might be nothing, but it could—"

"Be somethin' " Buck said, his eyes suddenly wide and bright. Gears groaned and whined as he forced the shift into first. The truck jerked forward just as Mark threw a hand up, signaling for Buck to wait.

"There's a decent size ditch running between the road and that field," Mark said, remembering the pothole that had nearly rent the pickup in two earlier. "And I don't see culverts or a drive. We might want to take this one on foot."

Not bothering to discuss the matter further, Buck pulled the truck over to the right side of the road, parking only inches away from the ditch. He killed the engine, grabbed Haley's shirt from the bench seat, then got out of the truck.

Knowing he'd be faced with the slope of the ditch and his lame leg the moment he'd open his door, Mark slid across the seat to the driver's side. He clambered out of the truck, cursing his pain and slowness.

By the time he reached the tailgate, Buck already had Stump in his arms and was placing him on the ground. Before he could press Haley's blouse to the dog's snout, Stump bolted for the field.

"Stump!" Buck called. "Doggone it, hold up!"

But Stump didn't hold up. He ran, ears flopping, short legs pounding ground until he eventually disappeared behind a thicket.

"Damn dog's got more nose than sense," Buck muttered, and tossed Haley's blouse into the bed of the truck. He quickly joined Mark, who was already making his way down the front end of the ditch.

Buck crossed over to the field first, then held a hand out to Mark as though knowing he wouldn't be able to maneuver the opposite slope of the ditch without taking on serious pain.

When they were both standing knee-high in weeds, Buck glanced about. "See that worthless hound anywhere?"

Mark shook his head, taking a moment to let the pain in his leg subside. "Last I saw, he shot past me like I was stapled to a tree."

"A'ight . . . guess we'll find him here in a bit."

They headed across the field side by side, following tire tracks. Each time they reached a tight cluster of trees, which seemed to be every five feet or so, Buck would shoulder into the lower branches, holding them in place until Mark passed through.

The sound of Stump's manic barking reached them before they cleared the last thicket.

"Prob'bly got 'im another rabbit. Vagrant'r somethin'," Buck said. He sounded almost nonchalant about it, but Mark saw hope spark in his tired blue eyes. It was as though he was forcing himself not to get too excited, playing it down—just in case.

Mark played along—until they emerged from the thicket and spotted Stump. The dog appeared out of control, barking, frantic, racing back and forth in front of another set of barn bay doors. Only this time, each time Stump circled back on the doors, he'd hurl his chunky body hard against it.

"What the hell?" Buck muttered.

Knowing—absolutely positive *this* place held the treasure they'd been seeking, Mark hobbled toward the barn as fast as he could. He lost awareness of Buck, concentrating solely on Stump. Each time the dog threw himself against the doors, Mark felt his blood turn to ice water. It sent chill after chill up his spine, finally culminating in his brain and forcing out the same thought he'd had hours earlier; *Old barns are good for a lot of things. . . .*

He knew the thought hadn't originated from within himself . . . at least not completely. Buck suddenly raced past him, and another strange thought came to mind. *All that trouble just to save a worthless hound.* Mark gave his head a quick shake to erase the stupid, spontaneous thought and doubled his efforts to catch up with Buck, with Stump. He wanted desperately to help them, help Haley, but wasn't sure how much longer he'd be able to last. As it was, he felt ready to keel over from the pain shooting through his leg.

A loud, deep moan suddenly echoed from inside the barn, and the sound yanked Mark to a halt. In a matter of seconds, the moan escalated in pitch and fervor until it finally burst into a howling wail.

Spontaneously, reflexively, surprisingly Mark threw his head back and responded in kind—or thought he had. As the wail ended, he glanced nervously over at Buck. The old man would probably think he'd lost his mind. But Buck was still speeding toward the barn, obviously not concerned about anything but getting there.

Stump still looked like an animal possessed, throwing himself violently at the barn door, as if he were both enraged and wild with pain. His barks were high-pitched, constant, and he'd occasionally let out a howl that matched the haunting, frightening sounds coming from inside the building.

When Buck reached the barn, he grabbed Stump's collar, tried pulling him away from the doors, but the dog turned on him, snapping and snarling until he finally broke free of Buck's grasp. In the next second, Stump was hurling himself against the bay doors again.

Buck kicked at the hound, yelling for him to shut up, to stop, then he grabbed Stump's collar with both hands and heaved him away from the door.

Oddly, Stump stopped cold, sitting on his haunches and staring at the door, his teeth bared and saliva dripping from his jowls as if daring anyone to come through it.

As Mark neared the barn, all but dragging his right leg behind him now, he saw Buck let go of Stump then grab hold to one of the bay doors with both hands and pull it open. Stump immediately jumped for the opening, but Buck knocked the dog aside and rushed through the door ahead of him. Stump stayed on his heels, and even from ten feet away, Mark could still hear him race through the barn, sniffing, barking, then breaking into a howl.

Having reached the barn door, Mark heard Buck's voice echoing inside the building.

"Haley? Haley, you here?"

Then another blood-curdling moan rumbled from the barn. As before, it started deep as if coming from the bowels of the earth, then increasing in pitch until it reached a screaming howl. The voice of hell itself.

Mark took hold of the bay door with trembling hands, wanting to open it wider in case they needed a more accessible escape route. It creaked open another inch or two then refused to budge any further. He wedged his body against it, braced his hands on the outside wall and pushed. The door sprang open all the way, surprising him. Mark let out a short gasp, stumbled backwards, heard Buck again . . .

"Haley? You here?"

Then the wail came again, but it sounded different to Mark this time, quieter, *more . . . human?*

He froze, listening, and picked up a familiarity in the tone . . . the voice . . . the wail.

It *was* human.

It was Buck.

CHAPTER TWENTY-EIGHT

Buck felt the wail die in his throat. He'd only heard himself make that sound once before. The day Justin died. He'd been sitting on the edge of the bed, counting each of his son's halting, gargled breaths, watching the small, blue swirls on the hospital gown that covered his emaciated chest rise—fall—rise—fall—fall . . . It had taken him a while to realize the gargling had stopped, and the swirls were no longer moving. When the reality of silence and stillness eventually hit him, Buck had to force his gaze away from the blue swirls to look at Justin's face. He didn't want to see what he knew he would. His son's blank stare, his partially opened mouth, the finality of death. In that moment, pain, much bigger than he, seemed to wrap itself into a tight, fiery ball in the center of his soul. And before he knew it, that ball was rolling up—up, gathering speed, collecting breath and power.

When it finally exploded past his lips, the sound it created had brought every nurse on the tenth floor running into Justin's room. There were no nurses here, however, just the horror lying before him and that sound's echo, which seemed trapped between the walls of the rundown old barn.

As soon as he'd forced his way into the building, Stump had jumped ahead of him, and for once Buck decided to trust his dog's lead. He'd followed him through the shadows, the hair on the back of his neck standing on end as they raced toward the north end of the barn. Although there was little light left in the day, enough pierced through the dust-covered windows and cracks in the walls to keep him from running headlong into injury. He'd suspected Stump was really onto something then, but he never expected that something to be this.

Haley, nearly naked, lay spread-eagled on the ground, clothes shredded about her, ankles wrapped in chains, her wrists bound with rope. It looked like she'd been painted with a narrow brush, and the colors of choice had been red and black. Both colors ran in squiggles and loops about her body, along with the blood that trickled from multiple scratches on her stomach, her thighs, her face. Haley's eyes were open but appeared unseeing and empty. Her mouth hung slack. There were no blue swirls for Buck to focus on as he had with Justin. Only blood and his granddaughter and the shallow, wheezing breaths that fell from her parted lips.

A few feet away from Haley lay a man with his chest splayed open like someone had taken a hacksaw to it. And blood—so much blood covered the man and the ground around him. His eyes were open, too, but unquestionably dead—and his mouth, oh, Jesus of Nazareth, the thing in his mouth . . .

Only then did the stench hit Buck full in the face. Blood—urine—sweat and dirt—feces—death. He didn't know what to do with it all. He felt his lips working—open—close—open, like that of a fish, felt his heart *kathunk* against its boney cage, felt his brain stumble over itself, trying to assimilate what his eyes dared to capture. *Haley . . . holy God . . . blood . . . so much . . . blood . . . the thing in his mouth . . .*

He tried to move, force himself forward—couldn't—had to reach her—untie—unchain. *So much blood!* His heart stuttered, then raced, and his body suddenly felt like it had taken on a thousand pounds. Waves of nausea washed over him, and cold sweat dribbled down his face. Buck clutched his chest and dropped to one knee with a groan. He sensed someone approaching from behind. *Haley . . . Justin . . . Mark! Gotta be Mark! God—so much—too much blood.*

Stump suddenly appeared beside him, a nervous prance to his step. He whined, nosed Buck's left cheek, then licked him repeatedly. Before Buck could gather the energy to push the dog away, he saw Mark emerge from the shadows near the front of the barn. The man looked shell-shocked, his gaze volleying between him and Haley and the man lying in so much blood.

"Y-you okay?" Mark asked, his eyes still roaming, apparently not ready to settle on any one victim. "You . . . what . . . she—"

"Go—go get 'er," Buck said, gesturing toward Haley. "I'm a' . . . a'ight."

"But you're—"

"Jus' get 'er!" The command seemed to suck what little air Buck had out of his lungs. He leaned over, drew in a shuddering, burning breath, felt the heaviness in his body lift slightly. Stump whined and nudged him on the ear with his snout. "It's a'ight, boy," Buck murmured, pushing him away. He peered up and saw Mark hobbling slowly toward Haley. He wanted to shout at him to hurry, but at the same time Buck understood the hesitation in the man's steps, the fear and worry on his face. It's what a person did when they stumbled onto a nightmare.

When Mark reached her, Buck felt tears well up in his eyes. He wanted to pray, but couldn't remember how. Nadine had always been the religious one in the family.

"Haley?" Mark called softly. He knelt beside her, and his hand shook visibly when he reached out and touched her face. She didn't move. He tucked a hand under her head, lifting it slightly. "Haley, it's Mark—Mark Aikman. Can you hear me? We're here, me and your grandpa, we're here for you."

When she didn't respond, Buck felt the weight of the world settle onto his shoulders. He tried to stand, but wound up dropping to his hands and knees. Tears spilled onto his cheeks as he crawled toward her. "Haley? You need to be a'ight now, you hear? It's Papaw. We came get you . . . so you need to be a'ight . . . please."

Mark threw him a quick glance, then started working on the ropes that bound her wrists. "I think she's in shock."

"But she ain't . . . she ain't . . . movin'." Buck came to a halt near Haley's feet. Stump inched up close to him, pressing against his right side.

"That happens when people are in shock." Having loosed her left wrist, Mark leaned over Haley to free her right. "Check the chains on her ankles. See what we're going to need to get them off."

Buck stared at the rusted links wound around his granddaughter's left ankle, at her left foot, which was dirty and shoeless. Her jeans, or what was left of them, looked like they'd been run through a shredder. Who could have done this to her? Who? How could anyone do something like this to an innocent girl? To his granddaughter? His baby granddaughter?

"Buck!"

Startled, Buck looked up. He saw Mark, now bare-chested, slip the t-shirt he'd been wearing over Haley's head, then quickly tuck her arms into the armholes.

"The chains," Mark said sternly. "Check them."

As though slapped awake, Buck jerked back onto his haunches. *Right, the chains. Gotta check the chains.* Stump chuffed an agreement, then sniffed Haley's right foot.

"I think she's going to be okay," Mark said, tugging the t-shirt over Haley's chest and stomach. "Her breathing sounds a little stronger. We just need to get her out of here."

Buck nodded, afraid to say anything lest he jinx that bit of good news. He fumbled with the links on her right ankle, his fingers stiff and uncooperative. He fumbled with the links on her left ankle. One end of the chain was attached to a metal stake that had an eyelet head, and the majority of its length had been wrapped around her ankle three times. Surprisingly, the opposite end of the chain had simply been looped and tucked beneath the wraps. Without the use of her hands, though, the links were just as good as padlocked together.

As soon he pulled the end of the chain out of hiding, Buck found himself working faster, his thoughts sharpening, racing. He needed to find a way to get the truck closer to the barn. They'd waste valuable time carrying her all the way back to the road.

Just as Buck removed the last of the chain from Haley's left ankle, Stump jumped to attention. Then he lowered his head, nose pointed toward the far back corner of the barn, and let out a long, low growl.

As if in response, a bone-chilling howl erupted from the darkness, and before either man could react, something flew through the air, striking

Mark in the left temple and knocking him backwards. Stump yelped like he'd been the one hit and ran off to hide, tail between his legs.

Instinct and reflex threw Buck into action, and he flung his body over Haley's to shield her. Mark was already scrambling to his feet, blood raining down from a gash in his temple.

A deep, gargling voice boomed out of the darkness. "Leave her! She's mine now, mine!"

Keeping his body tucked down low over Haley, Buck peered about, trying to find the voice's owner. All he saw was shadows. Pulsing, writhing, slithering shadows.

"Get away from her!" the voice commanded. "She's mine! *Get out!*"

"You *come out*, you chicken-ass motherfucker!" Mark shouted. He stood near Haley's head, feet widening into a fight stance, hands balled into fists.

A loud crash sounded from the back of the barn, wood, metal, glass, like someone had rammed a car into the building. Buck barely had time to gasp in surprise before a hideous *thing* sprinted out of the darkness about forty feet away. It looked to be about three feet tall and just as wide, with leathery skin and a head twice the size it should have been. Craggy teeth filled its wide, grinning mouth, and its small, dark eyes bore into them. Although two legged, like a man, it walked on cloven hooves, and dark, matted, hair swung across its stooped shoulders as it drew closer. "She is *mine!*"

As he gawked at the nightmare on hooves,

Buck heard Mark groan loudly. He glanced back, and saw him grab his right thigh with both hands. His face was contorted with pain, and he looked ready to keel over.

"Mark—Mark, you a 'ight?"

An ear-piercing shriek of laughter filled the barn, and Mark suddenly gasped and went wide-eyed as though he'd just been stabbed in the gut.

A chill ran through Buck. *Mark's gonna die. That thing's gonna kill 'im.* The thought carried such surety it was as if someone in the know had whispered it in his head. He began to shiver uncontrollably. If something happened to Mark, he'd be left alone with two dead men, an unconscious granddaughter, and a creature that appeared capable of killing someone without laying a finger on them. History would repeat itself. He'd fail Haley, just as he'd failed her father. And there wouldn't be a damn thing he'd be able to do about it.

Mark's gonna die.

Then, as if on cue, Mark doubled over and let out a long, blood-curdling scream.

CHAPTER TWENTY-NINE

Haley remembered struggling with Caster's creature and how the feel of him on top of her seemed to carry the bulk of so much more—the weight of her father's death, her mother's committal to a mental hospital, her foolishness in trusting Caster, how she'd betrayed her sister. In every case, all had been destined for death. Her father had died; her mother had died to the world; Haley's own faith in humanity and love had died; and her conscience and desire for life had died right along with her twin. It seemed only fitting that she should die, too. It was that simple.

Once she'd come to terms with that notion, she'd been prepared to give up, to stop fighting and let the creature take her, all of her. That way death would hurry and come. As far as she was concerned, it would actually be a victory of sorts. The timing of her death in her control.

So she'd let go, releasing her will, her mind, everything. And it had been easier than she thought. The moment Haley made the decision to stop fighting, it was like a dimmer switch began to turn, turn, slowly shutting off her life. Her arms went numb first, then her legs. The creature must have sensed the change because it stopped trying to force itself inside her and went still, as though waiting to see what would happen next. Thankfully her eyesight had begun to fade by this time, so all she'd been able to make out of its hideous face was a contorted, dark blur. Then it moved again, and just as she felt something wet and slimy press against the inside of her thigh, she heard a creaking sound— creaking—the groan of wood—the same sound the barn door made when it was being opened.

That was when the creature jumped off her, and she heard it scuttle away with a hurried *click-sfft-click* sound. But it had left a gift behind. Something slimy, crawling, twisting, writhing on her skin, on the inside of her thighs, working its way up, wanting inside her. Something flashed past her then, and for a second, Haley imagined it was Stump. She could've sworn she heard the dog's frenzied barking, felt him nuzzle the side of her face, her shoulder. Even if only in her imagination, she should have felt some sort of relief, the creature was gone. She could have widened that imagery to include rescuers. Someone had to be with Stump. The dog couldn't have gotten here on his own, which meant Papaw had come to save her. But her mind wouldn't allow the fantasy. It was too late for anyone to protect her now because of the worms—the snakes—whatever writhing wetness had been left by the creature.

No sooner had she considered that than she heard a long, drawn-out wail, and as odd as it seemed, she imagined it belonged to her grandfather. *But he'd never make a sound like that.*

Then another familiar voice—Mark Aikman's, filtered into her consciousness. *Imagination. Maybe I'm already dead. What would Mr. Aikman be doing here?* But Mr. Aikman didn't sound like Mr. Aikman. He wasn't saying things an art teacher would say. She sensed words: one sounding like her name; another sounding like Mr. Aikman saying his first name; then babble, babble, stuff she couldn't make out; and cursing, words she'd never heard him use before. She'd wanted to turn her head in the direction of the voice to check and see if it was really Mr. Aikman but couldn't make it move. Evidently whatever dimmer switch was turning off her life, didn't have a reverse mode. In fact, it felt stuck, like it had muted her senses but wasn't quite ready to shut them completely off. She could hear, but sounds were garbled, could feel an occasional breeze touch her skin but unable to close her eyelids or move so much as a fingertip. Her eyes could only take in what was directly in front of them, and even that was extremely blurry.

When she'd felt pressure against her ankles, heard the rattle of the chains that held her, she'd thought the creature was back, and a flutter of fear had stirred inside her. But it quickly died, the dimmer switch cutting off the emotion and replacing it with indifference.

Her art teacher's voice soon returned, joining the rattle of chains. Then another voice chimed in, one that sounded like Papaw's, and all of the sounds converged into a single action, a single scene in a movie that had no picture save for the ones that came to her mind's eye.

The art teacher saying something that sounded comforting—Papaw saying please—*Can't be Papaw. He never says please. Daddy? Daddy, is that you? Are you here?* And the movie in her mind gave her father the lead role, bringing his face right before the camera. Haley saw his smile, his beautiful blue eyes twinkling with happiness, the dark stubble that used to make her lip tickle every time she'd kissed his cheek. She wanted so much to run to him, throw her arms around his neck and never let go. But even her imagination wouldn't allow her to move, not even a smile. The one thing it couldn't stop, however, was the flood of warmth washing through her when she saw him—and heard him.

Papaw's here to help you. You've got to keep fighting. Don't stop fighting, baby girl. For me, okay? Don't give up, and I promise everything will be all right—for all of you.

Someone else joined the movie then—a girl— who looked so familiar—so—*Heather? Heather!* Her sister's face came into sharp focus, and she smiled at Haley. Smiled! *God, Heather I'm so sorry! Please, I'm so—*

Listen to Dad, Haley. Everything's going to be okay, but you can't—

At that moment another voice screeched in, shattering her newfound serenity, her sister's face, her father.

Leave her! She's mine now, mine! Get out! Get out!

Haley knew that voice and the stench that came with it. It was Caster's creature. Her heart sank. Not only would she die, so would Papaw, her daddy, her sister, and Mr. Aikman. They would all die along with her.

It's time . . . nearly over . . . I'm going to die . . . .

And the worms—the snakes—the writhing wetness turned the dimmer switch down lower. *Almost off now. Almost off.*

CHAPTER THIRTY

The creature that had invaded Mark's dreams since he'd been stabbed wasn't supposed to be real. He'd worked too hard to put the beast on a mental shelf, planning to keep it there for the rest of his life if possible, and labeling it as a figment of his imagination. With some effort, he might have convinced himself that his assailant had been a dwarf in some sort of costume and nothing more.

But no amount of effort geared toward positive thinking or denial could erase the hideous reality that grinned at him from only a few feet away. *It's real—the thing that stabbed me. Not a dwarf—not a dream.* And neither was the dead man lying on the floor. With so much blood on his face and his mouth opened wide and distorted by what looked like a large chunk of raw meat, the man was barely recognizable. Yet Mark instinctively knew it was the creep from the Curious Goods booth. And that the creature belonged to him.

Until the beast had jumped out of hiding, Mark had thought he'd been challenging and cursing a man, some sick asshole who'd kidnapped Haley and planned to do only-God-knewwhat to her. But a man didn't walk on cloven hooves. And a man couldn't cause excruciating pain in another being with only a thought—with a laugh.

The first shot of pain came the instant the creature revealed itself and spoke. For some reason, while it had been tucked away in the dark and he'd only been able to hear its voice, the only effect it'd had on him was anger. The moment it appeared, however, and shouted, "She's mine!" the words seemed to skewer Mark's brain. Then it felt like someone stuck an electric knife in his leg, right in the center of the stab wound and turned the damn thing on. Grinding— sawing—slicing. It felt so real he could almost hear the whine of the blade, the sound deepening as it strained against tendons and bone.

He vaguely recalled Buck asking if he was all right before the creature laughed, and that highpitched, maniacal shriek somehow sent that horrific pain searing through his body like a brushfire. He remembered screaming in agony and knew only a demon from the darkest pits could have discerned the defiant *Noooooo!* he'd imbedded in that scream. Despite the torment racking his body, he'd managed to remain standing, albeit doubled-over, refusing to let the sono-fabitch win the battle so easily.

Gasping, Mark forced himself upright. He squeezed his eyes shut, then opened them quickly to clear his vision. The creature stood in the same place, its grin fading, and the pain began to ebb from Mark's body.

"You will lose!" the creature shouted.

Mark glared at it and kept his voice quiet but determined. "Not today, asshole."

The creature snarled, then snapped his head to the left as though hearing a possible threat in that direction. When it turned back, it pointed a thick, gnarled finger at Mark. "You already lost—lost! I have the power, not you." It waved a hand toward the dead man on the floor. "Even him, the one who created me to do his bidding, wasn't as strong as me. I crushed him, look! I am the master now—her master. She belongs to *me!*"

Mark bit back a rebuttal, suddenly struck with thoughts that demanded attention. If the creature was so intent on destroying him, why was it just standing over there? Why didn't it attack? And if it had the ability to harm him with just a thought, why did it bother debating over who'd won or lost? Did it use physical force to attack him at the fair because that's what the man behind the booth wanted it to do? Was it *capable* of physically attacking without a master? Even its mental ability to inflict pain seemed limited. When Mark first saw the creature, he'd been so stunned it felt like his brain had lost

the ability to think. The beast had overtaken
him then. But for some reason when he'd stood
up to it, the pain in his body receded, and the
creature became boisterous like the only weapons
it had left were words.

Then there was the issue about the dead man
being its master. If that was true, it meant the
man had created it. But how? The damn thing
certainly wasn't made out of Play Doh. When
Mark considered the merchandise that had been
sold in the Curious Goods booth, only one logical explanation, which wasn't really logical at all,
seemed to fit. The creature had been designed
and given life with magic. Further reasoning
told him that since Haley had been hanging out
at the booth chances were pretty good that the
magic of choice had been Chaos.

Mark mentally scrolled through the multiple
articles he'd read on Chaos and came to an
abrupt halt when he recalled the section on sigils. He remembered reading that if a conjurer
wasn't sure about what they were doing when creating a sigil, especially for a large intention, it was
possible for that sigil to not only take on a life of
its own but to take over, or end, the life of its owner. If what he faced now was a conjuration, how
was he supposed to fight it? If its own creator,
who'd been at least twice the creature's height
and undoubtedly more agile, couldn't defeat it
or escape from it, how would they?

If memory served, there were only two ways to
destroy a wayward sigil. Either its master had to
end its existence or another sigil of equal or

stronger power had to be created to fight the first to the death. The first option wouldn't work since the creature's 'master' was dead. That left only the second—he'd have to conjure up a new, stronger sigil. He knew from his research how they were created, but he also knew it took time to create them, something they didn't have. *Unless I do something serious, really drastic—that might charge it quick . . . .*

The thought sounded on target, but it made Mark nervous. What if he screwed up and they wound up stuck with something weak and useless? Or worse—nothing at all? He sighed wearily, knowing it was a chance he'd have to take if they were going to get Haley out alive—and if any of them wanted to live a normal life again.

Buck was kneeling at his granddaughter's side, warily watching the creature, his body poised, seemingly ready to topple over the girl at the first sign of an attack. Mark called to him quietly. "Psst."

Buck glanced back at him.

"I might know how to get *it* back in the closet," Mark said in a loud whisper. He was certain the creature could hear him but hoped if he disguised his words, it might not understand. He kept his fingers crossed that Buck would catch on.

"What's 'at?" Buck cocked his head, a stunned expression on his face. "How'd you know about the closet?"

Now Mark was the one confused. "Huh?"

"What's 'at you said about a closet?"

Mark held his gaze, trying to tell him with his

eyes to listen carefully. "I said I might know how to get *it* back in there."

The wrinkles on Buck's face shifted as he clenched his jaw. Then a spark of understanding flashed through his eyes. "How you fig'rin' to do that?"

"By playing the same game."

Buck frowned, obviously lost to what Mark meant.

"Don't have time to explain the rules now. You'll have to trust me."

Worry lines deepened on Buck's brow, and he looked back at the creature. It sneered at them, arms held out at its sides, clicking fingers to thumbs like it was counting something. He turned back to Mark. "A'ight."

"What I've got to do is going to seem strange— very strange, so keep the trust thing in mind . . . okay?" As he spoke, Mark tapped his left hand on his upper right arm, then shot a glance at Haley, trying to signal for Buck to look at the girl's arm. In the class picture he'd taken, most of the fake tattoo on Haley's arm had been hidden beneath her shirtsleeve. Now the snake covered the entire length of her arm, its head resting right above her wrist. Mark couldn't think of a better indicator for just how weird things could get.

Buck pursed his lips and looked at Mark's arm—his eyes—his arm—then he finally peered over at Haley, and his eyes grew wide. When he turned back, his mouth was hanging open.

Mark nodded slowly "We've just got to put it back in the closet. Got it?"

The expression on Buck's face vacillated between fear and uncertainty. "And you know 'bout how you gonna do that?"

A boulder of pain suddenly rolled up Mark's thigh to his hip, and he grimaced. The creature must have finished counting. "Think so," he said through gritted teeth. "P-pocket knife—you got one?"

Buck slapped a hand on his right front pocket, then his left. "Damn thing ain't here."

Sweat trickled down Mark's face. The creature was playing pushy thought again. His right leg felt ready to burst. "Need some . . . something that cuts—anything."

Shaking his head, Buck turned first one way, then another as though visually searching the barn. "Ain't nothin' . . . don't know where— wait, hold up . . ." Already on his knees, he leaned forward, wincing, then crawled a couple feet to the right, patting and searching the ground with a hand. " 'Know I stepped on somethin' . . . here!" He quickly backtracked to Mark and held out a ten-penny nail. "This do?"

Mark took the nail and examined its rusted tip. "It'll do." Then before he had the chance to reconsider, Mark tucked the nail into his right fist, point sticking out past the heel of his hand, and turned to face the creature. *Need a symbol of the intent—symbol of the intent.* As if waiting on the sidelines to be summoned, an image immediately popped into Mark's mind. With a nod, he pressed the point of the nail against his left pectoral muscle, gritted his teeth, then drove the nail into his flesh. *Win!*

Fire seemed to envelope his chest as he dragged the nail downward at an angle to the bottom of his left rib cage. Rivulets of blood rolled down his body. *Win, goddammit! Win!* He heard Buck gasp loudly, and fought to keep his thoughts focused. *Win!* Taking a deep breath, he dragged the nail upward to the center of his chest. More fire—hell fire . . . Swallowing a scream that threatened to escape, Mark tore a path with the nail to the bottom of his right rib cage. *Win! Beat the sonofabitch! Win—win!* With a trembling hand and a scream that would no longer be contained, Mark yanked up on the nail and ripped a bloody trench all the way up to his right nipple.

Staggering back a step, he held the bloody nail out with one hand and pointed to the large *W* he'd just carved on his body with the other. "You got that, you ugly fuck?" he yelled at the creature. "Win! We're going to fucking win!"

The creature sneered and smacked its lips as though amused. "You can't win. You lost. You don't know what you're doing. Playing games, playing games."

Mark glared at the beast. *Win!* He concentrated hard, seeing past the creature until he got a mental image of the symbol on his body. *Win— win!*

Something stirred inside him. Fluttered.

Ignoring the pain in his body, the blood dripping from him, the horror locked on Buck's face, Mark closed his eyes. *Win!* He held both arms over his head and clenched his fists. *Win! Win!*

"Playing games! She's mine! I'm the master—me! Me!"

Mark hardly heard the creature. Something was happening inside him. A surging in his chest, like something pushing against it from inside. The pushing sensation grew insistent, then waned.

"You're not strong enough—playing games—you lost! You lost!"

As if the pain in his chest wasn't enough, the wound in Mark's thigh began to throb fiercely. Throb—throbbing—until it was in his head, pounding—knocking. . . . *That's it!* Nearly blinded by pain, Mark fumbled with the nail until he had a firm grip on it again. Then he aimed and plowed the nail through his jeans and into his thigh, right in the center of the stab wound. "W-WIN!"

He dropped to his knees, and the world and the pain fell silent. He saw Buck, or thought it was Buck—the face was wavering too much for him to be sure. It made him dizzy. Mark lowered himself to the ground, curled up on his right side, then immediately rolled onto his back. His chest hurt again, but it was a different hurt. Something was moving inside him, deep inside his chest. The same surging sensation he'd felt earlier started up again, only stronger, much stronger, and just when he thought his ribs would shatter from the pressure, it relented.

Before he had time to catch his breath, it came again, hard and fast. Mark quickly rolled to his side and vomited. He was still heaving bile when something shoved hard against him and slammed him onto his back on the ground. He gasped, felt his chest swell expansively, then white-hot pain blasted through his body. *The sigil! Oh, God, it's coming! Coming . . .*

He reached deep into his mind, narrowing his focus, *seeing* himself walking out of the barn with Haley . . . *feeling* the weight of her body in his arms . . . *hearing* Buck sigh with relief as he followed them out . . . *smelling* the thicket and brush as they headed for the truck, *tasting* victory with every step—then he mentally shouted, *Win!*

His chest swelled all the more, cutting his breath. *WIN! WIN!*

The surge that came next veritably lifted his body a few inches from the floor, then held him there—held him—held him. Without breath, unable to move, Mark wished, prayed, hoped his chest would explode and be done with it. It felt like every organ in his body wanted out through his sternum. Just when he thought he could bear no more, he was dropped unceremoniously to the floor, the pain in his chest abruptly gone.

A rush of wind swept across him, and he gulped greedily at the air. That's when Mark saw it—a massive, black form shaped like a W, hovering a few feet above him.

Win . . . he thought, and his eyelids drooped with exhaustion. *It's . . . it's here.*

"Get! Go on!"

Buck's shouting prodded Mark, demanding that he open his eyes.

"Go on, get away from 'im!"

Peering past heavy lids, Mark saw Buck standing, unsteady on his feet, batting the air with his hands.

"Buck, no—"

"Don't worry none, I got it," Buck said, throwing a high, right punch. "Big damn bat—somethin'—but I'll—"

Mark struggled to his feet. "No!"

A roar of anger boomed through the barn. The creature shook its head rapidly, obviously pissed off.

"Whatchu mean no?" Buck demanded. He lowered his arms.

"It's—it's going to help us," Mark said. "Remember I said weird? Trust?"

The creature bellowed again, louder, a heavy rumbling sound that vibrated through Mark's body like a clap of thunder. The beast was on the move now, slowly, hesitantly heading in their direction.

The air around them shifted with a thick *phoop!*, and both men looked up. Two smoke-gray, nearly translucent wings had been deployed by the thing overhead. They spanned at least six feet across and were webbed with thick, pink veins. Although the thing between the wings resembled a bat, it was almost as big as Stump but with a heavier coat of fur. It had wide translucent ears that narrowed into pointed tips and thick, black talons, similar to the creature. It let out a high-pitched shriek that pierced Mark's eardrums.

Gawking, Buck glanced back at the roaring creature, then up at the winged monstrosity hovering overhead. When he looked back at Mark, there was raw fear in his eyes. "What—"

"Watch over Haley," Mark said, and stepped away from him. He knew that whatever was about to go down wouldn't be pretty, and if it had to involve him, he wanted Buck and Haley at a safe distance.

"It's too late!" the creature shouted, inching closer, its eyes fixed on the wings, the needle-length teeth gleaming from the bat-thing's mouth. "You can't have her! She's mine! *All mine!*"

The air shifted again, *phoop!—phoop!*, and in a flash, wings and teeth and thick, pink veins swooped toward the creature.

CHAPTER THIRTY-ONE

Buck had only seen two picture shows in his life. *Lone Texas Ranger* with his best friend Larry Salon when he was eight and *Birdman of Alcatraz* back in the '60s, while on a date with Nadine. Both times he'd been mesmerized by the images projected on the large screens. The actors, the scenery, the sounds; everything seemed so real it was as if any breathing being in the Foxsboro Theater could just walk right up and jump into the action, into a whole new world. What he saw playing out before him now, however, put a whole new perspective on mesmerized. Only this was a world he wanted no part of—a squat, deformed creature with claws and split-hooves that stood upright like a man, talked like a man, smelled like something long buried in a swamp—now this winged thing that looked like a bat—this monstrous winged thing that he could have sworn rose from Mark's body like heavy, black smoke.

When Mark first took the nail to his chest, Buck thought for sure the man had lost his mind. Mark had asked him to trust, warned him that what he had to do would seem strange, but this—this stretched far past strange. It was every nightmare Buck ever had rolled into one.

The swoop of air from the bat-thing's wings sent dust swirling about, and Buck leaned over Haley. Protecting his granddaughter from dust was easy, but from this . . . ? Lifting his head, Buck saw the bat take to the rafters, then quickly disappear in the dark.

"Your tricks won't save her!" the creature screamed. "She's mine—you can't have her! Can't have—can't have—I'll kill her!"

Anger flared through Buck, and he was about to snap back a retort when he heard Mark shout.

"Win!"

The sound of that one word filled the barn like a living, swelling organ. It pushed toward the rafters, pressed against the walls, shoved against the ground, consuming every inch of space. The very force of it made Buck's insides quiver, and he glanced over his shoulder hesitantly, fearing what Mark might be doing now.

Covered in blood and looking like he'd been forced through a wood-chipper, Mark stood a few feet behind them, head raised, eyes closed, hands rolled into fists at his sides. "Win—win!"

Something about the determined set of his jaw and the ramrod stiffness of his stance sent fear and hope colliding in Buck's gut. Whatever Mark was doing had power in it, he felt it. But instinct

told him that that power had to go somewhere—
do something—and that the something could be
a kill-or-cure. And if it killed, the destruction
could very well include them all. He needed to
understand what was happening, had to know
what to expect.

"Mark?" Buck cringed, having spoken louder
than he'd intended.

Instead of answering, Mark unfurled his
hands, stretched his fingers out wide, and began
to chant. "Win . . . win . . . win!"

Realizing the man was lost in some sort of
trance, Buck held tight to Haley and whispered,
"Gonna be okay, baby girl. You hearin' me? It's
all gonna be a'ight." He never felt more like a
liar in his life.

"Not yours! I'll kill her—mine!" the creature
cried. It clawed at the air, then grabbed a handful of its own mangy hair and yanked it out by
the roots. "No, no, she's *mine*!"

Buck gritted his teeth, fighting an overwhelming urge to run over and dropkick the beast back
to the hellhole it had come from.

A mind-rending screech from overhead
stopped the creature in its tracks and sent Buck's
heart racing up to his throat. In that instant,
something flashed past him on the right and before he could turn to see what it was, a huge, wet
tongue lapped at his cheek.

"Stump!" Buck reached for his dog, needing
to bury his face in the warm familiarity of his fur,
even if only for a second.

He heard the *phoop!* of massive wings taking

flight and looked toward the rafters just as the
bat swooped overhead. It banked left near the
front of the barn, then circled back, flying low
and straight for the creature. For a moment,
Buck thought the bat intended to dive into its
midsection, but it pulled up at the last second,
talons extended, and ripped a bloody trench
across the crown of the creature's head. Clumps
of hair dangled from its talons as it flew up and
out of reach.

The creature howled and pawed furiously after the bat, blood running down its hideous face.
"You *can't win!*"

Stump let out a threatening growl, and Buck
grabbed the scruff of his neck to keep the dog
from bounding after the creature.

The beast suddenly froze, then turned ever so
slowly, like it suspected a rear attack. With a
heavy snort, it swung around again and twisted
its stout body from left to right, arms flapping
wildly as if batting away a swarm of bees. "No—
no—no!"

Phoop! Faster than seemed possible for its size,
the bat reappeared. This time it swooped down
on the creature and sliced through its left cheek.

With a fierce roar the beast threw a punch,
but the bat was already banking into a turn at the
other end of the barn. When it returned, striking again, it pierced the beast's right eye and
tore through its brow. Another *phoop!* and the
bat headed for the rafters once more.

The creature screamed, its voice now a gargle
of rage and agony. Its one remaining eye seemed

to jitter in its socket as it sought out the bat. "You will *fail!*" Then the beast turned and aimed a finger in their direction. "I am the master, and I will *destroy* her! Do you hear me . . . *Mark?*"

Buck's eyes grew wide. For some reason, hearing the creature call Mark by name compounded his fear, pulling it up close and naked. His hands began to tremble, and the sensation worked its way up through his arms and into his body. Soon he was shivering as if he'd been dunked in ice water. He glanced sidelong at Mark. The man stood in the same position he was in earlier, eyes closed, seemingly unaffected by the ruckus. "Mark—Mark, you heard 'at? You heard what it said?"

The furrows in Mark's brow deepened, but he didn't open his eyes: "Win . . . win . . . win!"

Stump nuzzled Buck's cheek nervously, then sidled up close to Haley. Suddenly, his head snapped to attention, and the fur on his back stood on end.

Mark's chanting grew louder, more insistent. *"WIN . . . WIN!"*

The creature lifted its head and bellowed, swatting its hands about blindly.

"WIN!"

The mantra seemed to call the bat from the rafters, for it appeared again and in one swoop it caught the creature on the right shoulder and gouged away three inches of flesh.

"No!" The creature stumbled sideways, and its arms flailed for balance. Once its hooves found purchase, the beast turned in tight, frantic circles and screamed, "I will destroy! Her—her—destroy her! Stop now—mine!"

As if challenged with a dare, the bat dropped down twice more in rapid succession, both times with a blood-curdling screech. When it soared for the rafters again, little remained of the creature's face. Instead of shrieking in pain and anger, though, the beast simply turned and steadied its good eye on Mark. Then it raised a hand, pointed at Haley, and shouted, "Die!"

Feeling his granddaughter's body jerk beneath him, Buck sat back quickly. Haley's eyes were still open, but they remained empty. Her body twitched harder, and she let out a deep, anguished moan.

Buck's heart wrenched in his chest, and he placed a hand on her forehead. "Gonna be a'ight, girl. Don't you worry none. Gonna be okay."

Phoop!

Buck looked anxiously about, familiar now with the sound of the bat's wings in motion. He spotted it coming in fast. *Kill it already, dammit!* he thought. *Finish it—go for its damn throat!*

Just as the bat reached its target, fate smiled on the bleeding creature. It swung around, caught the bat by the right wing, and slammed it to the ground.

As the screeching bat tried to right itself, Haley's body twitched again, then she began to jerk and buck like she was having a grand mal seizure. She gasped and lifted her arms, reaching out with trembling hands as though desperately begging for help. Then as quickly as it began the seizure stopped, and Haley fell limp. Fearing the worst, Buck grabbed her wrist and checked for a pulse. His shoulders sagged with relief when he felt one, albeit weak.

"We gotta get her outta here," Buck yelled, turning to Mark. He got no response. The man seemed oblivious to everything but the back of his eyelids. "Mark!"

"No, can't—no, can't." The creature's taunting sing-song was directed at the bat. It stood, rocking from side to side, watching its enemy. The second the bat worked itself upright the creature pounced on it from behind and knocked it back to the ground.

Amidst howls and hisses, shrieks and screams, the two entities fought for dominance. For a while, it appeared the creature had the upper hand when it clamped its teeth to the back of the bat's neck. But the bat pulled its wings in tight, did a strange arch and roll movement with its body, and before the creature could react, it wound up flat on its back on the ground. The bat wasted no time claiming its prize. With another twist of its body that seemed to defy logic, considering its wings and body mass, the bat landed on top of the creature and drove its talons into its abdomen. A guttural wail barely had time to escape the creature's mouth before the bat spread its wings and attempted flight.

The creature's body arched, its flesh bloodied and bowed like a fresh side of beef being lifted with meat hooks. It howled in pain, arms and legs flailing, head whipping from side to side.

Its prey obviously too heavy to lift, the bat toppled back onto the beast. Before it was able to position itself again for take off, the creature bucked hard, forcing the bat forward. Then it rammed its claws into the bat's chest. With a deafening squeal, the bat immediately jerked back, writhing and twisting, trying to free itself.

The vicious battle had Stump jittering beneath Buck's hand, and he tightened his grip, knowing the dog wanted in on the action. "Easy, boy." Hoping against hope they'd hurry and kill one other, Buck checked on Haley. No sooner did he turn to her than she started to flop about like a fish left to dry land. Her face paled dramatically, eyelids fluttering, eyes rolling to white. Her mouth opened wide, but if she uttered any sound, Buck couldn't hear it for the bat's screeching and the roar of the beast. Unsure of what to do, he let go of Stump and reached for her.

"WIN!" The sudden command blasted over the din as though an amplifier had been attached to Mark's vocal chords. He hadn't moved, but his eyes were open now and intently focused on the battle.

Before the echo of Mark's voice died away, the bat managed to tear itself away from the creature. It tumbled to the ground with a shriek. The beast rolled sideways and struggled to its feet. Both were drenched in blood and panting, and both moved much slower now. The bat stood a few feet away from the creature, one wing hanging at an awkward angle.

When the creature finally stood, instead of issuing another attack on the bat as Buck suspected, it turned toward them. "Warned you," the creature said, its voice hoarse, the words slightly garbled. A steady stream of blood ran from its face and chest and pooled on the ground. "*Warned* you—*warned* you. Now she . . . dies."

The calmness in the creature's voice when it spoke caused Buck to suck in a breath and reach for Haley. The instant he touched her arm, her body convulsed violently—relentlessly. Each time her body pounded the ground a whoosh of air escaped her lips.

"It's killin' her!" Buck cried. He didn't know what to do, where to hold her, or even *if* he should hold her. He thought he remembered reading somewhere that if a person had a fit you weren't supposed to hold them down, only move stuff out the way so they wouldn't get hurt. But he wasn't sure about that. He wasn't sure about anything anymore, which made him feel as useless as a slug on a rock. Tears welled up in his eyes. He thought about Justin, about Heather fighting for her life in the hospital— the granddaughter convulsing before him. He didn't want to fail his family again, but right now failure seemed as inevitable as dark was to night.

"We can't give up."

Startled by the closeness of the voice, Buck let out a small gasp and turned to see Mark leaning over him.

"If we give up, she'll die for sure," Mark said, his face grim.

As if to verify his words, Haley's entire body jerked violently, and she paled even more. She let out a tormented moan, and the sound wrapped itself around Buck's heart and squeezed so hard he thought it would burst. *They're killin' her . . . those damn things are killin' her . . . .*

Without forewarning, Mark stood and faced the sigil he'd created. Blood had coagulated along the jagged W on his chest, but he thumped the wound with a fist, causing the blood to flow once more. "Win!" he yelled.

The bat hissed vehemently, its damaged wing dragging the ground as it turned its full attention on the creature. It squawked loudly, shrieked, but didn't make a move toward the beast.

The creature cocked its mangled head in the bat's direction, uttered a series of clicking sounds, then let out a deep, winded howl. But it didn't move in for a fight either.

In response, the bat hissed again, a raspy, menacing sound that seemed to roll down Buck's spine like hot tar. The bat slowly rocked its head from left to right, then turned its dot-black eyes on them. The creature did the same.

"Oh, God . . ."

Not liking the note of disbelief in Mark's voice, Buck shot him a look. "Oh, God what?"

With his attention still locked on the bat and creature, Mark said quietly, I—I think they joined forces or something—called a draw maybe . . ."

"What's 'at mean?"

"It means we're in deep shit."

An involuntary shudder ran through Buck. Both the creature and bat stood bloodied and battle torn. They stared him down, saliva dripping from the corners of their mouths. In that moment, Buck heard Justin's voice clear and strong in his mind. *You've got to help her, Dad. You're all she's got. Please, help her.*

With a short nod and a grimace of pain, Buck struggled to his feet. It was time for this to end.

"What're you doing?" Mark asked, frowning.

Buck pushed past him. "Somethin'. Gotta do somethin'. Gotta help Justin . . . I mean Haley. Promised I'd—"

"Wait—"

"I ain't waitin' no more!" Buck snapped. "You stay with the girl—with Haley. *Stay* with her, you understandin' me, son?"

Before Mark could answer, Buck hobbled toward the bat and beast, his jaw clenched.

The creature gave a threatening snarl. The bat waggled its head as if in agreement, then let out a shrill screech.

"You shut the hell up!" Buck yelled, then slapped his palms on his chest. "You want somebody? Then you c'mere and get me, you goddamn bastards! C'merc and get me 'cause you sure as shittin' ain't gonna get her!"

"Buck!"

Ignoring Mark's cry of alarm, Buck slapped his chest again. "C'mon dammit!"

The creature growled, took a step toward him and looked ready to take another when Stump suddenly shot past Buck and launched himself at the beast.

With one swipe of its arm, the creature caught Stump on the side of the head and sent the dog flying into a dark corner a few feet away. Buck heard Stump land with a thud, then nothing more. Not even a whimper. It made his chest ache with grief.

Clenching his teeth, Buck glared at the entities.

They glared back.

The standoff lasted only a moment for the creature reared its head and bellowed.

The bat hissed, arching a wing.

Then both headed straight for Buck.

CHAPTER THIRTY-TWO

Mark could hardly believe his eyes. He didn't want to believe them. The sigil he'd created to defeat the creature was turning on them.

Evil begets evil. The thought came unbidden—as did another—*You can't fight darkness with dark.*

If creating another sigil wasn't the answer, then how in the hell were they supposed to fight back? He seriously doubted that a standoff with a seventy-year-old man was the answer, no matter how pissed off that man might be.

As the two sigils slowly advanced toward Buck, Mark racked his brain, trying to figure out a way to end this nightmare. But even thinking hurt. His entire body throbbed and burned like it had turned into one giant abscess.

"And it's going to hurt a lot more!"

Startled by the gravelly, familiar voice that yelled the proclamation in his mind, Mark peered over at the creature.

It came to halt and sneered back at him. *I told you—told you—interfere and you die—remember* . . .

Seemingly confused by the creature's actions, the bat stumbled to a stop alongside it and issued a short squawk.

Mark shook his head, narrowed his eyes, and threw his own thought back at the beast. *The only one who's going to die here is you, asshole.*

Lowering its head slightly, the creature growled. Mark braced himself, watching its one remaining eye shift from him to Buck, then to Haley. Instead of bounding after them as Mark suspected it would, the creature appeared to slowly melt. It shrank downward, knees hardly bending, then it twisted and dipped its body until it was on its belly and slithering laterally away from the bat.

Stunned by the creature's agility, it took a second for Mark to realize it was heading right for Haley. He was about to bolt for the girl's side when Buck sidestepped and blocked the creature's path.

"Ain't gonna happen," Buck declared.

The creature stopped short and in one fluid motion it stood upright again and roared with rage. Just as it appeared ready to charge, a monstrous *POP!* sounded from overhead—popped again—then the groan of twisting wood. Man and beast peered up in unison, but the rafters, where the sound seemed to be coming from, were hidden in darkness. A light shower of dust and straggles of hay drifted through the meager light remaining in the barn.

Suddenly a heavy creaking, splintering sound

called everyone's attention to the east wall of the building. Mark saw the wall bow out, contract, bow out again, then the panes from its only two windows exploded. Glass shards rained over the barn floor, and a few wallboards swung at odd angles where the windows used to be. Through those two new openings, dusk poked its head farther into the building, warning them that Brother Night would soon arrive and steal any notion of escape they might have entertained thus far.

As if to add to that warning, a larger section of the haymow on their far left abruptly gave way, collapsing with a horrendous crash to the barn floor.

Mark threw himself over Haley to protect her and instantly felt small shrapnel pepper his bare back and arms. For all the pain firing through his chest and thigh in that moment, a hand grenade could have detonated on his back and he probably wouldn't have felt it. When the debris settled, he quickly glanced up to check on Buck.

Except for a powdering of dust on his clothes, Buck appeared unmoved by the noise and chaos. He stood tall, arms at his side, chin locked at a defiant angle as he glared at the beast.

The bat as well as the creature seemed unaffected by the destruction. Both remained intently focused—and both were on the move again. When Mark saw them, a notion struck him—in all the time they'd been here, why hadn't the creature lived up to its threats? Any wild animal would have destroyed its prey by now. *Could* they even attack? It was obvious they were able to fight one another, but so far, even with all their vicious sound effects, neither beast nor bat had touched them. And considering the number of times the entities had advanced towards them, why did they always appear just as far in distance as when they began?

Another wide-mouthed hiss from the bat sent the questions flying out of Mark's mind. Whatever the reason for the constant distance and lack of physical contact, he just needed to be grateful and stay focused on helping Haley and getting them the hell out of here.

Keeping one eye on the approaching enemy, Mark pushed himself up and gasped with pain. He took a second or two to catch his breath, then slipped an arm under Haley's shoulder in an attempt to lift her. That's when he saw the bat's legs bend and its wings begin to expand from the corner of his eye. *It's going to attack!*

Another sharp *crack!* rang through the barn, and Mark heard his heart hammer in his ears. Soon they wouldn't have to worry about bats or beast. The barn would simply finish collapsing and kill them all. He lifted Haley's shoulders off the ground, and as her head flopped back, an image flashed through his mind. He saw himself lifting her, settling Haley over his shoulder in one easy motion—just as the bat shot forward. He saw—felt no pain in his chest and his leg withstood the extra weight as he stood with her in his arms. And as he pulled her close, the bat attacked—fangs sinking deep into Buck's throat—

ripping it open. The image was so real it sent waves of nausea washing over him. *Haley—at least I can save Haley . . .*

No matter how hard Mark tried to shake it off, the vision of the bat tearing at Buck's throat wouldn't leave him. *And Caster's creature . . . will attack from below.* No sooner did he complete that thought than his mind's eye produce the vision. He saw the creature clawing at Buck's stomach, spilling his entrails across the dirt floor. *Jesus, I've got to do something!*

Mark quickly settled Haley back on the ground and struggled to his feet. "Buck—Buck, come help me carry her—come—"

"You go on with her," Buck said with a sharp shake of his head. "Y'all both go on. I done made 'em a trade."

"No trade—all dead—too late!" the creature shouted. "DEAD!" Then it bounded after them at full speed. The bat immediately followed.

Mark was so shocked by the abrupt advancement he froze, unable to do anything but watch the distance between Buck and the entities evaporate.

A fierce snarl echoed from the back of the barn followed by the sharp snap of teeth. In the time it took Mark to look toward the sound, Stump suddenly appeared, bursting out of the darkness at full tilt. With his ears laid back, the dog ran straight for the bat's right leg and sank his teeth in deep. A loud *shhtapp!* told Mark he'd reached bone.

The bat's scream sounded almost human, and

it quickly folded itself over Stump. They rolled
as one toward the creature, who seemed taken
aback by the disruption. Teeth and claws ripped
through flesh, each followed by a shriek or howl
of agony. By the time bat and dog separated, the
bat looked worse for the wear. Stump took a
wobbly step back, then lowered his head threat-
eningly, blood dripping from his jowls, and
snarled.

The bat hissed in response, then sprang after
Stump with surprising speed.

Evidently not wanting to be left out of the action this time, the creature launched itself at the
dog as well. Stump held his ground, teeth bared,
seemingly undeterred by the two-sided attack.

Just as the animal and sigils collided, Mark felt
a strong gust of cool wind blow across his back.
Startled, he glanced back, then lost all sense of
place and time—when he saw Heather kneeling
behind him.

She smiled.

He frowned, utterly confused. This had to be
an apparition or a figment of his imagination.
Heather was supposed to be in the hospital fighting for her life. Yet here she was—looking freshly
scrubbed in a plain white dress and not a hair out
of place. How could that be?

As though hearing his thoughts, Heather's
smile broadened, and her face took on an an-
gelic glow. She leaned over, took hold of Haley's
left hand with her right, then extended her free
hand to Mark.

He looked at her palm, amazed to see it was as solid and pink as his own. "But . . . how can . . . ?"

Heather shook her head softly, offering her hand again.

Mark reached for it hesitantly, fearing it might be a trick, some new, deadly mind game from the land of Chaos and monsters. When he touched her, however, her palm quickly nestled against his as though it had always belonged there. It felt warm and dry to the touch, her grip sure. A soft, tingling current radiated from her curled fingers into his hand, then up his arm, slowly spreading throughout his body like butter left to a summer sun. Oddly, wherever the sensation traveled, it had an analgesic affect. The fierce pain in his chest and thigh calmed to a dull ache, and he felt stronger, more clear-headed, like he'd just awakened from a refreshing nap.

Sensing words were unnecessary he sought her eyes for understanding. She felt real, looked real, but *real* people didn't just *appear* out of nowhere. How did she get here? Heather's eyes didn't reveal the answer to that question. Instead, they took on an intensity that all but shouted, "Pay close attention, Mark!"

So he did.

And the instant he closed his mind to everything but her, he knew what needed to be done and that it needed to be done quickly.

Mark held out his free hand and yelled over the battle's din, "Buck!"

"I told y'all to get!" Buck shouted back, still oblivious to what was going on behind him.

"Grab my hand!

"What?" Buck turned to Mark with a scowl. As soon as he caught sight of Heather, his whole body seemed to sag with disbelief. His mouth dropped open as his gaze volleyed between her and Mark. "Wh-wha—"

"Just take my hand."

"But . . . she—how—"

A loud yelp echoed through the barn, and the sound carried the weight of intense pain. There was little doubt it belonged to Stump.

"Now, Buck! *Hurry!*"

As if sleepwalking, Buck stumbled toward Mark, his eyes fixed on Heather. When he drew near enough, Mark reached out, grabbed his right wrist, and pulled him closer quicker.

After locking Buck's hand into his, Mark dropped to his knees, tugging him along. "Get down here and take Haley's other hand."

"You—but you was in the hospital," Buck said, giving Heather a questioning look.

She nodded sadly, then looked down at her sister.

"Y-you was sick and—"

Mark turned and leaned in close so Buck was forced to look him full in the face. It took a moment for the old man's eyes to register his presence.

Once he had his attention, Mark said, "The questions have to wait. I need you to take Haley's hand, Buck—now. The *girls* need you to do it."

The mention of girls seemed to light a fuse in Buck, bringing him to life. His face grew hard and serious and turned a brilliant red. He pursed his lips and fell to his knees, his eyes squeezing shut momentarily when they hit the ground. He wasted no time reaching for Haley's hand.

As soon as Buck took hold of Haley, completing the circle of hands, a monstrous rumbling, like so many thunderclaps, rolled through the barn. The ground trembled beneath them.

Mark and Buck threw nervous glances at each other, then turned to Heather. She had her eyes closed as though concentrating and appeared no more concerned over what was going on around them than if she'd been in deep, meditative prayer.

The soft, tingling current that had flowed from her into Mark earlier now felt like something determined and directed—fully alive and vibrating. This time, instead of traveling throughout Mark's body, it seemed to be concentrated in their hands, his arms. And if the shocked expression suddenly widening Buck's eyes was any indication, it had already migrated into him.

A support beam that was anchored to a nearby T-post suddenly snapped in half, and a heavy cloud of dust thickened the air. What remained of the walls heaved with a wrenching, groaning of wood, then it settled—heaved again. Dust plumed, straw and wood slivers drizzled over them.

"Hold on!" Mark barely had time to issue the warning before part of the roof at the back of the barn collapsed. He squeezed Buck and Heather's hands tighter, fearing he'd made a mistake. Fearing they'd been tricked into staying here, into doing this ring-around-the-rosy, hand holding thing so they'd all be huddled together in one place and easier to kill. Fearing that Heather, or what looked like Heather, was in fact the harbinger of death.

The ground trembled beneath them again, and Mark shut his eyes and cringed, expecting to hear the crash and splinter of timber, to feel the rest of the building cave in on top of them, smashing them into the dirt. But none of that came. What did come were three words—each enunciated and spoken so loudly, it sounded as though they were shouted through a megaphone.

"POINT—OF—UNION!"

The voice sounded neither male nor female, young or old. It simply—*was.* And it seemed to capture something inside Mark's gut, something powerful—life-giving—eternal. It forced it up from his belly into his chest—up to his throat—up—until it burst from his lips—"WIN!"

Then the world exploded with brilliant white light.

CHAPTER THIRTY-THREE

Buck always figured when his time to die would come, he'd be ready. But he wasn't ready. Especially not right now. If he had to die today, he didn't want it to be because an old barn fell on his head like a wet sock. He'd rather his death come with a bit more dignity, from his having accomplished something, like protecting his grandbaby.

When he'd confronted the creature and offered his life for Haley's, he'd felt stronger and younger than he had in years. If the truth be told, he wouldn't have cared if the beast had torn him up with a thousand nasty claws. There was just something about confronting hell and damnation that made a man stand taller. And for him, it might have actually erased a little of what he'd screwed up with Justin. That alone would have given him reason to die smiling, no matter how ugly the death. He'd had that all settled in his

mind when he'd heard Mark calling for him.
Now, kneeling in the dirt, staring at his granddaughter who couldn't possibly be his granddaughter, Buck felt like a demented old man.
Certainly not a hero.

He was contemplating heroism when Mark
suddenly yelled, "WIN!" And the next thing
Buck knew, he was blinded by a brilliant white
light. For a second he was transported back to
Justin's childhood and Nadine snapping Christmas photos. She'd arrange father next to son beside the tree, then aim a clunker of a Polaroid at
them. The camera needed literal light bulbs for
its flash, and each time she took a picture, the
bulb went off with a *poof!* That bright light stole
their eyesight for a good minute, then left white
and black dots floating in front of their eyes for
at least another five. He'd always hated that damn
camera—until Justin was taken from them. Now
Buck would have suffered through a truckload
of flashing bulbs just to have the chance to stand
next to his son one more time.

But this wasn't Christmas and Nadine wasn't
here. And he sure as hell didn't know of any
camera, Polaroid or any other brand, that created that big a flash. It was as if the sun had
silently exploded not five feet away. In fact,
everything had gone completely silent. No shrieks
and howls, nothing. Was this death? All this
white and bright and quiet instead of black and
gloom like everyone assumed it to be? Somehow,
Buck didn't think so. For one thing, as intense as

all this light was, he felt not one speck of fear, and a person should feel at least a little instinctive, intuitive quiver if they were about to look death in the eye. But no quiver came, only something warm and big that started to fill him up on the inside—the same kind of warm and big he'd felt the first time he'd held Justin in his arms after he was born.

Squinting, but still unable to see past the bright white wall, Buck sat back on his haunches and tugged on Mark's hand. "Hey, you a'ight?"

"Y-yeah, I think . . . wait, where'd she go?"

Buck cocked his head, blinking rapidly. "Who?" At least the white wall had a black frame around it now, which meant, he hoped, it was shrinking.

"I . . . she was—Heather. I was holding her hand, but . . ." Mark let go of his hand, and Buck was surprised to find it left him feeling a bit naked. "Heather? Damn, I can't see shit! Heather, you still here?"

From the changing pitch in his voice, Buck knew Mark was leaning over, reaching and searching with his hands. The black frame was widening, but even as it grew, Buck couldn't make out more than a peripheral shadow. "Can't see nothin' neither."

Buck felt a little tug on his hand, and he was about to say, "What?" when it dawned on him that Mark wasn't holding his hand anymore and even if he had, the tug was on his *left* hand

"P-Papaw?"

"Wh—" Buck couldn't form the rest of the

word with his tongue. His brain was on lock-down
or melt down—had to be because he could have
sworn he heard—

"Papaw, is that you?"

"Haley?" Mark's voice sounded fluttery with
surprise, and Buck felt a wave of movement
around him.

"Where—where's my Papaw?"

Oh, God, Buck thought. *Can't be . . .* The black
border and white light suddenly changed to
dancing black and white dots.

"Where's—where's my sister? Where's
Heather?" Another tug on Buck's left hand. "Papaw?"

Blinking—blinking—Buck squinted and tilted
his head as if doing so would help him see
around the dots—and he saw—brown hair—a
small face—a nose just short of pug—*It's her! Haley!*

"P-Papaw?"

*She's sittin' up and ever'thin'! Okay—a'ight, have
to stay calm—don't want to be scarin' her none. Don't
need to be scarin' her . . . .*

"I'm right here, baby girl, Papaw's right here.
Ever'thin's fine. Don't you worry, it's all fine now."

No sooner did he finish reassuring her than
the dots disappeared, allowing everything back
into focus. Haley sat beside him, still holding
his hand. Aside from the scratches and ink
squiggles on her body, she looked perfect.
Mark was in the same place he had been in earlier, only now he had a huge shit-eating grin on
his face. But Heather was gone. Strangely, Buck

didn't feel panic over that. Somehow he knew his other granddaughter wasn't supposed to be here now—that she was safe and well back at Pine Lake Memorial. She'd only stopped by for a short visit so she could lend a hand—well, part of her had anyway. He still wasn't sure *what* part, though, since she'd looked so—so real.

"Heather?" Haley asked quietly.

"She's still in the hospital, honey," Mark said, getting to his feet. "But she's doing much better now." He gave her a knowing smile. "In fact, I'll bet you anything she's bossing doctors and nurses around right this minute."

Haley looked from him to Buck questioningly. "But she was here, right? She was right here with us, wasn't she?"

Buck nodded. "She was."

"Hey, y'all?" Mark said, walking away from them. His voice held a note of awe.

Buck looked up.

"There's nothing here." Mark raised his arms and held out his hands. "Look—I mean, nothing . . . it's gone—all of it. Not even a drop of blood anywhere."

Struggling to his feet, Buck scanned the barn. The haymow was still in pieces, so was the part of the roof that had caved in—but Mark was right. The creature was gone—there was no bat—no dead man lying on the floor with his chest torn open. Even the rope and chains that had bound Haley to the floor were gone, as were the stakes. And not one drop of blood remained as a testament to any of it.

Puzzled, Buck looked back down at Haley. Had they imagined everything? Had it all been some big hallucination? "Anythin' hurtin' you, baby girl? How you feelin'?"

"Okay." She touched her stomach through the t-shirt Mark had put on her. "Scratches just burn a little." The weary, used-up look in Haley's eyes confirmed that what she'd lived through hadn't come from anyone's imagination.

Suddenly, Buck heard a snuffle and snort, then something rammed into the back of his legs. A warm, wet tongue lapped at the hand he had dangling by his side.

"Stump!" Haley's face lit up, and she reached for the dog. He bounded into her arms, tail wagging, tongue slurping at her face.

This is almost better than Christmas pi'tures, Buck thought as he watched them.

"Think you can stand up?" Mark asked, making his way back to Haley. "Maybe walk?"

She opened her mouth to answer, and Stump swiped her bottom lip with his tongue. She laughed long and loud, and the sound of it was so pure and real it made Buck's heart swell. He hadn't heard that much happiness out of her since she and Heather had moved to Mississippi. Haley swiped the back of a hand over her mouth to clean off the dog slobber. "I think so, if Stump'll let me get up."

Buck snapped his fingers at the hound. "C'mere, boy." Stump just stared at him, tongue lolling out the side of his mouth. "C'mon now and quit actin' ign'rant. Get yourself out Haley's way."

"You called me Haley."

Afraid he'd named the wrong twin, Buck threw her a glance. "Ain't . . . ain't that your name—Haley?"

"Yeah." Haley shrugged. "But you used to always call me girl or . . . or, well, nothing. You'd just say what you had to say without using any name."

Peering down at his shoes, Buck gave a little nod. "Sorry 'bout that. Didn't mean—"

"No, no, it's all right," Haley said, and held out a hand to him. She smiled. "Least you're using it now."

Buck reached for her hand, but Mark suddenly stepped in and gripped his arm, giving him pause.

"Look what else disappeared," Mark said, and pointed to Haley's right arm.

The snake tattoo was gone.

CHAPTER THIRTY-FOUR

Blues and pinks, swirls of brown and tan, orange and yellow, then a steady pulse of white—white—white. . . .

"Oh . . . do . . ."

". . . get . . . God . . . up"

Thudump—thudump—thudump . . . the steady—beat—of—a heart?—a clock?—a voice—?

Heather frowned, felt her brows pull down tight and low, lower still. Why wasn't Haley turning off the alarm clock? It was too early for school. She wanted to sleep a little longer—just a little longer—until she smelled breakfast . . . Meemaw's buttermilk pancakes.

Thudump—thudump . . .

"Oh, my God, look!"

Meemaw? Heather opened one eye, wondering what her grandmother was doing in her room so early in the morning. Wait, wasn't it Saturday? They didn't have school on Saturday . . . *wanna*

*sleep for five more minutes . . . just five more . . . then
everyone will be happy . . . will be well . . .*

"Oh, my sweet Jesus, lookit!"

The jubilant sound of triumph, of hopes ful-
filled, of finding that best, first doll under the
tree on Christmas morning, discovering that
perfect dress—that swelling, ringing, tingling,
musical sound, reached deep inside Heather's
mind and pulled her from sleep.

*I have to open my eyes now . . . open them now . . .
open them?*

She heard the *squeak-toof—squeak-toof* of soft-
soled shoes hurrying towards her, then metal
scratching softly against metal, the same sound
a steel-ringed shower curtain made when you
pulled it along a metal rod.

Someone sniffled—sniffled louder—then the
distinct sound of a lot of snot being called back
to a runny nose.

"She's wakin' up!" Meemaw's voice, loud and
insistent. "My baby's wakin' up! Where's that
doctor at? Nurse, go fetch him now—hurry, go
fetch him!"

Squeak-toof of shoes again, many shoes heading
her way. Why were they running?

I've gotta wake up . . . have to wake . . .

Everyone well . . . everyone happy . . . The words
seemed to have arms for they wrapped around
her, gently tugging her farther from sleep. *Everyone will be happy . . . .*

Memories came—short flashes, hints of pho-
tographs once seen, now lost.

Thirsty . . .

Heather stirred, her tongue dry against the roof of her mouth. God, she was so thirsty . . . *gotta go to the bathroom* . . . her eyelids felt heavy . . . *hope nobody's in there* . . .

Then she remembered . . . Haley—safe. Papaw and Mr. Aikman—safe. There'd been so much blood, so much noise and blood and danger. She tried to focus on the dark ceiling overhead, then realized she was looking at the back of her eyelids. *Gotta open my eyes . . . gotta go to the bathroom . . . everyone will be happy . . . well . . .* As the thoughts rolled over and over in her mind like a looping tape, she saw light—more light. Then blurry colors.

Footsteps—closer now.

More colors—sporadic—lightning quick. For some reason they made Heather think of the snake drawing, that terrible, ugly sigil that had never matched anything she'd ever intended or could possibly have wished for. She had to get it off her arm. *Had* to. She'd use one of Meemaw's Brillo pads if she had to.

Heather concentrated on opening her eyes, not understanding why they felt so heavy, so impossible to open.

A flutter of light. Colors—not so blurry now. And white—white coat—dark pants. A man standing beside her.

He leaned in closer. "How're you feeling?"

The man's voice seemed to be the key needed to unlock her from sleep. The next thing Heather knew she was staring up at a bald man who wore wire-rimmed glasses. He smiled at her, then she heard a soft *click*, and a narrow beam of white light whipped across her right eye. Then her left.

"How do you feel?" he asked again.

Aside from being a little groggy and a lot thirsty, she felt fine, and she meant to tell him that, but her mouth felt stuffed with cardboard. She licked her lips. "Wh-where . . . who are you?"

"I'm Doctor Bresler, and right now you're in Pine Lake Memorial Hospital."

Hospital? Sick—God, she remembered being so sick—throwing up.

Blue pastel flashed beside the doctor's left shoulder, then a wobbling tangle of dark-gray hair. "Let me see. I gotta see my baby."

The doctor quickly stepped aside, and Meemaw's face suddenly loomed overhead. Her bloodshot eyes were filled with tears and worry. "Jesus of mercy you had us worried half to death, Puddin," she said, and cupped Heather's face with her large hands.

Heather licked her lips again, then gave her grandmother a small, reassuring smile. "I'm okay, Meemaw." Her voice sounded like it was being forced through thick wads of cotton.

Meemaw's face brightened. "Thank the lord—thank the—oh, look here—look who come see you. Papaw—Mr. Aikman—Brother Gerald from—"

"Haley? Is Haley—"

"Bless your heart, course she is. Lookit, your sister's right here. "Meemaw turned and extended an arm.

Haley burst into view, dressed in a hospital gown exactly like hers. She all but threw herself onto the bed, sobbing. She hugged Heather tight. "I'm so sorry. I'm so sorry for what I did. I was so awful, but you still saved me—you saved all of us. They brought me here—Papaw and Mr. Aikman—to make sure I was okay, but you were there—in that place. I saw—you were there."

For a moment, Heather recalled how she'd pushed through, forced herself past . . . something . . . something that had been separating them. Then there was that place—the blood—the fighting, crashing, crying—animal sounds, pain—their hands, the circle. Blinking away the memories, Heather tried to return her sister's hug but found her arms tethered to wires and soft plastic tubes. She caught one of Haley's hands and squeezed it. "You weren't awful, just confused—hurt and scared. Me, too."

Lifting her head, Haley looked at her for a long moment, tears streaming down her face. "I'm so sorry," she murmured.

Knowing her sister felt more guilt than could ever be appeased, Heather gave her a little nod and smiled. Haley hugged her again, and Heather closed her eyes, basking in the love that flowed between them.

Giving her shoulder a gentle nudge, Haley whispered, "Hey, check this out." She sat up and stuck a finger under the right sleeve of her hospital gown. Even before she lifted the material, Heather knew the snake drawing would no longer be there. After showing her an ink-free arm, Haley motioned to Heather's right arm. "Yours, too. Both gone—just like that. How'd that happen you think?"

At the moment, Heather didn't care about the how of anything. How she wound up in the barn from the hospital—how linking hands had gotten them here. How didn't really matter anyway. The most important thing was that they were all here together and safe.

She heard the scratch of metal shower rings again, and Dr. Bresler peered around one of the curtains that cordoned off both sides of the hospital bed. "Sorry to break this up, folks, but we need to do a more thorough check on our girl here. A lab tech'll be down in a few minutes to draw a little blood, then we'll take her up to x-ray."

With a sigh, Haley reluctantly got up from the bed.

"Can we at least say hello?" a man asked.

Following the sound of the voice, Heather glanced around her sister and saw Mark Aikman standing near the foot of the bed. He wore light gray sweatpants and what she thought was a t-shirt until she realized he was wrapped in white bandages from shoulders to waist. She remembered the W on his chest—he'd tried so hard to save her sister—to save them all.

"Thank you," Heather mouthed.

Mark gave her a little wink. "Keep feeling better, okay?"

She nodded, tears stinging her eyes.

"Think there's someone else here who wants to see you before they cart you off," Mark said, and motioned to someone she couldn't see.

"She decent?"

Mark grinned. "Yep, she's decent."

Tousled white hair and two anxious, lake-blue eyes peeked around a curtain flap. "So you okay now, huh, baby girl?"

Heather nodded, too choked up to say anything. God how she was grateful for her grandparents—for Papaw and his simple ways and the devotion he had for his family. Although he could be a bit tough and gruff at times, she knew he could have turned them away when they'd needed him most. Could have claimed he was too set in his ways and order of life to be strapped down with two teenagers. But he hadn't. He and Meemaw had taken them in without hesitation.

As though satisfied with her answer, Buck returned her nod, then inched toward the bed and stood by Mark. He folded his arms across his chest, then dropped them to his sides as if unsure which position was the proper etiquette for a hospital visit.

Heather wet her lips, wanting to make sure her words were clear when she spoke. "Thank you, Papaw. Thank you—for everything."

A stunned look flitted over Buck's face, then he tossed a hand in the air dismissively. "Just wanted to stop by and say hey. Doc says we gotta go, so—"

"What's that on your hand, Papaw?" Haley asked suddenly.

"Huh?" Buck glanced at the back of his hands.

"Your right one," Haley said, pointing. "On your palm."

Turning his right hand over, Buck's head jerked back slightly. "What the heck . . . ?"

"What?" Mark asked, leaning toward him. He reached out as if he planned on examining the find.

Buck lifted his right hand, palm out. A dark red spot about the size and shape of a penny looked like it had been burned into the middle of his palm. He motioned to Mark's extended hand with his chin. "Lookit—one on you, too."

Mark frowned, then checked his own palms. "I'll be . . ." He held up his right hand, revealing an identical red dot.

With his eyebrows collected into one hairy line, Buck jabbed the spot with a finger. "Doesn't hurt me none. You?"

Mark rubbed a thumbnail over the dot on his palm. "Nope."

Heather and Haley glanced at each other, then quickly checked their own hands and discovered the same red spot. As if synchronized, they immediately displayed right palms at the same time, both saying, "Us, too."

"What you figure it is?" Buck asked, looking from one to the other.

Mark shrugged. "Maybe we're all allergic to something?"

"In a hospital?" Heather asked. "And all of a sudden like that? They weren't there a minute ago, were they?"

"I didn't see nothin' earlier," Buck said.

Haley let out a little gasp. "I think I know what this is!" She looked up, eyes brimming with tears. "It's a circle, just like the one we made when we held hands, remember? Back at that place?"

Heather nodded slowly, feeling understanding creep up on her. She felt it best to keep quiet, to let Haley turn things over in her mind, then bring her thoughts up front where everyone could look at them and agree—because they would. She knew it.

"It's like a reminder," Haley continued. "that stuff comes back full circle sometimes. I mean, like I thought I had to control everything in order to get my old life back, but a person can't control everything. Sometimes stuff just happens for whatever reason, and it makes life go in a different direction. That doesn't mean life gets bad, it just gets different."

"What brings it back full circle, though?" Mark asked.

Haley pursed her lips and studied her hand. "I guess the full circle is when you come back around to knowing that the only thing you can control in life is you."

Mark nodded solemnly. "I think you're right."

Haley looked up at Buck. "You know stuff's going to happen sometimes whether we want it to or not. Sometimes that stuff's good, sometimes it's not so good. And sometimes you can do something about it, you know, make a situation change. Other times, though—"

"Other times nothin' you do changes nothin'," Buck said, a tear sliding down his cheek. He grinned, and the tear slid into his dimple. "But things can be a'ight if you let 'em . . . if you give 'em a chance. No matter how bad you fig're it is right then, sometimes it'll get different if you give it a chance to. Ain't that so, Haley girl? It can be a'ight can't it?"

Haley nodded and gave him a smile that reminded Heather so much of their father it took her breath away. "Yep, Papaw," Haley said. "It can definitely be a'ight."

DEBORAH LEBLANC

A HOUSE DIVIDED

Keith Lafleur, Louisiana's largest and greediest building contractor, thinks he's cut the deal of a lifetime. The huge old two-story clapboard house is his for the taking as long as he can move it to a new location. It's too big to move as it is, but Lafleur's solution is simple: divide it in half. He has no idea, though, that by splitting the house he'll be dividing a family—a family long dead, a family that still exists in the house, including a mother who will destroy anyone who keeps her apart from her children.

GRAVE INTENT

DEBORAH LEBLANC

In all their years at the funeral home, Janet and Michael Savoy have never seen anything like the viewing for nineteen-year-old Thalia Stevenson. That's because they have never seen a Gypsy funeral before, complete with rituals, incantations and a very special gold coin placed beneath the dead girl's hands....

When that coin is stolen, a horror is unleashed. If the Savoys don't find the coin and return it to Thalia's grave before the rising of the second sun, someone in their family—perhaps their little daughter—will die a merciless death. The ticking away of each hour brings the Savoy family closer to a gruesome, inescapable nightmare. Only one thing is certain—Gypsies always have their revenge...even the dead ones.

FAMILY INHERITANCE
DEBORAH LeBLANC

The dark, impenetrable bayous of Louisiana are filled with secrets that can never be revealed and mysterious forces that can never be understood. Jessica LeJeune left Louisiana, but she brought some of those mysterious forces with her—and now she's being called back home to her Cajun roots to confront a destiny she could not escape and a curse she might not survive.

Jessica's younger brother, Todd, has descended into a world of madness. His shattered mind is now the plaything of an unimaginable evil. But Jessica is not alone in her battle to save her brother's soul. For deep in the misty bayous, in an isolated wooden shack, lives the person who is their only hope....

RICHARD LAYMON

THE MIDNIGHT TOUR

For years morbid tourists have flocked to the Beast House, eager to see the infamous site of so many unspeakable atrocities, to hear tales of the beast said to prowl the hallways. They can listen to the audio tour on their headphones as they stroll from room to room, looking at the realistic recreations of the blood-drenched corpses....

But the audio tour only gives the sanitized version of the horrors of the Beast House. If you want the full story, you have to take the Midnight Tour, a very special event strictly limited to thirteen brave visitors. It begins at the stroke of midnight. You may not live to see it end.

ISBN 10: 0-8439-5753-0
ISBN 13: 978-0-8439-5753-2 $7.99 US/$9.99 CAN

RICHARD LAYMON
THE BEAST HOUSE

The Beast House has become a museum of the most macabre kind. On display inside are wax figures of its victims, their bodies mangled and chewed, mutilated beyond recognition. The tourists who come to Beast House can only wonder what sort of terrifying creature could be responsible for such atrocities.

But some people are convinced Beast House is a hoax. Nora and her friends are determined to learn the truth for themselves. They will dare to enter the house at night. When the tourists have gone. When the beast is rumored to come out. They will learn, all right.

Dorchester Publishing Co., Inc.
P.O. Box 6640
Wayne, PA 19087-8640

_____5749-2
$7.99 US/$9.99 CAN

Please add $2.50 for shipping and handling for the first book and $.75 for each additional book. NY and PA residents, add appropriate sales tax. No cash, stamps, or CODs. Canadian orders require an extra $2.00 for shipping and handling and must be paid in U.S. dollars. Prices and availability subject to change. **Payment must accompany all orders.**

Name: _____

Address: _____

City: _____ State: _____ Zip: _____

E-mail: _____

I have enclosed $_____ in payment for the checked book(s).

CHECK OUT OUR WEBSITE! www.dorchesterpub.com
_____ Please send me a free catalog.

OFFSPRING

JACK KETCHUM

The local sheriff of Dead River, Maine, thought he had killed them off ten years ago—a primitive, cave-dwelling tribe of cannibalistic savages. But somehow the clan survived. To breed. To hunt. To kill and eat. And now the peaceful residents of this isolated town are fighting for their lives....

ISBN 10: 0-8439-5864-2
ISBN 13: 978-0-8439-5864-5 $7.99 US/$9.99 CAN

EDGEWISE

GRAHAM MASTERTON

Lily Blake's first mistake is getting involved with dangerous forces she doesn't understand. But she is desperate. Her children have been taken. The police are no help. And George Iron Walker claims he can summon the Wendigo, a Native American spirit that can hunt anyone…anywhere…forever. She doesn't think he can really do it.

Then the man who took Lily's children is found—ripped to pieces. Lily's second mistake: she tells George Iron Walker that she can't keep her part of the bargain. Now she has become the prey, hunted by a spirit that will never rest until Lily is dead.

DEBORAH LeBLANC

Award-winning suspense author Deborah LeBlanc,
a Cajun native of Louisiana, has spent time in an
insane asylum (as a visitor!), been sealed in a coffin,
and helped embalm bodies, all for research. Prior to
writing chilling novels, she worked in the oil and
transportation industry and started two corporations.
She currently lives in Louisiana with her husband
and three daughters. You can find out more about
Deborah on her website, www.deborahleblanc.com.